D0114046

THE STAINLESS STEEL RAT GETS DRAFTED

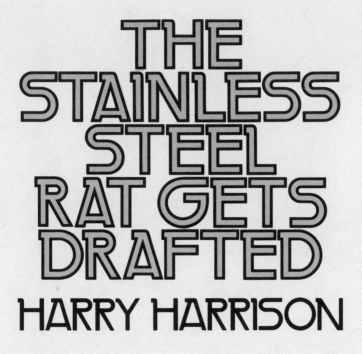

THE STAINLESS STEEL RAT GETS DRAFTED

HARRY HARRISON

SPECTRA

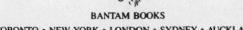

BANTAM BOOKS

TORONTO · NEW YORK · LONDON · SYDNEY · AUCKLAND

The Stainless Steel Rat Gets Drafted
A Bantam Spectra Book/October 1987

Library of Congress Cataloging-in-Publication Data

Harrison, Harry.
The stainless steel rat gets drafted.

(A Bantam spectra book)
I. Title.
PS3558.A667S7   1987   813'.54   87-47566
ISBN 0-553-05220-9

Published simultaneously in the United States and Canada

Bantam Books are published by Bantam Books, Inc. Its trade-
mark, consisting of the words "Bantam Books" and the por-
trayal of a rooster, is Registered in U.S. Patent and Trademark
Office and in other countries. Marca Registrada. Bantam
Books, Inc., 666 Fifth Avenue, New York, New York 10103.

PRINTED IN THE UNITED STATES OF AMERICA

FG   0   9   8   7   6   5   4   3   2   1

This book is for
Rog Peyton
and all the Brum gang.

CHAPTER 1

I am too young to die. Just eighteen years old—and now I'm as good as dead. My grip is weakening, my fingers slipping, and the elevator shaft below me is a kilometer deep. I can't hold on any longer. I'm going to fall . . .

Normally I am not prone to panic—but I was panicking now. Shaking from head to toe with fatigue, knowing that there was just no way out of this one.

I was in trouble, mortal trouble, and I had only myself to blame this time. All the good advice I had given myself down through the years, the even better counsel The Bishop had given me, all forgotten. All wiped away by sudden impulse.

Perhaps I deserved to die. Maybe a Stainless Steel Rat had been born—but a very rusty one was about to snuff it right now. The metal door frame was greasy and I had to hold on hard with my aching fingers. My toes barely gripped the narrow ledge—while my unsupported heels hung over the black drop below. Now my arches began to ache with the effort of standing on tiptoe—which was nothing compared to the fire in my throbbing forearms.

It had seemed such a logical, simple, good, intelligent plan at the time.

I now knew it to be irrational, complex, bad and moronic.

"You are an idiot, Jimmy diGriz," I muttered through my

tightly shut teeth, realizing only then that they were clamped into my lower lip and drawing blood. I unclamped and spat—and my right hand slipped. The great spasm of fear that swept over me rode down the fatigue and I grabbed a new hold with an explosion of desperate energy.

Which faded away as quickly as it had come, leaving me in the same situation. Tireder if anything. There was no getting out of this one. I was stuck here until I could no longer hold on, until my grip loosened and I fell. Might as well let go now and get it over with . . .

"No, Jim, no surrender."

Through the thudding of blood in my ears my voice seemed to come from a great distance, to be deeper in register than my own, as though The Bishop himself were speaking. The thought was his, the words might very well be his. I held on, though I didn't really know why. And the distant whine was disturbing.

Whine? The elevator shaft was black as the grave and just as silent. Was the maglevlift moving again? With muscle-tight slowness I bent my head and looked down the shaft. Nothing.

Something. A tiny glimmer of light.

The elevator was coming up the shaft.

But so what? There were two hundred and thirty-three floors in this government building. What were the odds that it would stop at the floor below me so I could step neatly back onto its top? Astronomical I was sure, and I was in no mood to work them out. Or perhaps it would come up to this floor and scrape me off like a bug as it went by? Another nice thought. I watched the light surge upward towards me, my eyes opening wider and wider to match the growing glow. The increasing whine of the centering wheels, the rush of air exploding at me, this was the end . . .

The end of its upward motion. The car stopped just below me, so close that I could hear the door swoosh open and the voices of the two guards inside.

"I'll cover you. Keep your safety off when you search the hall."

"You'll cover me, thanks! I didn't hear myself volunteer."

"You didn't—I did. My two stripes to your one mean you take a look."

One-stripe muttered complaints as he moved out as slowly as he could. As his shadow occulted the light from the open door I stepped down onto the car with my left foot, as gingerly as I could. Hoping that any movement to the car caused by my climbing onto it would be masked by his exiting.

Not that it was easy to do. My thigh muscle spasmed with cramp and my fingers were locked into place. I stepped slowly back with my vibrating right foot until I was standing on top of the elevator. My cramped fingers still gripped the frame: I felt very much the fool.

"Hall is empty," a distant voice called out.

"Take a reading from the proximity recorder."

There were muttered grumbles and clattering from outside as I wrenched my right hand free of the greasy metal, reached over with it to grapple with my still recalcitrant left hand.

"Got a reading for myself. Other than that the last movement in the corridor was at eighteen hundred. People going home."

"Then we do have a mystery," two-stripes said. "Come on back. We had a readout that showed this car going up to this floor. We called it back from this floor. Now you tell me that no one got out. A mystery."

"That's no mystery, that's just a malfunction. A glitch in the computer. The thing is giving itself instructions when no one else will."

"Much as I hate to agree—I agree. Let's go back and finish the card game."

One-stripe returned, the elevator door closed, I sat down as quietly as I could, and we all dropped back down the shaft together. The guards got out at the prison floor and I just sat there in creaking silence as I kneaded the knots out of my muscles with trembling fingers. When they were roughly under control again I opened the hatch that I was sitting on, dropped down into the car and looked out slowly and carefully. The card players were out of sight in the guardroom, where they belonged. With infinite caution I retraced the route I had taken during my abortive escape. Slinking guiltily along the walls—if I had a tail it would have been between my legs—making a fumbled hash of opening the locked corridor doors with my lockpick.

9

Finally reaching my own cell, unlocking and relocking it, slipping the lockpick back into my shoe sole—dropping onto my bed with a sigh that must have been heard around the world. I did not dare speak out loud in the sleeping silence of the cell block, but I did shout the words inside my head.

"Jim, you are the dumbest most moronic idiot who ever came down the pike. Don't, and I repeat, don't ever do anything like that again."

I won't, I promised in grim silence. That message had now been well drilled into my medulla oblongata. The truth was inescapable. I had done everything wrong in my eagerness to get out of prison. Now I would see if I could get it right.

I had been in too much of a rush. There should never have been any hurry. After he had arrested me, Captain Varod, strongman of the League Navy, had admitted that he knew all about the lockpick that I had hidden. He did not like prisons, he had told me that. Although he was a firm believer in law and order he did not believe I should be incarcerated on my home planet, Bit O' Heaven, for all of the troubles that I had caused there. Neither, for that matter, did I. Since he knew I had the lockpick I should have bided my time. Waited to make my escape during the transfer out of this place.

During the transfer. It had never been my intention of doing anything but serve my time here in this heavily guarded and technologically protected prison in the middle of the League building in the center of the League base on this planet called Steren-Gwandra—about which I knew absolutely nothing other than its name. I had been enjoying the rest, and the meals, a real pleasure after the rigors of war on Spiovente and the disgusting slop that passed for food there. I should have kept on enjoying, building my strength in preparation for my imminent freedom. So why had I tried to crack out of here?

Because of her, a woman, female creature briefly seen and instantly recognized. One glimpse and all reason had fled, emotion had ruled and I had attempted my disastrous escape. More fool I. I grimaced at the memory, recalling all too clearly how this idiot adventure had begun.

It had been during our afternoon exercise period, that wildly exciting occasion when the prisoners were let out of their cells and permitted to shuffle around the ferroconcrete yard under the gentle light of the double suns. I shuffled with the rest and tried to ignore my companions. Low foreheads, joined eyebrows, pendulous and drool-flecked lips; a very unsatisfactory peer group of petty criminals that I was ashamed to be a part of. Then something had stirred them, some unaccustomed novelty that had excited their feeble intellects and had caused them to rush toward the chainlink fence emitting hoarse cries and vulgar exhortations. Numbed by the monotony of prison life even I had felt a twinge of curiosity and desire to see what had caused this explosion of unfamiliar emotion. It should have been obvious. Women. That, and strong drink and its aftereffects, were the only topics that ever stirred the sluggish synapses of their teeny minds.

Three newly arrived female prisoners were passing by on the other side of the fence. Two of them, cut from the same cloth as my companions, responded with equally hoarse cries and interesting gestures of the fingers and hand. The third prisoner walked quietly, if grimly, ignoring her surroundings. Her walk was familiar. But how could it be? I had never even heard of this planet before I had been forcefully brought here. This was a mystery in need of a solution. I hurried along the fence to its end, cleared a space for myself by applying my knuckles to a hair-covered neck in such a manner that the neck's owner slipped into unconsciousness, took his space and looked out.

At a very familiar face passing by not a meter distant. Without a doubt a face and a name that I knew very well.

Bibs, the crewgirl from Captain Garth's spacer.

She was a link to Garth and I had to talk to her, to find out where he was. By kidnapping us and dumping us on the loathsome planet of Spiovente, Captain Garth had been responsible for The Bishop's death. Which meant that I would like to be responsible for his in return.

So, without further thought, and possessed only of a suicidal and impractical enthusiasm, I had foolishly escaped. Only the luck that watches over the completely witless had saved my life

11

and permitted my return, undetected, to my prison cell. I blushed now with shame as I thought about the stupidity of my plan. Lack of thought, lack of foresight—and the incredibly dumb assumption that all security in the giant building would be identical. During our daily exodus and return to the cell block I had noted the exceedingly simple locks on all of the doors, the absence of any alarms. I had assumed that the rest of the building had been the same.

I had assumed wrong. The car of the maglevlift had notified the guards when it had been used. I had spotted the detectors in the corridor at once when the door had opened on the top floor. That was why I had tried the escape hatch in the roof, hoping to find a way out through the mechanism at the top of the shaft.

Except that there had been no mechanism there—just another door. Opening into another floor that did not appear on the bank of buttons inside the car. Some secret location known only to the authorities. Hoping to penetrate this secret I had climbed onto the doorsill and searched for a way to open the door. Only to have the elevator vanish from behind me leaving me stranded on top of the empty shaft.

I had come out of this little harebrained adventure far better than I had deserved. Luck would not ride with me a second time. Cool planning was needed. I put this nearly-disastrous escapade behind me and thought furiously of schemes and ways to make contact with the crewgirl.

"Do it honestly," I said, and shocked myself with the words.

Honest? Me? The stainless steel rat who prowls the darkness of the night in solitary silence, fearing no one, needing no one.

Yes. Painful as the realization was, just this once honesty was indeed the best policy.

"Attention, foul jailers, attention!" I shouted and hammered on the bars of my cage. "Arouse yourself from your sweat-sodden slumbers and vulgar, erotic dreams and take me to Captain Varod. Soonest—or even sooner!"

My fellow prisoners awoke, calling out in righteous anger and threatened all sorts of unimaginative bodily harm. I returned

12

the insults with enthusiasm and eventually the night guard appeared, scowling with menace.

"Hi, there," I called out cheerily. "Nice to see a friendly face."

"You want your skull broke, kid?" he asked. His repartee just about as sharp as that of the inmates.

"No. But I want you to stay out of trouble by instantly taking me to Captain Varod since I have information of such military importance that you would be shot instantly if suspected of keeping it from the captain for more than a second or two."

He added some more threats, but there was a glint of worry in his eyes as he thought about what I had said. It seemed obvious, even to someone of his guttering intelligence, that passing the buck was the wisest fallback position. He growled some more insults when I pointed back down the corridor, but left in any case and went to his telephone. Nor was my wait a long one. A brace of overmuscled and overweight guards appeared on the scene within minutes. They unlocked my cell, clamped on the cuffs and hurried me into the maglevlift and up a few hundred stories to a bare office. Where they fastened the cuffs to a heavy chair and left. The lieutenant who entered a few minutes later was still blinking the sleep from his eyes and was not happy at being disturbed in the middle of the night.

"I want Varod," I said. "I don't talk to the hired help."

"Shut up, diGriz, before you get yourself into worse trouble. The captain is in deep space and unreachable. I am from his department and urge you to speak quickly before I bounce you out of here."

It sounded reasonable enough. And I had very little choice.

"Have you ever heard of a space-going Venian swine who goes by the name of Captain Garth?"

"Get on with it," he said in a bored voice, yawning to drive home the point. "I worked on your case so you can speak freely. What do you know that you haven't told us already?"

"I have information about our gun-running friend. You do have him in custody, don't you."

"DiGriz—you give us information, that is the way that it works, not the other way around." That was what he said, but his expression spoke otherwise. A fleeting instant of worry. If

13

that meant what I thought it meant then Garth had managed to escape them.

"I saw a girl today, a new prisoner being brought in. Her name is Bibs."

"Did you get me out of bed to describe some sordid sexual secret?"

"No. I just thought you should know that Bibs was a crewgirl on Garth's ship."

This caught his attention instantly, and not being as experienced as his commanding officer he could not conceal the look of sudden interest.

"You are sure of this?"

"Check for yourself. The information on today's arrivals should be readily available."

It was: he sat behind the steel desk and hammered away at the keys on the terminal there. Looked at the screen and scowled in my direction.

"Three women admitted today. None named Bibs."

"How very unusual." Scorn dripped from my voice. "Can it be that the criminal classes now use aliases?"

He did not answer but tapped away at the terminal again. The fax buzzed and produced three sheets of paper. Three color portraits. I dropped two of them onto the floor and handed the third back.

"Bibs."

He bashed some more keys, then slumped back and rubbed his chin as he studied the screen.

"It fits, it fits," he muttered. "Marianney Giuffrida, age twenty-five, occupation given as electrotechnician with deepspace experience. Arrested on a drugs possession charge, anonymous tip, swears she was framed. No other details."

"Ask her about Garth. Use persuasion. Make her talk."

"You have our thanks for your assistance, diGriz. It will go on your record." He tapped a number into the phone. "But you have been watching too many films. There is no way we can force people to give evidence. But we can question and observe and draw conclusions. They will take you back to your cell now."

14

"Gee, thanks for the thanks. Thanks for nothing. Can you at least do me the favor of telling me how long you intend to keep me here?"

"That should be easy enough to find out." A quick access of the terminal and a sage nod of the head as the door opened behind me. "You will be leaving us the day after tomorrow. A spacer will be stopping at a planet with the interesting name of Bit O' Heaven where, it appears, you have to answer some criminal charges."

"Guilty until found guilty, I suppose." I sneered and whined to hide the surge of enthusiasm that raced through me. Once out of here I really would be out of here. I ignored the rough clutch and muttered complaints of my warders and permitted myself to be docilely led back to my cell. I was going to be good, very, very good, until the day after tomorrow.

But I lay awake a long time after that, staring into the darkness, working out how I was going to pry the information I needed out of crewmember Bibs.

CHAPTER 2

"Sign here."

I signed. The ancient graybeard behind the desk passed over the plastic bag containing all of my worldly possessions, forcibly removed from me when I had been incarcerated. I reached for them but the fat guard reached even faster.

"Not yet, prisoner," he said, whisking them away from my clutching fingers. "These will be forwarded to the arresting authorities."

"They're mine!"

"Take it up with them. All set, Rasco?"

"My name's not Rasco!"

"Mine is. Shut up," the other guard said. A well-muscled and nasty individual whose right wrist was secured to my left by a pair of shining cuffs. He pulled hard on this connecting link so I stumbled toward him. "You do what I say and no backtalk or funny stuff."

"Yes, sir. Sorry."

I lowered my eyes in humility which caused him to smirk with assumed superiority. He should only know that I was using the opportunity to look more closely at the cuffs. Bulldog-Crunchers, sold throughout the known galaxy, guaranteed foolproof. Maybe proof against fools but I could open them in under two seconds. It was going to be a nice day.

16

Fatso walked on my right side, well-connected Rasco on my left. I marched in step with them, eager to leave the prison and examine the world waiting outside the League building. I had come here in a closed van and had seen nothing. Eagerness possessed me in expectation of a first glimpse of my new home; thoughts about my forceful removal from this planet may have preoccupied my guardians—but were the farthest thing from my mind at this moment.

Exiting the building was not easily done—and I gave myself another mental kick for even thinking of breaking out of this bunker-skyscraper. There were three doors to go out through, one after another, each sealed as tightly as an airlock. Our passes were slipped into computerized machines that hummed and clicked—then robot sensors examined our fingerprints and retinal patterns to make sure we matched the details on the passes. This was done three times before the outer portal hummed open and a wave of warm air, smell and sound washed in.

As we went down the steps to the street I gaped like a rube. I had never seen anything like this before. Of course my experience was strictly limited since this was only the third planet I had ever visited. My life on the porcuswine farms of Bit O' Heaven and my service in the swamps of Spiovente had not prepared me for the manifold impressions that bombarded me.

A wave of heat and dusty air washed over me. It was filled with pungent aromas, loud cries and a cacophony of strange noises. At the same time as my ears and nose were being assaulted my eyes bulged at the seething mass of humanity, the strange vehicles—and the four-legged alien creatures. One passed close by, a man sitting on its back, its great feet thudding on the ground, eyes rolling in my direction. Its mouth opened to reveal hideous yellow teeth and it squealed loudly. I drew back and my guards laughed aloud at this perfectly reasonable reaction.

"We'll protect you from the *margh*," Fatso said, and they chortled with dim pleasure.

Maybe it was called a *margh* in the local lingo, but it was still a horse to me. I had seen them in the ancient history tapes at school. The creatures had been used for farming when Bit

17

O' Heaven was first settled, but had soon succumbed to the deadly native life. Only the indestructible porcuswine had been able to survive. I looked more closely at the horse, at the obviously herbivorous teeth, and realized it posed no threat. But it was big. Two more of the creatures came up, towing a boxlike affair mounted on large wheels. The driver, sitting high above, pulled the thing to a stop when Rasco whistled to him.

"Get in," Fatso ordered, swinging open a door in the vehicle's side. I held back, pointed with distaste.

"It's filthy in there! Can't the League Navy provide decent transportation . . ."

Rasco kicked me in the back of the leg so I fell forward. "Inside—and no backtalk!" They climbed in after me. "It is Navy policy to use native transport when possible, to aid the local economy. So shut up and enjoy."

I shut, but I didn't enjoy. I looked unseeingly at the crowded street as we rumbled away, thinking of the best way to escape my captors while inflicting a bit of damage on my sadistic companion. Now would be as good a time as any. Strike like lightning, then leave them both unconscious in this vehicle while I slipped away in the crowd. I bent over and scratched furiously at my ankle.

"I've been bitten! There are bugs in here!"

"Bite them back," Fatso said and they both roared with juvenile laughter. Wonderful. Neither saw me slip the lockpick from my shoe and palm it. I turned toward Rasco with mayhem in mind just as the vehicle lurched to a stop and Fatso reached across and threw open the door. "Out," he ordered and Rasco pulled painfully on the handcuff. I gaped at the marble-fronted building before us.

"This isn't the spaceport," I protested.

"You got good eyes," Rasco sneered and dragged me after him. "A local version of a linear. Let's go."

I decided I wouldn't. I had had more than enough of their repellent company. But I had to stumble after them for the moment, looking about for some opportunity—and seeing it just ahead. Men, and only men, were entering and exiting a doorway

18

under a sign that proudly proclaimed PYCHER PYSA GORRYTH. Though I knew nothing of the local language I could figure this one out easily enough. I drew back and pointed.

"Before we get on the linear I gotta go in there."

"No way," Rasco said. Sadist. But I got unexpected aid from his companion.

"Take him in. It's going to be a long trip."

Rasco muttered disgustedly. But Fatso was obviously his superior because he pushed me forward. The pycher pysa was about as primitive as they come, a simple trough against one wall, a line of men facing it. I headed for a vacant position on the far end and fumbled with my clothing. Rasco watched me with obvious displeasure.

"I can't do anything with you watching," I wailed.

He rolled his eyes upward for a second. Just long enough for me to get his neck with my free hand. His look of surprise faded as I clamped down hard with my thumb. After this I had only to guide his unconscious fall to the tile floor. As he hit with a satisfactory thud I clicked open the cuff on my wrist. He snored lightly as I quickly frisked him, I had a reputation as a thief to live up to, and slipped his wallet from his hip pocket. It was safely hidden in my own before I stood and turned about. The row of men against the wall were all looking at me.

"He fainted," I said, and they gaped with incomprehension. "*Li svenas*," I added, which did not clarify it for them in any way. I pointed to the unconscious copper, to the door, then at myself. "I'm going for help. You lads keep an eye on him and I'll be right back."

None of them was in any position to follow me as I scuttled out of the entrance. Practically into Fatso's arms. He shouted something and reached for me—but I was long gone. Out of the station and into the crowd. There were some more outcries from behind me but they soon died away as I twisted between two horses, around a coach and down a dark alley on the far side of the street. It was that easy.

The alley opened into another street, just as crowded as the first, and I strolled along it, just a part of the crowd. Free as a bird. I actually whistled as I walked, staring around at the

19

sights, the veiled women and the brightly garbed men. This was the life!

Or was it? Alone on a primitive planet, not speaking the language, sought by the authorities—what did I have to be cheerful about? Black gloom descended instantly and I sneered aloud.

"That's it, Jim? You turn coward at the slightest setback. For shame! What would The Bishop say to this?"

He would say stop talking in public, I thought as I noticed the strange looks I was getting. So I whistled happily, not a care in the world, turned a corner and saw the tables and chairs, men sitting and drinking interesting beverages, under a sign that said SOSTEN HA GWYRAS which conveyed exactly nothing to me. But underneath it was printed NI PAROLOS ESPERANTO, BONVENUU. I hoped that they spoke Esperanto better than they wrote it. I found a table against the wall, dropped into a chair and snapped my fingers at the ancient waiter.

"*Dhe'th plegadow*," he said.

"*Plegadow* the others," I said. "We speak Esperanto. What's to drink, Dad?"

"Beer, wine, dowr-tom-ys."

"I'm just not in the mood for a dowr-tom-ys today. A large beer, if you please."

When he turned away I dug out Rasco's wallet. If my guards were supposed to encourage the local economy they should be carrying some of the local currency. The wallet clunked when I dropped it onto the table, heavy with little metal discs. I shook one out and turned it over. It had the number two stamped into one side, with *Arghans* on the other.

"That will be one Arghans," the waiter said, putting a brimming clay pot in front of me. I passed over the coin.

"Take that, my good man, and keep the change."

"You offworlders are so generous," he said, muffledly as he bit the coin. "Not mean, stupid, vicious like the locals. You want girl? Boy? *Kewarghen* to smoke?"

"Later perhaps. I'll let you know. Beer now and the heady pleasures of native life to come."

He went away muttering and I took a great slug of the beer. Instantly regretting it. I swallowed—and regretted that as well as the noxious brew bubbled and seethed its way through my digestive track. I pushed the jar away and belched. Enough of this tomfoolery. I had escaped, great, step one. But what came next?

Nothing that I could think of at the moment. I sipped at the beer, it still tasted just as repulsive, but even this heroic treatment produced no inspiration. I was grateful for the interruption when the waiter sidled over and whispered hoarsely behind the back of his hand.

"New shipment *kewarghen* fresh from the fields. You get high, stay up for many days. Want some? No? What about girl with whips? Snakes? Leather straps and hot mud . . ."

I interrupted since I wasn't sure that I enjoyed where the conversation was going. "I am sated, I tell you sated. All I wish are directions to return to the municipal edifice."

"Do not know what long words mean."

"Want to find building big, high, filled with plenty offworlders."

"Ahh, you mean the *lys*. For one Arghans I take you there."

"For one Arghans you give me instructions. I don't want to drag you away from your work." Nor did I want to be led astray to one of the many offers he had made. In the end he had to agree. I memorized the instructions, sipped some more of the beer and instantly regretted it, then slipped away when he had vanished into the back room.

As I walked a glimmer of a plan began to develop. I must think of a way to get to Bibs, the crewgirl from the freighter. Garth, the captain of her ship, had escaped, I was sure of that. But she might know more about him. She was my only link with this villain. But how could I get into the prison? I knew the name she had been arrested under, Marianney Giuffrida. Could I pass myself off as a concerned relative, one Hasenpeffer Giuffrida? The local identification should be easy to forge—if it existed at all. But would the computer identify me as an ex-prisoner when I entered the building? Or had I been wiped from its memory when I had left? Perhaps I had been, but would Fatso put me back in memory when he reported my escape?

These thoughts were rattling around in my head when I turned the next corner and found the gigantic edifice before me. It rose up from the low buildings of the city like a towering cliff—and looked just as impenetrable. I strolled by and looked up at the steps I had so recently descended, watched the doors open to admit a visitor. Then close again like a bank vault. My mind was still blank. I stood with my back to a brick wall across from the building. Which was perhaps not too bright, since I was still wearing prison garb. But such was the variety of local costume that my uniform drew no notice at all. I leaned and waited for inspiration to strike.

It didn't. But pure, random luck, a chance in a thousand did. The doors opened one more time and three people emerged. Two minions of the law, this obvious from the size of their boots, flanking a delicate female form. One thick wrist was manacled to her tiny one.

It was Bibs.

The suddenness of her appearance froze me in place. Kept me leaning against the wall as they descended to street level where one of the guards waved and whistled. In quick response two of the horsedrawn vehicles raced their way, one of them neatly cutting off the other. There were shouted curses and loud neighing as the horses reared up. This was quickly sorted out and the loser trotted off. The high body of the horsedrawn hulk blocked my view, but as clear as though it were transparent I knew what was happening. Door being opened, prisoner escorted inside, door closed . . .

The thing started forward as the driver's whip cracked, even as I was hurrying across the road. Getting up speed as I ran after it, jumped, got my feet on the step and hauled the door open.

"Out," the nearest guard said, turning toward me. "This cab is taken . . ."

We looked at each other in mutual recognition—he was the night guard from the prison. With a cry of anger he reached for me. But I reached quicker, jumping in on top of him. He was big and strong—but I was fast. I had a quick glimpse of the shocked look on Bibs's face as I turned all my attention to

avoiding his clutch and getting in a quick blow with the edge
of my hand.

As soon as he went limp I rolled over to face the other guard
and discovered that he had no interest in me at all. Bibs had
her free arm around his neck and was throttling him to death.
He flailed with his other hand but could do nothing because
it was manacled to her wrist.

"Just wait . . . until this one . . . is dead too," Bibs gasped.

I didn't explain that the guard I had taken care of was only
unconscious but reached over and grabbed her elbow hard, index
finger grinding into the big nerve there. Her arm went numb,
dropped away, and her face grew red with fury. But before she
could speak I silenced the gasping guard and unlocked the cuffs.
She rubbed her wrist and smiled.

"I don't know where you dropped from, buster, or why, but
I appreciate the help." She cocked her head and looked more
closely at me. "I know you, don't I? Yes, of course, you're the
midnight passenger, Jimmy something."

"That's right, Bibs. Jim diGriz at your service."

She laughed, loud and happily, while she removed all the
possessions of the two unconscious guards, then scowled when
I manacled them together.

"Better to kill them," she said.

"Better not to. Right now we're not important enough to
them to cause much fuss. But if we murdered two of their men
they would turn this planet over to find us."

"I guess you're right," she said with reluctant agreement—
then kicked both unconscious bodies with sudden fury.

"They can't feel anything."

"They will when they wake up. So where do we go from here,
Jim?"

"You tell me. I know absolutely nothing at all about this
planet."

"I know far too much."

"Then lead the way."

"Right."

She opened the door as our vehicle slowed and we slipped
out, stepped up onto the pavement as it lumbered from sight.

CHAPTER 3

Bibs tucked her arm through mine, which felt very cheering, as we strolled along the busy avenue. Anywhere else our gray prison clothes, tastefully decorated with blood-red broad arrows, would have certainly drawn attention—and apprehension. Not among the motley throngs crowding these streets, dressed in every manner possible. There were bearded men in fringed buckskins, women in layers of colored gauze, armed warriors in leather and steel; robes, gowns, chainmail, cuirasses, sashes—everything imaginable. Plus a few that defied the imagination. We drew no attention at all.

"Do you have any money?" Bibs asked.

"Just a few Arghans I lifted from one of my guards. Like you, I have just escaped."

Her eyebrows lifted at this—very attractive eyebrows arched above even more attractive eyes I noticed.

"Is that why you helped me out? What were you in prison for? All I know is that you and the old boy were left behind on Spiovente. Scuttlebutt had it that Garth sold you into slavery."

"He did, and my friend is dead because of that. I am a little bitter about Garth for a lot of reasons. I liked The Bishop. He helped me, taught me a lot, and I am happy to say that I was able to help him in return. We left our home world in a hurry, as you will remember, and paid Captain Garth a lot of money to get us away. But that wasn't enough for him. He earned more by selling us into slavery. I lived—but The Bishop died because of being a slave. As you can imagine I am not wildly pleased by his death. A number of loathsome things happened on that planet, the least of which was my being caught by the League Navy. They were returning me to my home planet to stand trial."

"On what charges?" There was keen interest in her voice.

"Bank robbery, criminal abduction, jailbreak. Things like that."

"Wonderful!" she said, laughing aloud with joy; she had very neat white teeth. "You did yourself an immense favor when you came to little Bibs's aid. I know this planet well, know where the money is. Know how to buy our way offplanet when we are done. You steal it, I'll spend it—and our troubles are over."

"Sounds reasonable. Could we talk about it over some food? It's been a long time since breakfast."

"Of course—I know just the place."

And she did too. The restaurant was small and discreet while the *felyon ha kyk mogh* tasted a lot better than it sounded. We washed it down with a great bowl of *ru'th gwyn* which turned out to be a satisfactory red wine: I memorized the name for future use. When we had eaten our fill I took one of the wood splinters from the jar on the table and worried bits of gristle from between my teeth.

"Do you mind if I ask you a question?" I asked, asking a question. Bibs sipped at her wine and waved permission. "You know why I was imprisoned. Would you consider it rude if I asked the reason for your incarceration?"

She slammed her mug down so hard that it cracked and oozed a carmine trickle. She was unaware of it; her face twisted with anger and I could hear her teeth grate together.

"He did it, I'm sure, it had to be him, the *bastardacfiulo!*" Which is about the worst name you can call anyone in Esperanto. "Captain Garth, he's the one. He knew the League Navy was after us for gunrunning. He paid us off here—and the next day I was arrested. He tipped them off and planted the *kewarghen* in my bag. With that evidence they busted me on a drugs charge, selling to the natives and all that. I want to kill him."

25

"So do I—for causing the death of my friend. But why did he want you arrested?"

"Revenge. I kicked him out of bed. He was too kinky for my liking."

I gulped and coughed and took a long slug of wine and hoped that she wouldn't notice that I was blushing. She didn't. Her eyes, still glazed with anger, stared past me into space. "Kill him, I really would like to kill him. I know that it's impossible but, oh how he deserves it."

"Why impossible?" I asked with some relief, glad to have the conversation back on comfortable topics like murder and revenge.

"Why? What do you know about this planet, Jim?"

"Nothing. Other than its name, Steren-Gwandra."

"Which means planet in the local lingo. They are not a linguistically imaginative lot. At least those here in Brastyr aren't. Like many other settled planets this one was cut off from galactic contact during the breakdown years. Brastyr, this continent, has few natural resources and over the centuries they managed to lose all of the old technology. They are so dim that most of them forgot Esperanto. Not the traders though, they had to deal with the offshore island. By the time that galactic contact was reestablished the locals had sunk into a sort of agricultural semi-feudalism."

"Like Spiovente?"

"Not quite. Just offshore is this damned great island I mentioned, separated from this mainland by a narrow strait. Almost all of the minerals, coal and oil in this hemisphere are located there. That's why it was settled first and why it was well developed before the second wave of immigrants arrived during the diaspora ages. None of the newcomers were allowed to settle there. Not that they cared, this entire continent was wide-open and bountiful and the arrangement suited all parties concerned. Industry and technology over there on Nevenkebla, farming and forestry here. I doubt if anything changed much during the breakdown years—I imagine the relationship was intensified if anything. That's why we are never going to get close enough to Garth to kill him."

26

"I don't understand. What has this got to do with him?"

"He's on the island. Unreachable." She sighed and rubbed her fingertip in circles in the pool of spilled wine. I was still puzzled.

"But Garth is a Venian, like you. The captain of a Venian ship. Why should they protect him?"

"Because he's not Venian, that's why. The Nevenkebla military bought the ship, he commanded it. We were happy to go along with the plan, they paid well. Venians are very flexible when it comes to money. But he is really something big in the military there. They run the place. All those guns we were smuggling were made on the island. It was a good racket, plenty of offplanet currency. But when the League Navy got too close they paid us off and closed the operation down. There is just no way to get at him on that island."

"I'll find a way."

"I hope that you do. I'll give you all the help that I can. But first things first, Jim. We will have to stay out of sight for a bit while they are looking for us—and that will take a pile of Arghans. How much do you have?"

She spread out the coins she had stolen and I added mine to the pile.

"Not enough. We need a lot for bribes, a safe place to get out of sight. I have contacts, a fence I used to peddle to. For the right price we can have him find a safe house . . ."

"No. Avoid the criminal classes at all counts. Too expensive and the first place that the authorities will look. Do they have hotels here? Expensive, luxurious hotels?"

"Not as such. But there are *ostelyow* where traveling gentry put up. But offworlders never go there."

"Even better. Can you pass as a native?"

"*Yredy*. You could too with a little effort. There are so many different accents and dialects here that no one will notice."

"Ideal. Let us then instantly steal a lot of money, buy some expensive clothes and jewelry and check in at the best *ostel*. Agreed?"

"Agreed!" She laughed out loud and clapped her hands together. "I swear, Jim, you are a breath of fresh air on this fetid planet. I like your style. But it won't be easy. They don't have banks here. All the cash is held by moneylenders called *hoghas*. Their places are like small forts. Plenty of guards, always from the moneylender's own family so they can't be bribed."

"Sounds good. Let's go check one out. Then we will go back tonight and crack it."

"Do you mean it?"

"Never more serious."

"I've never met anyone like you. You look like a kid—but you can really take care of yourself."

I did not like that kid remark but I stayed shut up and tried not to pout while she made plans.

"We'll take some of these Arghans, change them for Nevenkebla coins. This will take a lot of arguing over rate of exchange so you will have time to look around. I'll do the talking. You just carry the money and keep your mouth shut. We'll get you a bodyguard's club first, then they'll never even notice you.

"No time like the present. Let's find a club shop."

This was easily enough done. Most of the side streets were open markets, with stalls and tiny shops that sold an apparently endless variety of cloth, fruit, meals wrapped in leaves, knives, saddles, tents—and clubs. While the merchant extolled the value of his wares, muffledly and incomprehensively through the layers of cloth about his face and neck, I hefted the samples and tested their swing. I finally settled on a meter length of tough wood that was bound about with iron bands.

"This looks like what we want," I told Bibs. The weapon vendor nodded and took the coins and muttered some more. Bibs pointed inside.

"He insists that a year guarantee goes with every club and you must try it out before you leave."

The testing block proved to be a large upright stone that had been carved into human form, what might at one time have resembled a man in armor. But years of testing had taken their toll. Gouges, nicks and missing chunks defaced it; noseless, chinless with a single fragment of ear remaining. I hefted my club, tried a few practice swings—then stood with my back to the stone while I psyched up my muscles with some dynamic-tension contractions and a breathing mantra. I was chuffing as nicely as a Spiovente steam wagon, holding the club upright, when I felt ready.

Timed release, that's the secret. Not a secret really, just technique and practice. A single shout contracted my body all in an instant. In time with the sound I swung about with all of my weight and strength focused on the iron band on the end of the club. It whistled through a half-circle that terminated on the side of the rock head.

There was a ringing crack as the neck shattered and the stone head fell off. The club was still sound and the iron ring had a slight nick.

"This one will do," I said, as offhandedly as I could.

They were both very impressed, let me tell you. I was impressed myself. It had been a good blow, better than I had realized.

"Do you do that often?" Bibs asked in a hushed voice.

"If I have to," I said with a calm I did not feel. "Now take me to your *hogh*."

We found one just a few streets away, the identity of the business made known by a skeleton in an iron cage above the door.

"Some sign," I said. "You would think they would hang out a painting of a money bag or a wooden Arghans."

"This is more practical. That is the last thief they caught trying to steal from them."

"Oh, thanks."

"It's just a tradition, don't let it disturb you."

Easy enough for her to say—she wasn't going to rob this place. Disturbed, I followed her past two ugly weightlifters who leaned on their spears and scowled at us.

"*Hogh*," Bibs said, sniffing with disdain at the guards. They muttered something not too nice, but still knocked on the iron-bound door until it creaked open. Inside were more guardians from the same mould. Except these had swords. The door slammed shut and was locked behind us as we passed through a dark room into the courtyard beyond. There were spikes—as well as more guards—on the surrounding wall. Not a wall, really, but the roof of the buildings that surrounded the courtyard. The *hogh* himself sat on a large chest, shielded from the sun by a canopy, guarded by two more men—this time armed with pikes. The chest had a flat top and was covered with pillows.

"I suppose he sleeps on it at night," I said, a feeble joke to build the morale.

"Of course," Bibs said and the morale slumped even lower.

The moneylender was all smarmy gestures and oily voice. Bibs jingled our money at him and he smarmed even more. At the clap of his hands assistants cleared the pillows away and opened the lid of the chest. I looked in and the guards looked at me. It was neatly divided into sections and each section was filled with leather bags. More orders and handclapping produced a bag that was placed on top of the now reclosed chest. He sat back onto the lid with a happy sigh and cradled the bag in his lap, opened it and let a trickle of shining coins run through his fingers. The haggling began and I feigned boredom and looked around at the courtyard.

This was not going to be easy, not easy at all. The entrance door would certainly be sealed and guarded. If I came over the wall there were those spikes—and more guards as well. Then what? Sneak down into the courtyard and tip the old boy off into the dust, grab the bag. And get speared, stabbed, clubbed and so forth. Not an attractive proposition at all. We were going to have to get a new plan to raise funds. I could see no way to get into this place; brute strength was far more efficient than technology in this setup. And say I got in, say I lifted the loot—there was the little matter of getting out with it. Though that might not be too difficult . . .

I felt the glimmerings of an idea and held onto them and stirred them about. Keeping my expression as calm and stony as possible, with just a hint of a snarl as I looked at the guards, who snarled back. Negotiations were progressing well with plenty of wails of grief and snorts of disdain from both sides. I was only barely aware of this as I rough-fashioned my plan, ran it around and polished it a bit, then took it through slowly, step by step, to see if it would work. Given a little bit of luck it would. Was it the only plan? I sighed inwardly. Yes, all things considered, it was the only plan. I swung my club impatiently and called out to Bibs.

"Come on lady, don't take all day." She turned about and scowled.

"What did you say?"

"You heard me. You came to the bodyguard hiring hall and promised good pay for a short day. But the pay ain't that good and the day is too long."

If the *hogh* didn't understand Esperanto the plan would stop there. But I could see his ears perk up, listening and understanding everything we said. Bash on—no turning back now. Bibs didn't know what I was doing, but she was smart enough to play along, taking umbrage at my insults.

"Listen you muscle-bound moron—I can hire better than you for half the price. I don't need the static from a *malbonulo* whose eyebrows meet in the middle!"

"That does it!" I shouted. "I don't take that from no one!"

I swung my club at her in a wicked blow that just brushed her hair. It didn't touch her—so I let the butt end follow through with a light tap on the forehead that dropped her to the ground. With Bibs safely out of the picture I would now see if I could get away with what is usually referred to as a smash-and-grab.

My club swung again and knocked down one of the poles that held up the canopy. I stepped forward as it fell and chopped the *hogh* on the side of the neck as the cloth engulfed us.

Fast now, Jim. You have seconds—or less. I groped the bag of coins out of his lap and stuffed them inside my shirt. It wouldn't fit until I spilled some out. Seconds. Gone.

There was plenty of shouting now and struggling with the cloth. I pulled myself free—and walked away, calling back over my shoulder.

"I quit, lady. Get another bodyguard. Only poofters work for women anyway."

Two paces, three, four. The armed men looking from me to the heaving canopy as the guards there pulled it free. One of them emerged, dragging the unconscious *hogh*, shouting and screaming with anger. I did not need a translation. All of the other guards howled in rage and ran toward me.

I turned tail and ran in the opposite direction. Away from the only exit.

But toward the flight of wooden stairs that ran up to the roof.

The single guard there stabbed at me with his spear. I parried it with the club and kicked him hard where it would make the best impression. Jumped his falling body and bounded up the stairs two at a time and almost impaled myself on the sword of the man standing at the top. All I could do was dive under it, roll, crash into his legs and bring him down.

Catching him on the head with the butt of the club as I scrambled to my feet, coins jingling down about me.

Three other guards on the roof were screeching and lumbering toward me. I ran to the edge, looked at the drop, cursed aloud. The cobbled street was too far below. If I jumped I would break a leg. Turned and threw my club at the first of the attackers. It caught him nicely and the second man ran into him.

I saw no more because I was over the roof, holding onto the edge with both hands and letting myself down. Looking up at the third guard who was bringing his sword down on my hands.

I let go. Dropped. Hit and rolled. My ankle hurt but I did not even think about it. Spears and clubs cracked to the ground around me as I hobbled away, around the first corner and into a market street. Hobbling slower and slower as the howls behind me faded in the distance.

Around another corner where I stopped for breath, panting and wheezing. Then staggered on deeper into the city until I was sure I had lost my pursuers.

I dropped into a chair of the first bar and actually enjoyed drinking a mug of the terrible beer.

CHAPTER 4

The bag of coins sat uncomfortably on my stomach, straining the fabric of my prison jacket. I looked at the drab cloth with the big red arrows on it and realized that I was being kind of stupid. By now my description would have gone out and all the *hogh* minions would be looking for me. I would not be that hard to find. As I hammered on the table with a coin I felt the sweat beginning to form on my forehead.

At the sight of the Nevenkebla currency the waiter's eyes lit up and he seized it with shaking fingers and carried it away reverently. I received a great handful of Arghans in exchange, surely I was being cheated, still I scuttled away happily. Scuttled into the first shop I found that had garments displayed around the entrance. Esperanto was spoken badly here, but good enough to enable me to buy some baggy trousers and a cloak, along with a whicker basket to conceal the money bag. Feeling safe, at least for the moment, I shambled deeper into the city. Through the busy streets to a market where I purchased a widebrimmed leather hat with a colorful plume. Bit by bit I bought other clothes, until I was garbed anew, the basket with my prison clothes discarded, the money now safe in an elegant shoulder bag. By this time it was getting dark and I was completely lost.

33

And worried about Bibs. I had done all that I could to assure her safety, to distance her from myself and my crime. Had it been enough? I felt a quick surge of guilt and the need to contact her. Easier said than done. First I must find the League building, my only point of reference, and work back from there.

It was dusk by the time I located it—and I was getting very, very tired. Yet there was no choice, I must go on. Following the route the horse conveyance had taken with Bibs and her captors, finding the corner where we had emerged from it. From there it was easy enough to get to the restaurant where we had eaten, to drop into a chair with a sigh of relief. I could only hope now that she remembered the place and would think of coming here. I took off my hat and a hot band of pain circled my throat.

"Traitor," Bibs's voice hissed in my ear as I gurgled and groped but could reach nothing. Was this the end . . .?

It almost was. I was sinking into unconsciousness before the pain eased and the length of wire fell into my lap. I rubbed my sore, bleeding neck as Bibs pulled out a chair and sat down at the table. She weighed my shoulder bag, then looked inside. She had a black eye and some bruises around her mouth.

"I could have killed you," she said. "I was that angry, that was what I was going to do. But when I saw you had brought the money I realized you had planned the whole thing this way and had come here to meet me. But since they had worked me over I felt I owed you some of the same. I'll order some wine."

"Planned . . ." I croaked, then coughed. "Knocked you out—so they would think you weren't in on the robbery."

"It worked—or I wouldn't be here. They bashed me about a bit, then they all ran out after you. I went right behind them in the confusion. Just wandered around and stayed out of sight until dark. Hating you. I had no money, nothing. Other than this black eye. You're lucky I didn't throttle you all the way."

"Thanks," I said, then glugged down half a mug of wine when the waiter set it in front of me. "It was the only thing I could do. While you were talking to the old boy I looked at the defenses. There was no way in past them. But since we were

34

already inside I saw that there was a good chance of getting out. So I took the money."

"Tremendous. You might have told me."

"There was no way to. Knocking you out was the only thing I could think of that would not get you involved. I'm sorry— but it worked."

Bibs actually smiled as she ran her fingers through the coins. "You are right, Jim my boy. It was worth a few bruises to get this much loot. Now let's get moving. You've changed clothes and I must do the same thing."

"Then to the best *ostel* in town."

"For a hot bath and a real meal. You're on!"

The *ostel* was a sprawling building hidden behind high walls. Suites of rooms led off the central courtyard and we had the best, if the bowing and dry handwashing of the help meant anything. The wine was chilled and the finest I had ever tasted. I prowled around the carpeted rooms and nibbled the toasted tidbits that came with the wine, while Bibs burbled and splashed in the adjoining pool. She eventually emerged wrapped in a towel, glowing with health and growling with hunger. There was no nonsense about dining rooms or restaurants in this establishment. Servants brought the food on brass trays and we gorged ourselves. When they had cleaned up the leavings I threw the bolt in the outer door and filled Bib's crystal mug with more wine.

"This is the life," she said.

"It surely is." I sprawled on the cushions across from her. "A good night's sleep and I will be feeling human again."

She lay back on the couch and looked at me through half-closed eyes. Well, really one half-closed and one all the way closed where she had been bopped. She shook her head and smiled.

"You are something else again, Jimmy. Just a kid, really, yet you are sure a winner. You survived Spiovente, which is not easy. Took out those two cops—then you took on all the *hogh's* thugs—and got away with it."

"Just luck," I said. Enjoying the praise but not that "kid" remark.

"I doubt it. And you saved my neck. Got me out of the hands of the law and stole enough clinkers to get me off this planet. I would like to say thanks."

"You don't have to, not really. You are going to help me find Garth so that makes us even." I stood and yawned. "I want to ask you about him—but it can wait until morning. I need some sleep."

She smiled again. "But, Jim, I told you I would like to thank you. In my own way."

Was it chance that as she lay back the towel slipped a little? No it was not chance. Nor was it by accident that she was devastatingly naked underneath. Despite the black eye Bibs was a terribly, terribly attractive girl.

What does one do on an occasion like this?

What one does not do is talk about it to others. I'm sorry. This is a private matter between two consenting adults. Very consenting. You will excuse me if I draw the curtain over this day and insert a space in this text to denote the passing of a good many hours.

Never had the sun shone so warmly and brightly. The afternoon sun. I smiled back at it just as warmly, bereft of any guilt, filled full with happiness. Nibbling a bit of fruit and sipping some wine. Turning languidly from the window as Bibs reentered the room.

"You mean it?" she asked. "You won't go offplanet with me? You don't want to?"

"Of course I want to. But not until I have found Garth."

"He'll find you first and kill you."

"Perhaps he might be the one who gets killed."

She cocked her head most prettily to one side, then nodded. "From anyone but you I would think that bragging. But you might just do it." She sighed. "But I won't be here to see it. I rate survival ahead of vengeance. He put me into jail—you got me out. Case closed. Though I admit to a big bundle of curiosity. If you do get out of this, will you let me know what happened? A message care of the Venian Crewmembers' Union

36

will get to me eventually." She passed over a slip of paper. "I've written down everything that I remembered, just like you asked."

"General," I read. "Either Zennor or Zennar."

"I never saw it spelled out. Just overheard one of the officers talking to him when they didn't know I could hear them."

"What is Mortstertoro?"

"A big military base, perhaps their biggest. That's where we landed to take on cargo. They wouldn't let us out of the spacer, but what we could see was very impressive. A big limousine, all flags and stars, would come for Garth and take him away. There was a lot of saluting—and they always saluted him first. He is something big, high-up, and whatever he is involved with has to do with that base. I'm sorry, I know it's not much."

"It's a lot, all I need now." I folded the paper and put it away. "What next."

"We should have identification documents by tonight. They are expensive but real. Issued by one of the smaller duchies that needs the foreign exchange. So I can ship out on any spacer I want to. As long as the League agents don't recognize me. But I've managed to bribe my way onto a trade delegation that made their flight arrangements months ago. One of them has been well paid to get ill."

"When do you leave?"

"Midnight," she said in a very quiet voice.

"No! So soon . . ."

"I felt the same way—which is why I am leaving. I am not the kind of person that gets tied down in a relationship, Jimmy."

"I don't know what you mean."

"Good. Then I am getting away before you find out."

This sort of conversation was all very new and confusing. I am reluctantly forced to admit that up until the previous evening my contact with the opposite sex had been, shall we say, more distant. Now I was at an unaccustomed loss for words, indecisive and more than a little bewildered. When I blurted this out Bibs had nodded in apparent complete understanding. I realized now that there was an awful lot I did not know about women, a mountain of knowledge I might never acquire.

"My plans aren't that fixed. . ." I started to say, but she silenced me with a warm finger to my lips.

"Yes they are. And you're not going to change them on my account. You seemed very certain this morning about what you felt you had to do."

"And I am still certain," I said firmly, with more firmness and certainty than I felt. "The bribe to get me over to Nevenkebla was taken?"

"Doubled before accepted. If you are going to go missing then old Grbonja will never be permitted to go ashore there again. But he has been ready to retire for years. The bribe is just the financial cushion he needs."

"What does he do?"

"Exports fruit and vegetables. You'll go along as one of his laborers. He won't be punished if you get away from the market—but they will take away his landing pass. He won't mind."

"When do I get to see him?"

"We go to his warehouse tonight, after dark."

"Then . . ."

"I leave you there. Are you hungry?"

"We just ate."

"That is not what I mean," she answered in a very husky voice.

The dark streets were lit only by occasional torches at the corners, the air heavy with menace. We walked in silence; perhaps everything that might be said had already been said. I had bought a sharp dagger which hung at my waist, and another club that I slammed against a wall occasionally to be sure any watchers knew it was there. All too soon we reached our destination, for Bibs knocked on a small gate let into a high wall. There were some whispered words and the gate creaked open. I could smell the sweetness of fruit all about us as we threaded through the dark mounds, to the lamplit corner where an elderly man slumped in a chair. He was all gray beard and gray hair to his waist, where the hair spread out over a monstrous paunch held up by spindly legs. One eye was covered by a cloth wound round his head, but the other looked at me closely as I came up.

"This is the one you are taking," Bibs said.

"Does he speak Esperanto?"

"Like a native," I said.

"Give me the money now." He held out his hand.

"No. You'll just leave him behind. Ploveci will give it to you after you land."

"Let me see it then." He turned his beady eye on me and I realized that I was Ploveci. I took out the leathern bag, spread the coins out on my hands, then put them back into the bag. Grbonja grunted what I assumed was a sign of assent. I felt a breeze on my neck and wheeled about.

The gate was just closing. Bibs was gone.

"You can sleep here," he said pointing to a heap of tumbled sacks against the wall. "We load and leave at dawn."

When he left he took the lamp with him. I looked into the darkness, toward the closed gate.

I had little choice in the matter. I sat on the sacks with my back to the wall, the club across my legs and thought about what I was doing, what I had done, what we had done, what I was going to do, and about the conflicting emotions that washed back and forth through my body. This was apparently too much thinking because the next thing I knew I was blinking at the sunlight coming through the opening door, my face buried in the sacks and my club beside me on the floor. I scrambled up, felt for the money—still there—and was just about ready for what the day would bring. Yawning and stretching the stiffness from my muscles. Reluctantly.

The large door was pulled wider and I saw now that it opened onto a wharf with the fog-covered ocean beyond. A sizable sailing vessel was tied up there and Grbonja was coming down the gangway from the deck.

"Ploveci, help them load," he ordered and passed on.

A scruffy gang of laborers followed him into the warehouse and seized up filled sacks from the pile closest to the door. I couldn't understand a word they said, nor did I need to. The work was hot, boring, and exhausting, and consisted simply of humping a sack from the warehouse to the ship, then returning for another. There was some pungent vegetable in the sacks that soon had my eyes running and itching. I was the only one who seemed to mind. There was no nonsense about breaks either. We carried the sacks until the ship was full, and only then did we drop down in the shade and dip into a bucket of weak beer. It had foul wooden cups secured to it by thongs and after a single, fleeting moment of delicacy I seized one up, filled and emptied it, filled and drank from it once again.

Grbonja reappeared, as soon as the work was done, and gurgled what were obviously orders. The longshoremen became sailors, pulled in the gangplank, let go the lines and ran up the sail. I stood to one side and fondled my club until Grbonja ordered me into the cabin and out of sight. He joined me there a few moments later.

"I'll take the money now," he said.

"Not quite yet, grandpop. You get it when I am safely ashore, as agreed."

"They must not see me take it!"

"Fear not. Just stand close to the top of the gangplank and I will stumble against you. When I'm gone you will find the bag tucked into your belt. Now tell me what I will find when I get ashore."

"Trouble!" he wailed and raked his fingers through his beard. "I should never have gotten involved. They will catch you, kill you, me too . . ."

"Relax, look at this." I held the money bag in the beam of light from the grating above and let the coins trickle between my fingers. "A happy retirement, a place in the country, a barrel of beer and a plate of porkchops every day, think of all the joys this will bring."

He thought and the sight of the clinking coins had great calming affect. When his fingers had stopped shaking I gave him a handful of money which he clutched happily.

"There. A downpayment to show that we are friends. Now think about this—the more I know about what I will find when I get ashore the easier it will be for me to get away. You won't be involved. Now . . . speak."

"I know little," he mumbled, most of his attention on the shining coins. "There are the docks, the market behind.

40

All surrounded by a high wall. I have never been past the wall."

"Are there gates?"

"Yes, large ones, but they are guarded."

"Is the market very large?"

"Gigantic. It is the center of trade for the entire country. It stretches for many myldyryow along the coast."

"How big is a *myldyryow?*"

"*Myldyr, myldyryow* is plural. One of them is seven hundred *lathow.*"

"Thanks. I'll just have to see for myself."

Grbonja, with much grunting and gasping, threw open a hatch in the deck and vanished below, undoubtedly to hide the coins I had given him. I realized then that I had had enough of the cabin so I went out on deck, up to the bow where I would not be under foot. The sun was burning off the morning haze and I saw that we were passing close to an immense tower that rose up from the water. It was scarred, ancient, certainly centuries old. They had built well in those days. The mist lifted and revealed more and more of the structure, stretching up out of sight. I had to lean back to see the top, high, high above.

With the remains of the fractured bridge hanging from it. The once-suspended roadway hung crumpled and broken, dipping down into the ocean close by. Rusted, twisted, heaped with the broken supporting cables which were over two meters thick. I wondered what catastrophe had brought it down.

Or had it been deliberate? Had the rulers of Nevenkebla destroyed it to cut themselves free from the continent that was slowly sinking back into barbarism? A good possibility. And if they had done this they showed a firmness of mind that made my penetration of their island that much more difficult.

Before I could worry about this a more immediate threat presented itself. A lean, gray ship bristling with guns came thundering up from ahead. It cut across our bow and turned sharply around our stern; our sailing ship bobbed in its wake and the sails flapped. I emulated the sailors and tried to ignore the deadly presence, the pointed weapons that could blow us

41

out of the water in an instant. We were here on legitimate business—weren't we?

The gunboat's commander must have believed this as well because, with an insulting blare on their horn, the vessel changed course again and blasted away across the sea. When the ship had dwindled into the distance one of the sailors shook his fist after them and said something bitter and incomprehensible that I agreed with completely.

Nevenkebla rose out of the mists ahead. Cliffs and green hills backing an immense, storied city that rose up from a circular harbor. Factories and mineheads beyond, plumes of smoke from industry already busy in the early morning. And forts at the water's edge, great guns gleaming. Another fort at the end of the seawall as we entered the harbor. I could feel the glare of suspicious eyes behind the gunsights as the black mouths of the barrels followed us as we passed. These guys were not kidding.

And I was going to tackle this entire country single-handed?

"Sure you are, Jim," I said aloud with great braggadocio, swinging my club so that it whistled in tight arcs. "You'll show them. They don't stand a chance against fighting Jimmy diGriz."

Which would have been fine if my voice had not cracked as I said it.

CHAPTER 5

"Down sails," an amplified voice roared. "Take our line aboard."
A high-prowed tug came chuntering up with its loudhailer
bellowing. Grbonja swiftly translated the commands to the crew.

Nothing was left to chance in Nevenkebla: all matters were
highly organized. Even before the sail was down we were secured
safely to the tug and being towed to our berth at the crowded
wharfside. Sailing craft of interesting variety and form were
already unloading cargo there. We were moved into a vacant
berth among the others.

"They come long ways," Grbonja wheezed, stumbling up
beside me, pointing at the other ships. "From Penpilick,
Grampound, even Praze-an-Beeble—may everyone there suffer
from a lifetime of *dysesya!* Tie up outside harbor at night. You
give me the money now, too dangerous on shore!"

"A deal's a deal, grandpop. Too late to back out now."

He sweated and muttered and looked at the land coming close.
"I go ahead first, talk to freightmaster. Only then we unload.
They take your papers and give you dock badge. After that you
will see me. Give me the money."

"No sweat. Just keep your mind on the sunny future of happy
retirement."

Two armed guards glowered down at us as we tied up. A
steam winch dropped the gangway into place and Grbonja

43

puffed up the incline and onto the dock. To turn me in? Maybe I should have paid him in advance? My heart gave a few quick thuds as it shifted into worry mode.

In a few minutes—or was it centuries?—Grbonja had returned and was shouting instructions at the crew. I left my club in the cabin and put the dagger inside my shirt where it couldn't be seen. My lockpick and remaining coins were in a pouch inside my shirt as well. I was ready as I was ever going to be. When I came out of the cabin the sailors were already starting to unload. I picked up a bag and followed the others up the gangway. Each of them held out his identity papers: I did the same. As they reached the dock the officer there took each man's papers and stuffed them into a box. Then pinned an identification tag to the man's clothes. He looked bored by the job. I tried not to tremble as I came up to him.

It was just routine. "Next," he called out, whipped the papers from my hand and pinned the tag to my chest. Or rather pinned it through the fabric into my skin. I jumped but kept my mouth shut. He grinned, with a touch of sadism in the turn of his mouth, and pushed me on.

"Keep moving, lunkhead. Next."

I was safely ashore and undetected. Following the bent back of the man ahead of me into the dark warehouse. Grbonja was standing by the growing pile of sacks. When he saw me he called out an incomprehensible instruction and pointed to the next bay.

"The money, now," he burbled as I dumped the sack. I slipped it to him and he staggered away muttering with relief. I looked around at the solid cement and steel walls and went back for another sack.

By the time I had carried in my third sack I was getting desperate. After a few more trips the ship would be unloaded and that would be the end of that. I would have had an expensive round trip and done some hard work. Nothing more. Because I could see no way out of the building—and no place to hide within it. They obviously did not relish uninvited visitors to Nevenkebla. I needed more time.

"Call a beer break," I whispered to Grbonja as I passed him at the head of the gangway. The checker-inner had gone but the

44

two unsmiling guards still stood watch.

"We never stop—it is not the custom."

"It is today. It's a hot day. You don't want me to tell them you were hired to smuggle me here?"

He groaned aloud, then called out. "Beer, we stop for beer!"

The crew asked no questions at this unexpected treat, only chattered together with pleasure as they gathered round the barrel. I had a good slug of the stuff then went and sat on the gunwhale beside the gangway. Looked up at the boots of the guard who stood above me. Looked down at the water and saw the space between the pilings there.

My only chance. The guard above me moved out of sight. Grbonja had his back turned while the sailors had their attention focused on the barrel. A difference of opinion over the rationing appeared to break out. There were angry shouts and a quick blow. The crew watched these proceedings with great interest. No one was visible on the dock above.

I dropped a length of line over the side, swung my legs over and climbed down it. No one saw me go. With my legs in the sea I used my dagger to cut the line above my head and dropped silently into the water. With noiseless strokes I swam into the darkness under the pier.

Slime-covered boards connected the wooden piles. When I reached for one of them something squealed and vanished in the darkness. And it stank down here. Nameless rubbish bobbed in the water around me. I was beginning to regret my impetuous swim.

"Chin up, Jim, and move along. This is the first place they look when they find out you are missing."

I swam. Not far, for there was a solid wall here that ran back into the darkness. I groped along it until I reached the outer piles again. Through the openings between them I saw the hull of another sailing ship, tied close. There was no room to pass between the planks of the ship and the piles. Trapped so soon?!

"This is your day for panic," I whispered aloud, the sound of my voice covered by the slapping of the waves. "You can't go back, so carry on you must. The hull of this ship has to curve

45

away. Just dive down and swim along it until you find another opening between the piles."

Ho-ho. Sounded very easy to do. I kicked my boots off and breathed deep. But my trepidition grew with each shuddering breath that I drew in. When my head was swimming with oxygen intoxication I let out the last lungful and dived.

It was a long, dark and apparently endless swim. I ran my left hand along the ship's hull to guide me. Collecting some heroic splinters at the same time. On and on with no glimmer of light in front or above. This must be a very big ship. There was fire in my lungs and desperation in my swimming before I saw light ahead. I came up as quietly as I could by the ship's bow. Trying not to gasp as I exhaled and drew in life and fresh air.

Looking up at a sailor standing on the rail above, turning towards me.

I sank out of sight again, forcing myself deep under the water, swimming on with my lungs crying out for air, until I saw the black bulk of the next ship ahead of me, forcing myself to swim on to the last glimmer of light before floating up the surface again.

Catching my head nicely between hull and piling, to fight down the rising panic as I fought to free myself—getting some splinters in my scalp this time. My groping fingers found a gap between the pilings so I surfaced there, hung on, sucked in lungful after lungful of the stinking fug, enjoying it more than the freshest air I had ever breathed.

This was the beginning of a very long and very tiring day. I did not keep track of the number of ships I passed, but it was a lot. At first I searched under the various docks but soon gave that up since they were all the same, each firmly separated by an underwater wall from the next. Some of the ships had finished unloading and had left, for I came to gaps in the continuous wall of vessels. All I could do when this happened was to breath deep, dive deep—and swim like crazy to reach the next ship before my breath ran out.

It was afternoon before I reached the last ship and the end of the docks. The tide was ebbing, the vessels were now down

46

below the dock level so there was more concealment from above. I was very tired but very proficent by this time. One more time I breathed deep, dove down at the bow, swam the length of the hull and surfaced in the shadow of the rudder.

To look at a solid wall of jointed stone stretching out before me.

Holding onto the rudder, my eyes just above the surface, I peered around it. And realized that I was looking at the harbor wall that stretched unbroken out to the fort built at its far end. I drew back into the shadow of the rudder and found that my heart was sinking so fast it was pulling me under the water.

"Any bright ideas, Jim?" I asked, then found that I was waiting a long time for an answer.

Think, don't despair I ordered myself. I still felt despair. Could I go back? No, that was out. After all I had gone through today I was not going to surrender that easily. Hide under one of the docks? Possibly. But they would be thoroughly searched as soon as I was missed, I was certain of that. What else? Climb up onto the dock? No way. The warehouses here were sure to be as barren of hiding places as the one I had left. Then what?

"Turn the problem on its head, that's what The Bishop had always said."

What would that be in this situation? I was trying to get away from the soldiers, fleeing them, knowing they would be looking for me. So I should go to them. But that would be suicide. But where could I possibly go that would be totally unexpected?

Why, the fort on the end of the harbor wall of course.

"Without a doubt the most insane idea you have ever had," I muttered in disgust, peering around the rudder again. Above me there were shouted oaths from the sailors and the thud of feet on planking. I had the feeling that this ship would be leaving soon as well, taking my protection with it. The solid stone blocks of the jetty stretched unbroken to the fort at the end. Some debris washed against the stone and sea birds fought over the edible bits. Other than that—nothing. No cover at all. If I tried to swim out there I would be seen at once by anyone who glanced that way. Above me tackle creaked as the sail was lifted; the ship was getting under way.

I had to get clear of it—or did I? No tug had appeared. Was it possible the ships were only towed into harbor? That they permitted them to sail out on their own? It was. I peered around the rudder again and saw two of the cargo vessels standing out toward the entrance. Light poured down from the growing gap above me and I sank under the surface before I could be seen.

It was not easy—but it could be done. I held tight to the rudder as it came over, almost pulling itself out of my hands. I stayed under the surface as long as I could so I would not be seen from the shore. The sailing ship was moving along smoothly and it took all my strength to shift my grip from the front to the back of the rudder. Holding on was easier now. When I finally was forced to lift my face up to breathe I found myself in a rush of foam, inhaled some and fought not to cough. As we drew away from the dockside I saw an armed guard there. His back turned with indifference.

It was almost easy after that. The rush of the waves held me against the rudder post. I breathed easily with my head out of the water, unseen from the shore and invisible to anyone on the deck above. We tacked twice and each time I changed sides to keep the rudder between me and the fort that was now growing larger and larger ahead. When we went about for the last time I saw that this tack would take us close to the fort and past it on into the open ocean. I watched as the stone wall came closer and closer until I could see the sea beyond the end of it. Only then did I take a last breath, let go and dive deep.

Yes, I was tired. But this should also be my final little swim for the day so I wanted to make it a good one. The seaweed-covered harbor wall was clear ahead, the end rounded where it met the open ocean. There was a strong swell coming in that I had to fight against, swimming close to the stone where its force was weakest. Farther and farther until I had to breathe or inhale water. Floating up to the bright surface and through it, looking up at the stone wall with the projecting gun barrels above. Holding on against the waves and breathing deep. Clutching into the cracks between the stones and working my way around to the far side until I could peer down its unbroken length at the shore beyond. Pleasure craft dotted the water here, power and sail, and I would certainly be seen if I tried to swim its length. Then what? I couldn't stay here in the water where I could be seen by any passing ship. I looked up at the great stone blocks and thought.

Why not? The only ships in sight now where vanishing seaward. At the outermost swell of the fort I could not be seen from the shore. And the space between stones provided ample grip for toe and finger. So climb.

Climb I did. It was not easy—but I had little choice. Up the vertical wall, scrabbling and clinging, midway between two of the largest seaward-facing guns. They projected through embrasures in the solid wall, shining steel, polished and deadly. I clung on and rested when I reached their level, the heaving surface of the sea a good ten meters below. The ocean was still empty—but for how long?

"Give me a light, will you Jim?"

I started so hard I almost lost my grip and fell back into the water.

Fragrant cigar smoke blew over me and I realized it was coming from the gun embrasure close by. I hadn't been seen, no one here knew my name. It had just been coincidence. The gunners were there, that close, looking seaward and smoking on duty which I was sure was frowned upon strongly. I did not dare move. I could only hold on and listen.

"This new captain, he has got to go."

"He is the worst. Poison in his coffee?"

"No. I heard they did that up north and they decimated the entire regiment. You know, shot one guy out of ten."

"That is the real old cagal and you know it. Nothing but cagal-house rumor. Like fragging. Everyone talks about it, no one does it . . ."

"Captain coming!"

A cigar butt sailed by my head and there was the quick slap of retreating feet. I climbed again, before my arms came out of their sockets. Forcing myself up the last few centimeters until I reached the edge and hauled myself painfully onto the flat roof of the fort. A seabird cocked a cold eye at me, screeched and flapped off. I crawled slowly across the sun-baked bird

49

droppings of centuries, to the very center of the round building. I lay flat on my back and could see nothing but sky and the top of a distant hill. This meant that in turn I could not be discovered except from the air. I would chance that, since I had seen only one distant aircraft the entire day. I closed my eyes against the glare of the sun and instantly, without intending to, fell sound asleep.

I awoke with a start and a rapidly beating heart. A cloud had crossed the face of the sun and I was chilled in my wet clothes. It had been stupid, falling asleep like that, yet I had gotten away with it. I had not been seen. The sun was closer to the horizon and since I had been safe here so far I might still be safe until dark.

And hungry and thirsty. The demands of the body are insatiable, always after something. But this time it was going to be mind over matter and I was going to stay on the roof, unmoving, until nightfall.

Which was slow in coming. I smacked my dry lips and ignored the angry rumblings in my gut. The suns always set. It was just a matter of patience.

Dusk finally crept over the land, the first stars came out as it slowly grew dark. Lights came on in the fort below and I could hear the hoarse shouting of military orders. Very slowly I crawled to the inner edge and peered over. Into a courtyard where some sort of maneuver was being engaged in. Soldiers marched back and forth in little groups with much screeching from the officers. Eventually one group entered the fort and the other marched back toward the land along the broad top of the harbor wall, their way lit by evenly spaced lights. They got smaller and smaller in the distance until they reached the distant shore and vanished from sight.

Then all of the lights went out.

I lay, blinking into the sudden darkness, and could not believe my good luck. Had the lights been extinguished to enable me to sneak safely ashore? Probably not. There were guns below and if they meant to use them, as they obviously did, the gunners would not want to be blinded by their own lights. Good thinking, guys!

50

I waited until I could see my way by starlight, then climbed down the outside wall to the rail around the courtyard, stepped carefully onto it and down onto the stone flagging. A single door in the wall was sealed and silent. On tiptoe I scuttled landward as fast as I could. The dark bulk of the fort grew small behind me and I strolled more easily, resisting the impulse to whistle with pleasure. The dark forms of the pleasure boats were visible off to the left. There were lights in the cabins of a few of them and I heard distant laughter across the water. I relaxed, strolled, the rough stone cool beneath my bare feet. I had the world to myself and safety lay close ahead.

Then I ran headlong into the metal fencing that cut off the top of the harbor wall and all the lights came on in a searing blaze of illumination. Lights stretching ahead and behind, lights above revealing the wire fence and sealed metal door in front of me.

CHAPTER 6

I bounced back from the wire, looked around wildly, hurled myself flat on the wall waiting for the sound of shots.

But nothing happened. The lights burned down brightly; the harbor wall behind me stretched emptily back to the fort. On the other side of the barrier the wall extended as far as the warehouses above the harbor where more lights revealed a small marching group. Coming towards me.

Had I been seen—or was I invisible in the shadows? Or had I triggered some alarm that turned on the lights and revealed my presence? Whatever had happened there was no point in my waiting around in order to find out. I crawled quickly to the outer edge of the wall facing the ocean—I had had enough swimming in the harbor, thank you—and dangled my legs backward over the edge. Groped with my bare feet for a toehold on the rough stone. Found one and eased myself down into the darkness. The tide was coming in again and my legs were engulfed by the sea. Above me on top of the wall the tramping feet grew louder. Below me the water was cold, black and unattractive.

Why didn't I just stay here out of sight until they had gone by above?

As soon as this cowardly thought had trickled through the synapses of my brain I recognized it for the dumb idea that it was. A flick of a flashlight and my presence would be revealed. I had not gone through all of the strenuous efforts and dangers of the day to be grabbed now because I was afraid of getting wet. Or eaten by unseen monsters. The ocean here must be safe or the fleets of pleasure craft would not have been drifting around all day.

"Swimmies, Jim, swimmies," I muttered and slid down into the sea.

By the time the soldiers had reached the gate I was treading water well away from the wall, ready to dive instantly if they pointed any lights my way. They didn't. I could see one of them unlocking the gate, then relocking it again after they had all passed through. Then they all marched on again. A relief party, surprise inspection perhaps, or some other uninteresting military maneuver. I turned about and began to swim toward shore.

What next? The lights of a promenade grew closer and my problem grew bigger. How was I a barefoot, sodden stranger with no knowledge of this land whatsoever, how was I to go ashore and make my way about unnoticed? Not easily, that was obvious. A dark shape came between me and the lights. A craft of some kind. Salvation of some kind?

I swam slowly between the moored pleasure boats. In the distance I could see that some of them were illuminated, but only darkness prevailed here. Were they occupied? They didn't appear to be; it was too early for any occupants to be asleep. Which hopefully meant that the jolly sportsmen had gone ashore after a strenuous day at play.

A thin mast moved against the stars. A sailboat, a small one. I wanted something larger. I swam on until a darker form rose up above me. No masts, which meant that it was a powered craft of some kind. I swam alongside it to the stern, where my groping fingers found the ladder that was secured there. Rung by rung I climbed, dripping, out of the sea and into the craft. There was enough light from the stars and the illumination along the shore to make out cushioned seats, a wheel—and a door that might lead below. I went to it, found the handle and tried to turn it. Locked.

"Good news indeed, Jim. If it is locked there is something here worth stealing. Best to look and see."

I did. Darkness is no handicap for an efficient locksmith. I felt out the tumblers of a very simple lock with delicate touches of my lockpick. Lifted them aside and pushed the door open.

What followed was slow work. If there were lights I did not want to turn them on. I did it all by touch. But there is a certain logic to any small craft that must be followed. Berths in the bow along the hull. Lockers below, shelves above. After a good deal of rattling, fumbling, head-banging and cursing I gathered my treasures in a blanket and took them up on deck and spread them out.

What had felt like a bottle with a screwcap was a bottle with a screwcap. Which I unscrewed and sniffed. Then dipped in a finger and tasted. A very sweet wine. Not my normal tipple, but paradisical after all the sea water I had swallowed. There was a metal box with stale bread or biscuits of some kind that almost broke my teeth. They softened a bit when I poured wine over them, then wolfed them down. I belched deeply and felt better.

I groped through the rest of my loot. There were books and boxes, unidentifiable forms, and strange shapes. And clothing. A very sheer skirt that was just not my thing. But other sartorial items were. I sorted out all of the other bits that appeared to be clothing not instantly identifiable as being intended for the fairer sex, stripped and tried some of it on. I had no idea of how well they matched, but it was an outfit of sorts. The trousers were too large by far, but a length of line in place of a belt took care of that. The shirt was a better fit, and if the jacket came down to my knees perhaps it was intended to be that length. The shoes were too big but stayed on my feet after I had stuffed cloth into their toes. It was the best I could do. Then I undressed and put my own wet clothing back on, put my new outfit into the can the bread had been in, wrapped this in turn in what I hoped was waterproof plastic.

The air was beginning to be chill and it was time to get moving. I was tired, slowed down by the exertions of the day and badly in need of some sleep. I wasn't going to get any. I

54

finished the wine, put the empty bottle and everything else I had removed back into the cabin, then relocked the door. Before I could change my mind I put the bundle on my head and slipped over the side.

The shore was close and the beach empty as far as I could see. Which was a major blessing since swimming with one hand while balancing a can of clothing on the head with the other is not an exercise to be recommended. I emerged from the sea and scuttled to the shelter of some large rocks, stripped and buried my unwanted clothing in the sand. I quickly dressed in the dry clothes, tucked my small bag of possessions into my belt, slipped my dagger into the side of my shoe and I was ready to conquer the world.

I really wanted only to find a quiet place to curl up for a nap—but knew better. These people took their security seriously and the shore was their first line of defense as the fort had proved. I must get into the city itself.

There were lights on the promenade above, the sound of voices, but shadow below where I moved in silence. A flight of stairs rose up from the beach. I rose up as well—but dropped back again even more swiftly at the sight of two uniformed and armed men close by. I lurked and counted backward from two hundred before I peeked again. The uniforms were gone and there were just a few evening strollers in sight. I merged and strolled and took the first turning that led away from the shore. There were street lights here, open windows and locked doors. My clothing must not have looked too garish for a couple passed without even glancing my way. I heard music ahead and soon came to a bar over which a sign proclaimed DANCING AND DRINKING—COME AND GET STINKING. An invitation almost impossible to resist. I pushed the door open and went in.

There is a power that shapes the bars of this universe. There has to be because form follows function. Function: to get containers of alcoholic beverages to people. Form: chairs to sit in, tables to rest containers on. I entered, pulled out a chair and sat at a vacant table. The other occupants ignored me just as I ignored them. A plump waitress in a short skirt came toward me, ignoring the whistles from the group of youths at the next table, skilfully avoiding their snapping fingers as well.

"Whadilitbe?" she asked, flaring her nostrils at them as they raised beer mugs in her direction and toasted her loudly.

"Beer," I said and she moved off. When it came it was pungent and cold. She made her own change from the coins I had spread on the table, this seemed to be the local custom, then went back behind the bar.

I drank deep and wiped the foam from my mouth just as another young man came through the door and hurried to the adjoining table.

"*Porkaĉoj!*" he whispered hoarsely. Two of the youths stumbled to their feet and hurried toward the rear of the bar.

I put down my beer, scraped up my coins, and hurried after them. There was trouble here, though I did not know what kind. What he had said could be translated as bad-pigs, and must surely be local slang since I did not imagine some mucky swine were on their way. Pigs as an epithet for police is a common usage—and the reactions of the two men seemed to bear this out. And I would lose nothing by being cautious. They hurried down a hallway and when I reached it a door at the far end was just closing. I had my hand on its knob when a loud siren sounded from the other side and a glare of illumination shone in through the cracks between door and frame.

"What's this?" a coarse and loud voice said. "You boys maybe slipping out through the backdoor because we got a patrol out front? Let's see your identification."

"We've done nothing wrong!"

"You've done nothing right so far. C'mon, the ID."

I waited, unmoving, hoping the bad-pig outside was not joined by his stymates from the bar. The coarse laughter from the other side of the door was anything but humorous.

"Hello, hello—both out of date? Not thinking of avoiding the draft, are you boys?"

"A clerical error," a pale voice whimpered.

"We get a lot like that. Let's go."

The light went away and so did the footsteps. I waited as long as I dared, then opened the door and exited the bar. The

56

alley was empty, pig and prisoners were gone. I went myself, as quickly as I could without running. Then stopped. What was I running from? Once the police had left, the bar would be the safest place in the city for me. I stopped in a dark doorway and looked back at the rear entrance. No one else came out. I counted to three hundred, then to be safe backward again to zero. The door remained closed. Cautiously, ready to flee in an instant, I went back into the bar, peered into the barroom. No police—but the glimmerings of an idea.

The four young men at the table looked up as I came back in, the newcomer sitting at one of the recently vacated seats. I shook my head gloomily and dropped into a chair.

"The *porkaĉoj* got them. Both."

"I told Bil he needed new papers, wouldn't listen to me," the blond one said, the one who had come with the warning. He cracked his knuckles then seized up his beer. "You got to have good papers."

"My papers are out of date," I said gloomily, then waved to the waitress.

"You should have stayed in Pensildelphia then," one of the others said, a spotty youth in an ill-fitting gold and green shirt.

"How did you know I was from Pensildelphia?" I protested. He sneered.

"Rube accent like that, were else you from?"

I sneered back and glowed with pleasure inside. Better and better. I had a peergroup of draft dodgers, one of them who might be working with the police, and a home town. Things were looking up. I buried my nose in my beer.

"You ought to get new ID," the friendly-warner, possible police informer, said. I sniffled.

"Easy to say here. But you can't do it in Pensildelphia."

"Hard to do here too. Unless you got the right contacts."

I stood up. "I gotta go. Nice meeting you guys."

Before leaving I checked to make sure that the police were gone. Then I exited and waited. My new friend came out a moment later and smiled at me.

"Smart. Don't let too many people know what's going on. My label is Jak."

57

"Call me Jim."

"Good a name as any, Jim. How much you got to spend?"

"Not much. I had a bad year."

"I'll put you in touch with the man himself for three sugarlumps. He'll want twenty."

"ID not worth more than ten. You get one-fifty."

"They're not all dumb in the backwoods, are they. Slap it in my hand and we"re on our way."

I paid him his cut and when he turned I put the tip of my knife against his neck just under his ear and pushed just hard enough to break the skin. He stayed absolutely still when I showed him the knife with the fresh drop of blood.

"That is a little warning," I said. "Those pigs were waiting for whoever you flushed out. That's not my worry. My skin is. I got a feeling that you play both sides. Play the right side with me or I will find you and slice you. Understand?"

"Understood . . ." he said gruffly, with a tremor in his voice. I put the knife away and clapped him on the shoulders.

"I like you, Jak. You learn easy."

We went in silence and I hoped that he was making the right conclusions. I don't like threats and when threatened I do the opposite of what I am requested. But my experience of the petty criminal led me to believe that threats tended to work with them. Part of the time.

Our route took us past a number of other bars and Jak looked carefully into each one before going on. He struck paydirt in the fifth one and waved me in after him. This place was dark and smokefilled, with jangling music blasting from all sides. Jak led the way to the rear of the room, to an alcove where the music was not quite as loud, at least not as loud as the striped outfit the fat man was wearing. He leaned back in a heavy chair and sipped at a tiny, poisonous green drink.

"Hello, Captain," my guide said.

"Get dead quickly, Jak. I don't want your kind here."

"Don't say that even funning, Captain. I got good business for you here, a mission of mercy. This grassgreen cutlet is a step ahead of the draft. Needs new ID."

The tiny eyes swiveled toward me. "How much you got, cutlet?"

"Jak says one-fifty for him, ten for you. I already paid him his."

"Jak's a liar. Twelve is the price and I give him his cut."

"You're on."

It was an instant transaction. I gave him the money and he passed over the grubby plastic folder. Inside there was a blurred picture of a youth who could have been anyone my age, along with other vital facts including a birthdate quite different from my own.

"This says that I am only fifteen years old!" I protested.

"You got a baby face. You can get away with it. Drop a few years—or join the army."

"I feel younger already." I pocketed the ID and rose. "Thanks for the help."

"Any time. Long as you got the sugarlumps."

I left the bar, crossed the road and found a dark doorway to lurk in. It was a short wait because Jak came out soon after me and strolled away. I strolled behind him at a slightly faster stroll. I was breathing down his neck before he heard my footsteps and spun about.

"Just me, Jak, don't worry. I wanted to thank you for the favor."

"Yeah, sure, that's all right." He rolled his eyes around at the deserted street.

"You could do me another favor, Jak. Let me see your own ID. I just want to compare it to mine to make sure the Captain didn't give me a ringer."

"He wouldn't do that!"

"Let's make sure." My dagger blade twinkled in the streetlight and he rooted inside his jacket then handed me a folder very much like my own. I turned to look at it under the light, then handed it back. But Jak was the suspicious type. He glanced at it before putting it away—and dropped his jaw prettily.

"This ain't mine—this is yours!"

"That's right. I switched them. You told me that ID was good. So use it."

His cries of protest died behind as I walked uphill away from the shore. To a better neighborhood without a criminal element. I felt very pleased with myself. The ID could have been good—in

59

which case Jak would lose nothing. But if it were faulty in any way it would be his problem, not mine. The biter bit. A very evenhanded solution. And I was going in the right direction. Once away from the waterfront things did get better, the buildings taller, the streets cleaner, the lights brighter. And I got tireder. Another bar beckoned and I responded. Velvet drapes, soft lights, leather upholstery, better-looking waitress. She was not impressed by my clothes, but she was by the tip I passed over when my beer arrived.

I had very little time to enjoy it. This was a well-policed city and the bad-pigs came in pairs. A brace of them waddled in through the door and my stomach slipped closer to the floor. But what was I worrying about? My ID was fine.

They circuited the room, looking at identification, and finally reached my table.

"Good evening, officers," I smarmed.

"Knock off the cagal and let's see it."

I smiled and passed over the folder. The one who opened it widened his nostrils and snorted with pleasure.

"Why look what we got here! This is Jak the joike strolled away from his home turf. That's not nice, Jak."

"It's a free world!"

"Not for you, Jak. We all know about the deal you made with harbor police. Stay there and rat on your friends and you get left alone. But you strayed out of your turf, Jak."

"I'll go back now," I said rising with a sinking feeling.

"Too late," they said in unison as they slapped on the cuffs.

"Far too late," the nostril-flarer said. "You're out of business, Jak, and in the army."

This really was the biter bit. This time I had been just a little too smart for my own good. It looked like my new and exciting military career had just begun.

CHAPTER 7

The cell was small, the bed hard, I had no complaints. After the strenuous day I had just finished, sleep was the only thing that I wanted. I must have been snoring as I fell toward the canvas covers, with no memory of my face ever touching the stained pillow. I slept the sleep of exhaustion and awoke when a gray shaft of light filtered in through the barred window. I felt cheered and rested until I realized where I was. Dark depression fell.

"Well, it could be worse," I said cheerily.

"How?" I snarled dispiritedly. There was no easy answer to that. My stomach rumbled with hunger and thirst and the depression deepened. "Cry-baby," I sneered. "You've had it much worse than this. They took the dagger but nothing else. You have your money, your identification." And the lockpick I added in silence. The presence of that little tool had a warming affect, holding out hope of eventual escape.

"I'm hungry!" a youthful voice cried out and there was a rattling of bars. Others took up the cry.

"Food. We're not criminals!"

"My mom always brought me breakfast in bed . . ."

I was not too impressed by this last wail of complaint but sympathized with the general attitude. I joined the cry.

"All right, all right, shut up," an older and gruffer voice called out. "Chow is on the way. Not that you deserve anything, bunch of draft dodgers."

"Cagal on that sergeant—I don't see your fat chunk in the army."

I looked forward to meeting the last speaker; he showed a little more courage than the rest of the wailers. The wait wasn't too long, though it was scarcely worth it. Cold noodle soup with sweet red beans is not my idea of the way to start the day. I wondered how it would end.

I had plenty of time for wondering because after feeding time in the zoo we were left strictly alone. I stared up at the cracked ceiling and slowly began to realize that my ill fortune wasn't that bad when closely examined. I was alive and well in Nevenkebla. With a promising career ahead of me. I would learn the ropes, find out all I could about this society, maybe even get a lead on Garth—or General Zennor if Bibs had overheard the name correctly. He was in the army and I would very soon be in the army, which fact might work to my advantage. And I had the lockpick. When the right moment came I could do a little vanishing act. And how bad could the army be? I had been a soldier on Spiovente, which training should come in handy . . .

Oh, how we do fool ourselves.

Somewhere around midday, when my cowardly peer group were beginning to howl for more nourishment, the crash of opening cell doors began. The howls changed to cries of complaint as we were ordered from our cells and cuffed wrist to wrist in a long daisychain. About a dozen of us, similar of age and gloomy of mein. The unknown future lay darkly ahead. With much stumbling and curses we were led from the cell block to the prison compound where a barred vehicle waited to transport us to our destiny. It moved away silently after we had been herded aboard, battery or fuel cell powered, out into the crowded city streets. Clothes were slightly different, vehicles of unusual shapes, but it could have been any world of advanced technology. No wonder they had cut themselves off from the rest of this decadent planet. Selfish—but understandable.

62

No effete amenities like seats were provided for hardened criminals: so we clutched to the bars and swayed into each other at the turns. A thin, dark-haired youth secured to my left wrist sighed tremulously, then turned to me.

"How long you been on the run?" he asked.

"All my life."

"Very funny. I've had six months since my birthday, six short months. Now it's all over."

"You're not dying—just going into the army."

"What's the difference? My brother got drafted last year. He smuggled a letter out to me. That's when I decided to run. Do you know what he wrote—?"

His eyes opened wide and he shivered at the memory, but before he could speak our transport slammed to a halt and we were ordered out.

The street scene was one to give joy to the eyes of any sadist. Varying forms of transport had converged on the plaza before the tall building. Emerging from them were young men, hundreds, perhaps thousands of them, all wearing upon their faces a uniform expression of despair. Only our little band was manacled—the rest clutched the yellow draft notices that had dragged them to their destiny. A few of them had the energy to make mock of our manacled state, but they shrunk away under the chorus of our jeers. At least we had made some attempt, no matter how feeble, to escape military impressment. Nor did it appear to make any difference to the authorities. They did not care how they had managed to grab the bodies. Once inside the doors our chains were stripped away and we were herded into line with all the others. The faceless military machine was about to engulf us.

At first it did not seem too bad. The lines of youths crept forward toward desks manned by plump maternal types who might have been our moms or teachers. All of them had gray hair and wore spectacles, which they looked over the tops of when they weren't two-fingeredly hammering their typewriters. I finally reached mine and she smiled up at me.

"Your papers please, young man."

I passed them over and she copied dates and names and incorrect facts into a number of forms. I saw the cable leading from her typewriter to a central computer and knew that everything was being recorded and ingested there as well. I was happy to see the false identity entered; when I un-volunteered I wanted to drop from sight.

"Here you are," she said, and smiled, and passed over a buff file of papers. "You just take these up to the fourth floor. And good luck in your military career."

I thanked her, it would be churlish not to, and started back toward the front doors. A solid line of unsmiling military police blocked any chance of exit.

"Fourth floor," I said as the nearest one eyed me coldly and smacked his club into his palm.

The elevator cars were immense, big enough to take forty of us at a time. Nor did they leave until they were full. Jammed and miserable we rose to the fourth floor where a little taste of what awaited us awaited us. As the doors sighed open a military figure, all stripes and decorations, medals and red face came roaring toward us.

"Get out! Get out! Don't stand around like a bunch of poofters! Move it! Snap cagal or you'll be in the cagal. Take a box and a small transparent bag from the counter on the right as you pass. Then go to the far end of this room where you will UNDRESS. That means take all of your clothes off. AND I MEAN ALL OF YOUR CLOTHES! Your personal effects will go into the plastic bag which you will keep in your left hand at all times. All of your clothing will go into the box which you will take to the counter at the far end where it will be sealed and addressed and sent to your home. Where you will retrieve it after the war, or it will be buried with you, whichever comes first. Now MOVE!"

We moved. Unenthusiastically and reluctantly—but we had no choice. There must be a nudity taboo in this society because the youths spread out, trying to get close to the walls, huddled over as they stripped off their clothes. I found myself alone in the center of the room enjoying the scowled attention of the stripe-bearing monster: I quickly joined the others. So reluctant

64

were they to reveal their shrinking flesh that dawdle as I might I was still first to the counter. Where a bored soldier seized my box and quickly sealed it, slammed it down before me and pointed to thick pens hung from the ceiling on elastic cords.

"Name-address-postcode-nearest-relative."

The words, empty of meaning through endless repetition, rolled out as he turned to seize up the next box. I scrawled the address of the police station where we had been held and when I released the pen the countertop opened and the box vanished. Very efficient. Plastic bag in left hand, folder in my right I joined the shivering group of pallid, naked young men who hung their heads as they waited their next orders. With their clothes gone all differences of identity seemed to have fled as well.

"You will now proceed to the eighteenth floor!" was the bellowed command. We proceeded. Into the elevator, forty at a time, doors closed, doors opened—into a vision of a sort of medical hell.

A babble of sound, shouts for attention, screamed orders. Doctors and medical orderlies garbed in white, many with cloth masks over their faces, poked and prodded in a mad mirror-image of medical practice. Senses blurred as event ran into event.

A physician—that is I assume he was a physician since he wore a stethoscope around his neck—seized my folder, threw it to an orderly, then clutched me by the throat. Before I could seize him by the throat in return he shouted at the orderly.

"Thyroid, normal." The orderly made an entry as he squeezed my stomach wall.

"Hernias, negative. Cough."

This last was an order to me and I coughed as his rubber-clad fingers probed deep.

There was more, but only the highlights stand out.

The urinalysis section where we stood in shivering ranks, each holding a recently-filled paper cup. Our file slowly wending forward, on tiptoe for the floor was aslosh, to the white-clad, white-masked, booted and rubber-gloved orderly who dipped a disposable dropper into each cup, dropped a drop into a section of a large, sectioned chemical tray. Discarded the dropper into

65

an overflowing container, eyed the chemical reaction. Shouted "Negative, next!" and carried on.

Or the hemorrhoidal examination. Good taste forbids too graphic a description, but it did involve rows of youths bent over and clutching their ankles while a demonic physician crouched over as well and ran along behind the rows with a pointed flashlight.

Or the injections, ahh, yes the injections. As this particular line crept forward I became aware that the youth in front of me was a bodybuilder of some sort. Among the pipestem arms and knocking knees his bronzed biceps and polished pects stood out as a monument to masculinity. He turned to me with a worried expression on the knotted muscles of his face.

"I don't like needles," he said.

"Who does," I agreed.

Not nice at any time, positively threatening in mass attack. I watched, horrified, as I approached the point of no return. As each shivering body came into position an orderly on each side injected each upper arm. No sooner were the needles hurled aside than the victim was pushed in the back by the uniformed supervising brute. After tottering a few paces forward two more injections were made. Arms curled with pain the subject leaned on the nearby counter. Where he was vaccinated. Very efficient.

Too efficient for the weightlifter. As he stepped into position his eyes rolled up and he slumped unconscious to the floor. This, however, was no obstacle to military efficiency. Two needles flashed, two injections were made. The sergeant seized him by the feet and dragged him forward where, after receiving the rest of his injections, he was rolled aside to recover. I gritted my teeth, tried stoically to accept the puncturing barrage, and sighed.

At some point the mass medical examination ended with a final assault on whatever shards of personal dignity the victims might still have left. Still nude, still clutching our plastic bags in our left hands, our thickening folders in our right, we shuffled forward in yet one more line. A row of numbered desks stretched across the width of the room, very much like the reception hall of an airport. Behind each desk sat a dark-suited gent. When it

66

was my turn the sergeant-herdsman glanced over his shoulder and stabbed a stumpy figure at me.

"You, haul it to number thirteen."

The man behind the desk wore thick-framed glasses, as did all of the others I noticed. Perhaps our eyes were going to be examined and this was what we would be like if we failed. My folder was seized yet one more time, another printed sheet inserted—and I found tiny red eyes glaring at me through the thick lenses.

"Do you like girls, Jak?"

The question was completly unexpected. Yet it prompted a sweet vision of Bibs that obscured the medical mockery around me.

"You bet I like girls," was my instant response. An entry was made.

"Do you like boys?"

"Some of my best friends are boys." I began to have a glimmering of what this simpleton was up to.

"Are they?" Slash of pencil. Then, "Tell me about your first homosexual experience."

My jaw fell with disbelief. "I can't believe that I'm hearing this. You are doing a psychiatric examination from a *checklist?*"

"Don't give me any cagal, kid," he snarled. "Just answer the question."

"Your medical degree should be taken away for incompetence—if you ever had one. You're probably not a shrink at all, just a time-server dressed like one."

"Sergeant!" he shouted in a cracked voice, his skin flushing. There was a thunder of feet behind me. "This draftee is refusing to cooperate."

Sharp pain slashed the backs of my bare legs and I Yowed! and jumped aside. The sergeant raised the thin cane again and licked his lips.

"That will do for the moment," my examiner said. "If my questions are answered correctly."

"Yes, sir," I said, snapping to attention. "No need to repeat the question. "My first experience of that kind was at the age of twelve when, with the aid of large rubber bands, I and fourteen other boys . . ."

I continued on in this vein while he scribbled happily and the sergeant muttered with frustration and waddled away. When the form had been completed with the last work of fiction, I was released and ordered on to join the others. It was back to the elevators again, jammed inside in nude groups of forty. The doors closed for the descent. The doors opened.

At what was obviously the wrong floor. Before our horrified eyes there was displayed a vista of desks and typewriters. With a young lady laboring away at each of them. There was a fluttering sound as all of the folders were swung forward over the vitals. The air temperture rose as everyone turned bright red. All we could do was stand there in carmined embarrassment, listening to the endless rattle of typewriter keys, waiting for heads to turn, gentle female eyes to peer our way. After about fourteen and a half years the doors slowly closed again.

There were no females present when the doors opened this time, just the now-familiar form of another brutish sergeant. I wondered what twisted gene in the population had produced so many thick-necked, narrow-browed, pot-bellied sado-masochists.

"Out," this one bellowed. "Out, out, groups of ten, first ten through that door. Next ten next door. Not eleven! Can't you count, cagal-head!" Followed by a yipe of pain as discipline was enforced yet again. My ten victims shuffled into a brightly lit room and were ordered into line. We faced a white wall that was hung with a repulsive puce-green flag distastefully decorated with a black hammer. An officer with little golden bars on his shoulder strutted in an stood before the flag.

"This is a very important occasion," he said in a voice heavy with importance. And occasion. "You young men, the fittest in the land, have been chosen as volunteers by your local draft boards to defend this country we love against the evil powers abroad that seek to strip away our freedoms. Now the solemn moment that you all have been waiting for has arrived. You entered this room as fun-loving youths. You will leave it as

68

dedicated soldiers. You will now be sworn in as loyal members of the army. Raise your right hands and repeat after me . . ."

"I don't want to!"

"You have that choice," the officer said grimly. "This is a free country and you are all volunteers. You may take the oath. Or if you chose not to, which is your right, you may leave by the small door behind me which leads to the federal prison where you will begin your thirty-year sentence for neglect of democratic duties."

"My hand's up," the same voice wailed.

"You will all repeat after me. I, insert your own name, of my own free will . . ."

"I, insert your own name, of my own free will."

"We will do it again, and we will do it correctly, and if we don't get it right next time. There is going to be *trouble.*"

We did it again, and correctly. Repeating what he said and trying not to hear what we were saying.

"To serve loyally . . . to show respect to all of the senior officers . . . death if I show disloyalty . . . death if I should desert . . . death if I sleep on duty . . ." and so on to the very end, which was "I do swear this in the name of my mother and father and the deity of my choice."

"Hands down, congratulations, you are all now soldiers and subject to military law. Your first order is that each of you will volunteer voluntarily a liter of blood since there has been a sudden call for transfusions. Dismissed."

Weak with hunger and fatigue, dizzy from loss of blood, cold noodle soup still sitting leadenly in the stomach, we reached the end of the line. We hoped.

"Fall in. Move it along. You will each be issued with a disposable uniform which you will not dispose of until ordered. You will don the uniforms and proceed up these stairs to the roof of this building where transportation is waiting to take you to Camp Ŝlimmarĉo where your training will begin. You will turn in your folders before you receive your uniforms. You will each receive an identity disc with your name and service number on it. These discs are grooved across the center so they may

69

be broken in half. Do not break them in half because that is a military crime and will be punished."

"Why make them to break in half if you don't break them in half?" I muttered aloud. The youth beside me rolled his eyes and whispered.

"Because when you're dead they break them in half and send one half to death registrations and put the other half in your mouth."

Why was it that as I shuffled forward to get my uniform I had a very strong metallic taste in my mouth?

CHAPTER 8

Under any other circumstances I would have enjoyed the ride in this unusual airship. It was shaped like a large cigar and undoubtedly contained light gas of some kind. Slung beneath the lifting body was a metal cabin tastefully decorated outside with a frieze of skulls and bones. Ducted fans on the cabin were angled to force it aloft and forward: the view from the window must have been fascinating. But the windows that we had glimpsed from the outside were all forward in the pilot's compartment, while we draftees were jammed into a windowless metal chamber. The seats were made from molded plastic surfaced with uneven bumps and hideously uncomfortable—but at least they were seats. I dropped into one and sighed with relief. In all the hours at the reception center the only time we had been off our feet was during the bloodletting. The plastic was cool through the thin paper fabric of the purple disposable uniform, the deck hard through the cardboard soles fastened at the end of its legs. The only pocket in this hideous garment was a pouch at the front into which we had shoved our bags of personal possessions so that we all resembled demented purple marsupials. I felt depressed. But at least I had company. We were all depressed.

"I never been away from home before," the recruit to my right sniveled, then sniffed and wiped his damp nose on his sleeve.

"Well I have," I said in my heartiest, most jovial tones. Not that I felt either hearty or jovial, but bucking up his spirits might help mine as well. "And it is a lot better than home."

"Food will be rotten," he whined self-indulgently. "Nobody can cook like my Mom. She makes the best cepkukoj in the whole world."

Onion cakes? What sort of bizarre diet had this stripling enjoyed? "Put that all behind you," I chirped. "If the army bakes cepkukoj they will be foul, count on that. But think of the other pleasures. Plenty of exercise, fresh air—and you can curse all the time, drink alcohol and talk smutty about girls!"

He blushed ardently, his splayed ears glowing like banners. "I wouldn't talk about girls! And I know how to drink. Me and Jojo went behind the barn once and drank beer and cursed and threw up."

"Whee . . ." I sighed and was saved from future futile conversation by the appeerence of a sergeant. He slammed open the door from the front cabin and roared his command.

"Alright you kretenoj—on your feet!"

He assured instant obedience by hitting a button on the wall that collapsed our seats. There were screams and moans of pain, writhing purple confusion on the deck as the recruits fell on top of each other. I was the only one standing and I caught the full force of the sergeant's sizzling glare.

"What are you—a wise guy or sometin'?"

"No, sir! Just obeying orders, sir!" Saying this I leaped into the air slapping my arms to my sides, stamping my feet heavily as I landed, then delivered a snappy salute—so snappy I almost put my eye out. The sergeant's eyes bulged in return at this display before he was lost from sight by the rising, milling bodies.

"Quiet! Attention! Hands at sides, feet together, stomachs in, chests out, chins back, eyes forward—and stop breathing!"

The purple ranks swayed and writhed into this absurd military stance, then were still. Silence descended as the sergeant glared around with dark suspicion.

"Did I hear someone breathe? No breathing until I tell you to. The first cagalhead who breathes gets my fist where it will do the most good."

The silence lengthened. Purple figures stirred as incipient asphyxiation took hold. One recruit moaned and fell to the deck; I breathed silently through my nostrils. There was a gasp as one of the lads could hold out no longer. The sergeant surged forward and the spot where a fist will do the most good turned out to be the pit of the stomach. The victim screamed and fell and all the others gasped in life-giving air.

"That was a little lesson!" the sergeant screeched. "Did you get the message?"

"Yes," I muttered under my breath. "You're a sado-masochist."

"The lesson is that I give the orders, you obey them—or you get stomped." Having delivered this repulsive communication his face writhed, his lips pulled back to reveal yellowed teeth; it took a long moment for me to realize this was supposed to be a smile.

"Sit down men, make yourselves comfortable." On the steel deck? The seats were still stowed. I sat with the rest while the sergeant amicably patted the roll of fat that hung over his belt. "My name is Klutz, Drill-sergeant Klutz. But you will not address me by my name which is for the use of those of equal rank or higher. You will call me sergeant, sir, or master. You will be humble, obedient, reverent and quiet. If you are not you will be punished. I will not tell you what the punishment will be because I have eaten recently and do not wish to upset my stomach."

A stir of fear passed through the audience at the thought of what might possibly upset that massive gut.

"One punishment is usually enough to break the spirit of even the most reluctant recruit. However, occasionally, a recruit will need a second punishment. Still more rarely a hardened resister will require a third punishment. But there is no third punishment. Would you like to know why there is no third punishment?"

The red eyes glared down and we all wished that we were someplace, anyplace, else at this moment.

"Since you are too dim to ask why, I will tell you. Third time is out. Third time is being stuffed, kicking and screaming and begging for your mommy, into the dehydration chamber where

73

ninety-nine point nine nine percent of all your precious bodily fluids will be removed with a dry whishing sound. Do you know what you will look like then? You will look like *this!*"

He reached into his pocket and took out a tiny dehydrated figure of a recruit in a tiny dehydrated uniform, the features on its tiny face fixed forever in lines of terror. Moans of fear sighed from the soldiers and there were a number of thuds as the weakest dropped unconscious. Sergeant Klutz smiled.

"Yes, you will look just like this. Your tiny dry body will then be hung on the barracks bulletin board for a month as a warning to the others. After that your body will be put in a padded mailing envelope and sent to your parents, along with a toy shovel to assist in burial. Now—are there any questions?"

"Please, sir," a quavering voice asked. "Is the dehydration process instant and painless or drawn-out and terrible?"

"Good question. After your first day in the army—do you have any doubt which it will be?"

More moans and unconscious thuds followed. The sergeant nodded approval. "Alright. Let me tell you what happens next. We are going to the RTCS at MMB. That means the Recruit Training Camp Ŝlimmarĉo at Mortstertoro Military Base. You will take your basic training. This training will turn you from feeble civilian wimps into sturdy, loyal, reverent soldiers. Some of you will wash out of basic training and will be buried with full military honors. Remember that. There is no way back. You will become good soldiers or you will become dead. You will understand that the military is hard but fair."

"What's fair about it?" a recruit gasped and the sergeant kicked him in the head.

"What is fair is that you all have an equal chance. You can get through basic or wash out. Now I will tell you something." He leaned forward and breathed out a blast of breath so foul that the nearest draftees dropped unconscious. There was no humor in his smile now. "The truth is that I *want* you to wash out. I will do everything I can to make you wash out. Every recruit sent home in a wheelchair or a box saves the government money and lowers taxes. I want you to wash out now instead of in combat after years of expensive training. Do we understand each other?"

If silence means assent, we certainly did. I admired the singleminded clarity of the technique. I did not like the military, but I was beginning to understand it.

"Any questions?"

My stomach rumbled loudly in the silence and the words popped from my mouth.

"Yes, sir. When do we eat?"

"You got a strong stomach, recruit. Most here are too sickened by military truth to eat."

"Only thinking of my military duty, sir. I must eat to be strong to be a good soldier."

He shuffled this around about in his dim brain, little piggy eyes glaring at me the while. Finally the projecting jaw nodded into the rolls of fat beneath the chin.

"Right. You just volunteered to get the rations. Through that door in the aft bulkhead. Move."

I moved. And thought. Bad news: I was in the army and liked nothing about it. Good news: we were going to Mortstertoro base where Bibs had last seen Captain Garth-Zennar-Zennor or whatever his name was. He was on top of my revenge list—but right now I was plugging away at the top of my survival list. Garth would have to wait. I opened the door which revealed a small closet containing a single box. It was labeled YUK-E COMBAT RATIONS. This had to be it. But when I lifted the box it seemed suspiciously light to feed this shipload of incipient soldiers.

"Pass them out, kreteno, don't admire the box," the sergeant growled, and I hurried to obey. the Yuk-E rations did appear pretty yuky. Gray bricks sealed in plastic covers. I went among my purple peers and each of them grabbed one out, fondling the bricks with some suspicion.

"These rations will sustain life for one entire day," the rasping voice informed us. "Each contains necessary vitamins, minerals, protein and saltpeter that the body needs or the army wants you to have. They are opened by inserting your thumb nail into the groove labeled thumbnail-here. The covering will fall away intact and you will preserve it intact. You will eat your ration. When you are finished you will go to the wall here and

75

to the water tap at this position and you will drink from the plastic cover. You will drink quickly because one minute after being moistened the cover will lose its rigidity and will shrink. You will then roll up the cover and save it for display at inspection because it will now be transformed into a government issue contraceptive which you will not be able to use for a very long time, if ever, but which you will still be responsible for. Now—eat!''

I ate. Or tried to. The ration had the consistency of baked clay but not half as much flavor. I chewed and gagged and swallowed and managed to choke it all down before rushing to the water spigot. I filled the plastic cover and drank quickly and refilled it, emptying it just as it went limp and flacid. I sighed and rolled it up and stowed it in my marsupial pocket and made room for the next victim at the tap.

While we had been gnawing our food the collapsed seats had snapped back into position. I eased myself carefully into the nearest, but it did not give way. It appeared impossible, but the combination of food and near-terminal exhaustion worked their unsubtle magic and I crashed. I could hear myself snoring even before I fell asleep.

The bliss of unconsciousness ended just as I might have expected; the seats fell away and dropped us into a writhing, moaning mass on the deck. We stumbled groggily to our feet under the verbal lashing of the sergeant and were trying to stand in a military posture as the deck vibrated beneath our feet and became still.

"Welcome to the first day of the rest of your new life," the sergeant chortled, and wails of anguish followed his words. The exit sprang open, admitting a chill and dusty blast, and we stumbled out wearily to see our new home.

It was not very impressive. One of the red and pallid suns was just setting into the cloud of dust on the horizon. I could tell by the thin and chill air that the base had been built at some altitude, a high plateau perhaps. Which guaranteed good flying weather and maximum discomfort for the troops. The ground trembled as a deepspacer took off in the distance, its exhaust blast brighter than the setting sun. The sergeant snarled us into a ragged formation and we shivered in the downblast of our departing airship. He waved a clipboard in our direction.

"I will now call the roll. You will be called by your military name and will forget that you ever had any other. Your military name is your given name followed by the first four numbers of your serial number. When your name is called you will enter the barracks behind me and proceed to your assigned bunk and await further instructions. Gordo7590—bunk one . . ."

I looked crosseyed at my dogtag until I could make out the number. Then stared numbly at the mud-colored barracks until the voice of our master called out Jak5138. With dragging feet I passed through the doorway over which was inscribed THROUGH THIS PORTAL PASS THE BEST DAMNED SOLDIERS IN THE WORLD. Who, as the expression goes, was kidding whom?

The floor was stone, still damp from the last scrubbing. The walls concrete, clean and still wet. I let my horrified gaze move up to the ceiling and, yes, it was damp as well, the light bulbs still dripping. How this maniacal cleansing was carried out I had no idea—though I was certain that I would find out far too soon.

My bunk was, naturally, the top one in a tier of three. It was strung with wire netting, though a bulky roll at its head hinted at softer pleasures.

"Welcome to your new home," the sergeant grated with false jollity as we drew our fatigued bodies up into an imitation of attention. "Note how your bedding roll is stowed when you unroll it, because it will be rolled in that stowed position at all times except when your sleeping—which will be the minimum amount of time needed to stay alive. Or less. Your footlockers are imbedded in the floor between the bunks and are opened and closed by me with this master switch."

He touched a stud on his belt and there was a grating sound as the mini-graves opened up in the floor. One recruit, who was standing in the wrong position, screamed as he fell into his.

"Lights out in fifteen minutes. Bedding to be unrolled but not utilized before that time. Before retiring you will watch an orientation film that will acquaint you with tomorrow's orders of the day. You will watch and listen with full attention, after which you will retire and pray to the deity or deities of your choice and cry yourselves to sleep thinking about your mommies. Dismissed.''

Dismissed. The door slammed behind our striped overseer and we were alone. Dismissed was the right word for it. Dismissed from the warmth and the light of the real world, sent to this gray military hell not of our choosing. Why is mankind so inhuman to its own species? If you were caught treating a horse in this manner you would probably be put in jail, or shot. Rustling cut the silence as we opened our bedrolls. To reveal to each of us a thin mattress and even thinner blanket. A pneumatic pillow as well that could only be inflated with lusty puffing which, I was sure, would go flat by morning. While we were unrolling and blowing TV screens dropped down silently behind us in the passageway between the bunks. Brassy military music blared and the image of an officer with a severe speech impediment appeared and began to read out totally incomprehensible instructions which we all ignored. I dumped the contents of my marsupial pocket into the subterranean footlocker and climbed and crawled, still dressed, into the bunk. My eyes blurred with fatigue as the voice droned on and I was nine-tenths asleep when a blast of light and sound jerked me awake. A grim military figure in black uniform glared angrily from the screen.

"Attention," it said. "This program has been interrupted, as have all programs throughout Nevenkebla on all stations, to bring you the following important announcement." He scowled at the sheet of paper he held and shook it angrily.

"A dangerous spy is at large in our country tonight. It is known that he entered the harbor of Marhaveno yesterday morning disguised as a laborer on one of the ships from Brastyr. A search was made of the harbor but he was not found. The search was extended today and it was discovered that the spy entered a pleasure vessel in the adjoining harbor and stole a number of items."

A deathly chill stirred the hairs on the nape of my neck as he held up a bundle of clothes.

"These were found buried in the sand and have been identified as the clothing worn by the spy. The entire area has been sealed, curfew declared and every building is now being carefully searched. The public is ordered to be on the lookout for this man. He may still be wearing these items of clothing that he stole. If you have seen anyone dressed like this notify the police or security forces at once."

His image vanished and was replaced by a carefully done computer simulation of the clothing I had borrowed from the boat. These rotated slowly in space—then appeared on a man's figure which the computer strolled about the screen. The face was a blank but I knew all too well what face would soon appear there.

How long would it take them to identify me, to track me down, discover that I was now in the army, to follow me here?

There was a grating thud as the barracks door locked and the lights went out. The chill spread down my body and my heart thudded with panic and I stared, sightless and horrified into the darkness.

How long?

CHAPTER 9

I would like to say that it was nerves of steel and fierce self-control that enabled me to fall asleep, after hearing the announcement that the entire country was turned out and searching for me. But that would be a lie. Not that I mind telling a lie or two, white lies really, to further myself in this universe. After all a disguise is a lie and continuous lying, sincere lying, is the measure of a good disguise. That went with the job. But one must not lie to oneself. No matter how distasteful the truth it must be faced and accepted. So, no lies; I fell asleep because I was horizontal in the dark, fairly warm and totally exhausted. Panic ran way behind exhaustion in the sleepy-time race. I slept, hard and enthusiastically, and awoke in the darkness only when a strange noise cut through my serious sack time.

It was a distant rustle, like waves on the beach—or leaves blowing in the wind. No, not that, but something else equally familiar. An amplified sound I thought numbly, like an ancient and worn recording being played, just the background scratching without the recording itself.

Theory was proved correct an instant later as a blurred and distorted recording of a bugle thundered through the barracks just as all the lights came on. The barracks door crashed open and, as though summoned from some dark hell by this hellish sound and light, the sergeant entered screaming at the top of his lungs.

"Get out and get under! Off your bunks and on your feet! Roll bedding! Dip into your footlockers! Remove shaving gear! Then on the double to the latrine! You're late, you're late! Barracks will be washed in twenty seconds precisely! Move it— move it—move it!"

We moved it, but we really didn't have enough time. I fought my way through the latrine door with the other frenzied purple figures just as the footlockers slammed shut and the barracks wash-heads let go. At that precise instant the sergeant stepped backward and slammed the door. From all sides torrents of cold water gushed forth, catching at least half of the recruits still on the run. They followed us into the latrine, soaked and shivering, their disposable uniforms beginning to dispose in long rents and tears. Crying and sniveling they pushed forward like sheep. Sheep struggling for survival. There was a limited number of sanitary facilities and all were in use. I forced my way through the mob until I could glimpse my face in the corner of a distorted mirror, almost did not recognize myself with the dark-circled eyes and pallid skin. But there was no time to get organized, take stock, to think coherently. At some lower level I realized that it had all been planned this way, to keep the recruits off-balance, insecure, frightened—open for brainwashing or destruction. This realization percolated up to a slightly more conscious level and with it a growing anger.

Jimmy diGriz does not destruct! I was going to beat them at their own game, until I beat it out of here. It didn't matter that the entire country was looking for me—until they tracked me to this military cesspit all I had to do was survive. And survive I would! The supersonic razor screeched in my brain as it blasted my overnight whiskers free. Then, while the automated toothbrush crawled around inside my mouth, I managed to get a hand under a running faucet, scrubbed my face clean, ignored the air-dryer and pelted back to my bunk over the puddled floor. I stowed my kit away just as the footlocker flew open, then spun about as Sergeant Klutz popped through the door again.

"Fall out for rollcall!" he bellowed as I rushed by him into the night. I snapped to attention under the single glaring light as he turned and approached me with grim suspicion.

"Are you some kind of joker or something?" he shouted, his face so close to mine that that his spittle dotted my skin.

"No, sir! I'm raring to go, sir. My daddy was a soldier and my grandaddy and they told me that the best thing to be was a soldier and the highest rank in the army was sergeant! That's why I'm here." I stopped shouting and leaned forward and whispered. "Don't tell the others, sir, they'll only sneer. But I wasn't drafted—I *volunteered.*"

He was silent and I risked a quick look at his face. Could it be? Was it, there, a drop of liquid in the corner of one eye? Had my tissue of lies touched some residual spot of emotion buried deep with the alcohol-sodden, sadistic flesh of his repulsive body? I couldn't be sure. At least he did not strike me down on the spot, but turned on his heel and rushed into the barracks to boot out the stragglers.

As the moaning victims stumbled into line I put some thought to my future. What should I do? *Nothing*, came the quick answer. Until you are tracked down, Jim, stay invisible in the ranks. And learn all that you can about this military jungle. Watch and learn and keep your eyes open. The more you understand about this operation the safer you will be. Then, when you run, it will be plan not panic that guides you. Good advice. Hard on the nerves to follow, but good advice nevertheless.

After repeated mumbled mistakes, mispronunciation of names—is it really possible to mispronounce Bil?—the sergeant finished stumbling and muttering his way through the rollcall and led the way to the messhall. As we approached it, and the smells of real food washed over us, the splattering of saliva on the pavement sounded like rain. Other recruits stumbled up through the night and joined us in the long line leading into the warmth of this gustatory heaven. When I finally carried my heaped-high tray to the table I found it hard to believe. All right so maybe it was grundgeburgers with caramel sauce, but it was food, hot, solid food. I didn't eat it—I insufflated it and went back for more. For one moment I actually thought that the army was not so bad after all. Then I instantly banished the thought.

They were feeding us because they wanted to keep us alive. The food was nasty and cheap—but it would sustain life. So if we washed out it would not be because of the diet but because of our own intrinsic insufficiency or lack of will. If we got through basic training each of us would supply one hot and relatively-willing body for the war machine. Nice thinking.

I hated the bastards. And went back for thirds.

Breakfast was followed by calisthenics—to aid the digestion or destroy it. Sergeant Klutz double-timed us to a vast, wind-swept plain where other recruits were already being put through their paces by muscular instructors. Our new leader was waiting for us, steely-eyed and musclebound, the spread of his shoulders so wide that his head was disproportionately small. Or maybe he just had a pinhead. Speculation about this vanished as his roar rattled the teeth in my jaw.

"What's this, what's this? You kretenoj are almost a minute late!"

"Pigs, that what they is," our loyal sergeant said, taking a long black cigar from his pocket. "Little trotters in the trough. Couldn't tear them away from their chow."

Some recruits gasped at this outright lie, but the wiser of us were learning and stayed silent. The one thing that we could not expect was justice. We were late getting here because our porcine sergeant could not move any faster.

"Is that so?" the instructor said, his beady eyes swiveling in his pinhead like glowing marbles. "Then we will see if we cannot work some of that food off of these malingering cagal-kopfs. ON THE GROUND! Now—we do fifty pushups. Begin!"

This seemed like a good idea since I usually did a hundred pushups every morning to keep in shape. And the chill wind was blowing through the rents in our disposable uniforms. Five. I wondered when we would be issued with something more permanent. Fifteen.

By twenty there was plenty of wavering and grunting around me and I was warming up nicely. By thirty over half of the pipe-stemmed striplings had collapsed in the dust. Sergeant Klutz dropped cigar ashes on the nearest prostrate back. We continued. When we reached fifty just I and the muscular lad who hated injections were the only ones left. Pinhead glared at us.

"Another fifty," he snarled.

The weightlifter puffed on for twenty more before he groaned to a halt. I finished the course and got another glare and a snarl.

"Is that all, sir," I asked sweetly. "Couldn't we do another fifty?"

"On your feet!" he screamed. "Legs wide, arms extended, after me. One, two, three, four. And one more time . . ."

By the time the exercises were finished we had worked up a good sweat, the sergeant had finished his cigar—and two of the recruits were collapsed in the dust. One of them lay beside me, groaning and clutching his midriff. The sergeant strolled over and pushed him with his toe which elicited only some weak moans. Sergeant Klutz looked down with disgust and screamed his displeasure.

"Weaklings! Faggots! Momma's boys! We'll weed you out fast enough. Get these poofters out of my sight. Man to each side pick up the malingerers, bring them to the medic tent. Then fall back in. Move!"

I bent and seized one arm and lifted. I could see that the recruit on the other side was having difficulty so I shifted my grip to take most of the weight and heaved.

"Get his arm around your shoulder—I'll do the carrying," I whispered.

"My . . . thanks," he said. "I'm not in such great shape."

He was right, too. Thin and round-shouldered with dark circles under his eyes. And older than the others I noticed, in his mid-twenties at least.

"Morton's the name," he said.

"Jak. You look kind of old for the draft, Mort."

"Believe me, I am!" he said with some warmth. "I almost killed myself getting through university, keeping top of the class to keep out of the army. So what happens? I'm so overworked I get sick, miss the exams, wash out—and end up here anyway. What do we do with this dropout?"

"That tent there, I guess, where they're bringing the others."

The limp form hung between us, toes dragging in the dust.

"He doesn't look too good," Morton said, glancing at the pallid skin and hanging head.

"That's his problem. You have to look out for number one."

"I'm beginning to get that message. A crude communication but a highly effective one. Here we are."

"Drop him on the ground," a bored corporal said, not deigning to even look up from his illiterate comic book. When he touched the page little voices spoke out and there was a mini scream. I looked at the four other unconscious forms stretched out in the dirt.

"What about some medical treatment, corporal. He looks in a bad way."

"Tough cagal." He turned a page. "If he comes to—it's back to the drill field. Stays like that the medic will look at him when he gets here tonight."

"You're all heart."

"That's the way the kuketo crumbles. Now get the cagal out of here before I put you on report for cagaling off."

We got. "Where do they get all these sadistic types from?" I muttered.

"That could be you or I," Morton said grimly. "A sick society breeds sickies. People do what they are ordered to do. It is easier that way. Our society lives on militarism, chauvinism and hatred. When those are the rules there will always be someone eager to do the dirty work."

I rolled my eyes in his direction. "They taught you that in school?"

He smiled grimly and shook his head. "The opposite, if anything. I was majoring in history, military history of course, so I was allowed to do research. But I like to read and the university library is a really old one and all the books are there if you know how to look, and how to crack some simple security codes. I looked and cracked and read—and learned."

"I hope you learned to keep your mouth shut as well?"

"Yes—but not always."

"Make it always or you are in big trouble."

Sergeant Klutz was just leading our squad off the field and we fell in behind them. And marched to the supply building to

85

get outfitted at last. I had heard that clothing came in only two sizes in the army and this was true. At least most of mine were too big so I could roll up the cuffs. In addition to clothing there were mess kits, webbing belts, canteens, sewing kits, assassination kits, foxhole diggers, backpacks, VD testers, bayonets, scrokets and more items of dubious or military nature. We staggered back to the barracks, dumped our possessions and hurried to our next assignment.

Which was something called Military Orientation.

"Having possessed our bodies they now seek to take over our minds," Morton whispered. "Dirty minds in military bodies."

He was sure bright this Morton, but not bright enough to keep his mouth shut. I hissed him into silence as Sergeant Klutz glared in our direction.

"Talking is forbidden," he graveled. "You are here to listen, and this here is Corporal Gow who will now tell you what you got to know."

This Gow was a smarmy type, all smooth pink skin, little ponce's moustache and fake grin. "Now sergeant," he said, "this is orientation, not orders. You men will become good soldiers by following orders. But good soldiers also should know the necessity of these orders. So get comfortable, guys. No chairs of course, this is the army. Just sit down on the nice clean concrete floor and give me your attention, if you please. Now—can any of you tell me why you are here?"

"We was drafted," a thick voice said.

"Yes, ha-ha, of course you were. But why is the draft necessary? Your teachers and your parents have let you down if this has not been made completely clear. So let me take this opportunity to remind you of some vital facts. You are here because a dangerous enemy is at our gates, has invaded our precious land, and it is your duty to defend our inalienable freedoms."

"This is the old cagal if I ever heard it," I muttered, and Morton nodded silent agreement.

"Did you say something, soldier?" The corporal said, staring right at me; he had good ears.

"Just a question, sir. How could a broken-down, unindustrialized society like they got over there, how could they ever

86

invade a modern, armed and equipped country like ours."

"That is a *good* question, soldier, and one that I am happy to answer. Those barbarians across the channel would pose no problem if they were not being armed and equipped by *offworlders*. Greedy, hungry strangers who see our rich land and want to take it for themselves. That is why you lads must go willingly to the service of your country."

I was shocked at the magnitude of the lie, angered. But I struggled hard and followed my own advice and kept my mouth shut. But Morton didn't.

"But, sir, the Interplanetary League is a peaceful union of peaceful planets. War has been abolished . . ."

"How do you know that?" he snapped.

"Common knowledge," I said breaking in, hoping that Morton would shut up now. "But you know that is the truth, don't you, sir?"

"I know nothing of the sort and I wonder just who has been feeding you lies like that. After our orientation session I want to talk to you, soldier. You and that recruit next to you. This free country is fighting the interplanetary forces that wish to destroy us. No sacrifice is too great to defend that freedom which is why I know that you will all do your duty, happily. And become good soldiers in a good team. Look to the good Sergeant Klutz as you would to your own father, for he is here to be your mentor and guide to your military life. Do what he says and you will grow strong and prosper and become first-class soldiers in the service of your country. But I know that you will at times find things confusing, even worrying, for this military experience is a new experience for all of you. That is when you must think of me. I am your counselor and guide. You can call upon me for advice and help at any time. I would like to be your friend, your very best friend. Now I am going to pass out these orientation pamphlets and you have ten minutes to read them. We will then have a question and answer session to help acquaint you with the details. While you are doing that I am going to have a nice friendly chat with these recruits who appear to be badly misinformed about the political realities of our land." The finger was pointing at me, then at Morton.

"That's right, you two. We will step outside, get a bit of sun, have some good old jaw-jaw."

We rose with great reluctance—but had no choice at all. All eyes were upon us when we went to the door that Gow was holding open. I could feel the heat from Sergeant Klutz's burning glare as I passed him. Corporal Gow closed the door behind us and turned to face us. His smile as insincere as ever.

"Kind of warm now since the sun came out."

"Sure is. Feels nice."

"Where did you get that subversive cagal you were spouting in there? You first." He pointed at me.

"I sort of, well, sort of heard it somewhere."

He smiled happily and stabbed a stubby finger at Morton.

"I knew it. You have been listening to the illegal radio, haven't you? Both of you. That is the only possible place you could heard such outrageous lies."

"Not really," Morton said. "Facts are facts and I happen to be right."

He was digging his own grave with his jaw. I broke in; this radio dodge sounded like a possible out. If there were such a thing we might just wriggle from under this creepo's thumb. I lowered my eyes and twisted my toe in the dirt.

"Gee, corporal, I don't know how to say this. I was going to lie or something—but you're too smart for me. It was, you're right, the radio . . ."

"I knew it! They pump that poison down from their satellite, too many frequencies to jam, too defended to shoot down. Lies!"

"I just did it that once. I knew I shouldn't have, but it was a dare. And it sounded so true—that's why I spoke out like that."

"I'm glad you did, recruit. And I imagine that you did the same?" Morton did not rise to the bait but the corporal took silence for assent. "I think that you did. But at least it shows the poison didn't take, that you two wanted to talk about it. The devil always has the best tunes. But you must turn away from the siren song of such slimy untruths and listen to the authorities who know far better than you do." He smiled warmly upon us and I grinned with wide insincerity.

"Oh I will, sir," I said quickly before Morton could open his mouth again. "I will. Now that you have told me this, and didn't punish us or anything . . ."

"Did I say that?" The warm grin suddenly had a cold and nasty edge to it. "You'll get your punishment. If you were civilians you would each get a year at hard labor. But you are in the army now—so the punishment should be worse. It has been nice talking to you, recruits. Now get back inside for the rest of this orientation session. That will give you plenty of time to contemplate your crimes and their inevitable punishment. In the future, if you have a future, you will not contradict me or any other officer."

He waved us inside ahead of him: we went like sheep to the slaughter. I whispered to Morton. "Is it true what he said about the radio broadcasts."

"Of course. Haven't you ever listened? Pretty boring stuff for the most part. Heavy on propaganda and low on content. But it doesn't matter that you admitted listening. He was out to get us no matter what he said. Military justice!"

"Do we just stay here and wait?!"

"Where's to run," he said, with utmost gloom.

Where indeed? There was no place to flee to.

Sergeant Klutz glared his best glare at us and we shut up. I sank to the floor with a sigh. Wondering just what possible punishment the military could dream up that could be worse than recruit training. I had the sinking feeling that I would find out soon enough.

CHAPTER 10

A distant buzzer sounded like a stifled eructation and Sergeant Klutz's eyes came back into focus and the expression of dull vacuity vanished to be replaced by his normal sneer of anger.

"On your feet you cagal-kopfs! You had a whole hour of cagaling off and you will now pay for it. Double time! The next session will be small arm instruction and short arm inspection. Move it!"

"I'm holding onto these two," Gow said, separating us out from the others. "I'm putting them on report for spreading sedition."

Klutz nodded happily and slashed a line through our names on his roster sheet. "Suits me, Gow. As long as I got the roll call right you can eat them for breakfast for all I care."

The door closed and Gow and I stood there eyeball to eyeball. Morton slumped to one side, drooping with apathy. I was beginning to get angry. Corporal Gow took out his notebook and pencil and pointed at me.

"What is your name soldier?"

"ScrooU2."

"That is your military name, Scroo, and not a complete one at that. I would like your entire name."

"I'm from Pensildelphia, corporal, and we were taught never to give our names to strangers."

90

His eyes narrowed with hatred. "Are you trying to make fun of me soldier?"

"That would be impossible, sir. You are a walking joke as it is. Selling lies to the peasantry. You know as well as I do that the only threat to this country is the military that control it. This is a military state kept in operation only for the benefit of the military."

Morton gasped and tried to wave me to silence. I was too angry for that now. This cagaling corporal had gotten under my skin. He smiled coldly and reached for the telephone.

"If you won't tell me your name the Military Police will find it out quickly enough. And you are wrong about only the military benefiting from a military state. You are forgetting the industrial corporations that profit from the military contracts. One cannot exist without the other. They are mutually interdependent."

He said this calmly, smiling, and shocked me into silence. "But . . ." I finally mumbled as he dialed the phone. "If you know that—why are you selling that line of old cagal to the troops?"

"For the simple reason that I am the scion of one of those industrial families and quite happy with the situation as it is. I fulfill my military obligations by selling this line of old cagal, as you so quaintly put it, and in a few months will return to the life of luxury which I greatly enjoy. The number is engaged. I've enjoyed our talk as well, and in return for the pleasure I derived from the novelty of our conversation I wish to give you a gift."

He put the phone down turned and opened a drawer in the desk behind him and I was numb enough to let him do it. When the coin finally dropped it was too late. As I jumped forward he spun about with a large weapon in his hand, aimed and steady.

"I wouldn't, if I were you. I hunt, you know, and I am a first-class shot. I would also have no slightest compunction in shooting you. In the back if needs be," he added as I turned away. I turned around again and smiled.

91

"Well done, corporal. Intelligence was concerned about the quality of your orientation talks and I was sent here to, you know, try to irritate you. And I promise not to repeat your remarks about the industrial-military complex. I come from a poor family so I do not enjoy any of your advantages."

"Is that true?" Morton gasped.

"It is—and you are under arrest. There, one traitor caught, Gow, so some good has come of our conversation."

His eyes narrowed but the gun never moved. "Do you expect me to believe that?"

"No. But I can show you my identification." I smiled and reached into the empty back pocket of my new uniform.

He might have been a good shot when it came to blasting helpless animals or paper targets, but he had no combat experience. For a single instant his eyes looked down toward my moving hand. Which was all the time I needed. My other hand was already chopping the inside of his wrist, moving the gun aside. It hissed once and something slammed into the wall behind me. Morton screeched with fright and jumped aside. Before Gow could fire again my knee came up into his stomach.

The gun dropped to the floor and he dropped beside it. I took a deep and shuddering breath and let it out with a sigh.

"Well done, Jim," I said, and reached over my shoulder and patted myself on the back. "All the reflexes working fine."

Morton bulged his eyes at me, then down at the silent form of the corporal. "What's happening . . . ?" he gurgled in confusion.

"Exactly what you see. I've rendered the corporal unconscious before he did us bodily harm. And you are not under arrest since that was just a ruse. So now, quickly before someone comes, push that desk up against the entrance since you can see that the door has no lock."

I bent and retrieved the weapon in case the scion of millions came to earlier than planned. And what was I going to do with the poor little rich boy? I looked down at his recumbent form and inspiration struck.

"You are a genius," I bragged aloud. "You deserve another pat which you will get later because now speed is of the essence."

I bent and began to unbutton his uniform. "The uniform, that is the key, the uniform. They will be looking for a ragged recruit in baggy fatigues. Not a spiffy corporal in tailormades. You have earned this promotion, Jim. Go to the head of the class."

I tore off his shoes and pulled his trousers free—and whistled. His underpants were woven of gold thread. Rich is as rich does. It was chance, pure chance, that he was a little overweight from a lifetime of good living. My muscles took the place of his fat and the uniform could have been made for me. Except the shoes; he had very tiny feet. My boots would have to do. I emptied his pockets and found, in addition to a great deal of money and a container of sinister looking black cigarettes, a small pocketknife. This worked admirably in cutting my discarded clothing into strips with which I bound the corporal securely, wadded more of the cloth into a gag. He was breathing easily through his nose so my conscience was clear that he would not die of suffocation.

"Are you going to kill him?" Morton asked.

"No, but I want him quiet until I put the next part of the plan into operation." I'm glad that Morton didn't ask what that was since I didn't know yet. There were no closets in the room so the corporal could not be stuffed out of sight. The desk—that was it!

"Morton," I ordered. "Stand with your back to the door and think like a lock. If anyone tries to open it lean hard against it."

While he leaned and thought lockish I dragged the desk back into position and wedged the bound corporal under it. By reflex I went through the desk drawers, which were all empty except the top one which had a folder of papers. I tucked these under my arm. Then I stepped back and examined my handiwork. Admirable. The corporal was well out of sight. Anyone who glanced into the room would think it empty.

"Now—what next?" I said cheerily. Then felt the smile slip from my face.

"Yes!" Morton agreed eagerly. "What happens next?"

I shook myself, took a brace and tried to think positively. "For one thing—there is no going back. So let us seek out a way forward. When they find the corporal they will find out our names quickly enough. By which time we must have new names. Which means we go to the personnel section and make a few changes."

Morton was blinking very rapidly now. "Jak, old friend, don't you feel well? I don't understand a word that you are saying."

"Doesn't matter—as long as I do." I unloaded the gun, put the power charge in my pocket and the empty weapon back in the drawer. "March ahead of me, do as I command. Go! As soon as you have opened the door a crack to see if the coast is clear."

It was. We marched out, stamping and striding in a very military fashion, me clutching my sheaf of papers, Morton hopefully clutching to his few remaining shards of sanity. One, two, one, two. Around the corner and almost into the arms of a red-capped military policeman.

"Squad halt! Stand at ease!" I screamed. Morton halted with a decided sway and shudder, showing the whites of his eyes as he rolled them toward the MP. "Eyes front!" I shrieked. "I gave no orders for you to move your eyes."

The MP, wise in military ways, paid us absolutely no attention until I called out to him. "Just hold it, there, private."

"Me, corporal?" he asked, stopping and turning.

"You are the only thing moving that I can see. Your pocket is unbuttoned. But this is my generous day. Just point us toward the Personnel Building and keep moving."

"Straight ahead, right on the company street, past the bandstand, left at the torture chamber and there you are." He scurried away, groping at his shirt pockets to find the open one. Morton was shivering and sweating and I patted him on the back.

"Relax, my friend. As long as you have the rank you can do what you want in the army. Ready to go on?"

He nodded and stumbled forward. I marched after him, shouting commands at the corners, marking time, being noisy, obnoxious and abusive so I would not be noticed. A sad commentary indeed on the reality of military life.

The Personnel Building was large and industrious with plenty of to-ing and fro-ing from the front entrance. As we started

94

toward it Morton came to a halt and stood at attention, swaying. "W-what are you going to do?" He whispered huskily and I saw that he was shaking with fear.

"Relax old buddy, all is under control," I said, leafing through the handful of papers to cover this unmilitary pause. "Just follow me, do as I say, and in a few minutes we will have vanished without trace."

"We'll really vanish without trace if we go in there! We'll be caught, tortured, killed . . ."

"Silence!" I shouted into his ear and he leaped as though he had been shot. "You will not talk. You will not think! You will only obey or you will be in the cagal so deep you will never see the light of day again!"

A passing sergeant smiled and nodded approval so I knew I was on the right track. I hated to do this to Morton but it was the only way. "Left face—forward march!"

His skin was pale, his eyes rolled up, his mind empty of conscious thought. He could only obey. Up the steps we went and through the entrance toward the armed military policemen stationed there.

"Halt, at ease!" I shouted and spun toward the MP, still shouting. "You—where do I find the Transport Section?"

"Second floor, room two-oh-nine. Could I see your pass corporal?"

I glared at him coldly as I shuffled through the papers I was carrying, let my eyes travel slowly down to his boots, then back up again. He stood at attention, shivering slightly, and I knew he was new at this game.

"I don't think I have ever seen dirtier boots," I hissed. When his eyes glanced down I held out the turned-back papers. "Here's the pass." When he glanced up again I let the papers slap shut.

He started to say something, I turned up the the power of my glare and he wilted. "Thank you, corporal. Second floor."

I turned smartly away, snapped my fingers at Morton, then stamped away toward the stairs. Trying to ignore the fine beading of sweat on my brow. This was very demanding work— and it wasn't over yet. I could see that Morton was definitely shivering as he walked and I wondered how much more of this

95

he could take. But there was no turning back now. I threw open the door of 209 and waved him in. A bench ran along the wall and I pointed him towards it.

"Sit there and wait until you"re called," I said, then turned to the reception clerk. He was on the phone and waved vaguely in my direction. Behind him rows of desks and laboring soldiers stretched the length of the room. All totally ignoring me, of course.

"Yes, sir, get onto it at once, sir," the reception clerk smarmed. "Computer error, possibly, captain. We'll get right back to you. Very sorry about this."

I could hear the phone disconnect loudly in his ear. "You crock of cagal!" he snarled and threw the phone back on the desk, then looked up at me. "What's up, corporal?"

"I'm up here, corporal, and I'm here to see the transport sergeant."

"He's home on compassionate leave. His canary died."

"I do not wish to hear the disgusting details of his personal life, soldier. Who's sitting in for him?"

"Corporal Gamin."

"Tell the corporal I'm coming in."

"Right, right." He picked up the phone. I stamped past him to the door marked TRANSPORT SERGEANT—KEEP OUT and threw it open. The thin, dark man at the computer terminal looked up and frowned.

"You are Corporal Gamin?" I said, closing the door and flipping through the papers one more time. "If you are I got good news for you."

"I'm Gamin. What's up?"

"Your morale. The paymaster says they found a cumulative computer error in your pay and you are owed possibly two hundred and ten big ones. They want you there to straighten it out."

"I knew it! They been deducting double for insurance and laundry."

"They're all cagal-kopfs." My guess was right; there cannot be anyone alive, particularly in the army, who isn't sure there are errors in his payslip. "I would suggest you get your chunk over and collect before they lose the money again. Can I use your phone?"

"Punch nine for an outside line." He pulled up his necktie and reached for his jacket—then stopped and took the key out of the terminal; the screen went black. "I bet they owe me more than that. I want to see the records."

There was a second door behind his desk and, to my satisfaction, he exited that way. The instant it closed I had the other door open and poked my head through. When the reception clerk looked up I turned and called back over my shoulder.

"Do you want him in here as well, corporal?" I nodded my head and turned back. "You, recruit, get in here!"

Morton jumped at the sound of my voice, then scurried forward. I closed and locked the door behind him.

"Get comfortable," I said, pulling off my boot and rooting about inside it for the lockpick. "No questions. I have to work fast."

He slumped into a chair, eyes bulging in silence as I gently tickled the lock until the terminal came to life.

"Menu, menu," I muttered as I hammered away on the keys.

It all went a lot smoother and faster than I had hoped. Whoever had written the software had apparently expected it to be accessed by morons. Maybe he was right. In any case I was led by the hand through the menus right to the current shipping orders.

"Here we are, leaving at noon today, a few minutes from now. Fort Abomeno. Your full name and serial number, Morton, quickly."

I had my own dogtags spread out as I punched in all the requested information. A bell pinged and a sheet of paper slipped out of the printer.

"Wonderful!" I said, smiling and letting some tension out of my muscles: I passed it over to him. "We're safe for the moment since we have just left for Fort Abomeno."

"But . . . we"re still here."

"Only in the flesh, my boy. For the record, and records are all that count to the military, we have shipped out. Now we

97

make the flesh inviolate." I read through the shipping orders, checked off two names, then turned back to the terminal and entered data with some urgency. We had to be long gone before the corporal returned. The printer whiffled gently and one sheet slipped out, then another. I grabbed them up, relocked the terminal, and waved Morton to his feet.

"Here we go. Out the back door and I'll tell you what is happening as soon as we are clear of this building."

Someone was coming up the stairs, a corporal, and my heart gave a little hip-hop before I saw that it wasn't the corporal in question. Then it was down the hall to the front door and yes, there was Corporal Gamin coming up the stairs with a very nasty cut to his jib!

"Sharp right, recruit!" I ordered and we turned into the first doorway with military precision. A lieutenant was combing his hair in front of a mirror there. Her hair I realized when she turned about and glared at me.

"What kind of cagal-head are you, corporal? Or doesn't the sign on the other side of this door read female personnel only?"

"Sorry, sir, Ma'am, dark in the hall. Eye trouble. You, recruit, why didn't you read the sign correctly? Get the cagal out of here and march straight to the MPs."

I pushed Morton out ahead of me and closed the door. The hall ahead was empty.

"Let's go! Quick as we can without attracting attention."

Out the door and down the steps and around the corner and another corner and the pace was beginning to tell. I leaned against a wall and felt the sweat run down my face and drip from my nose. I wiped it with the sheaf of papers I still carried—then held up the two new sheets of orders and smiled; Morton gaped.

"Freedom and survival," I chortled. "Shipping orders, or rather cancellation of shipping orders. We are safe at last."

"I haven't the slightest idea of what you are talking about."

"Sorry. Let me explain. As far as the military is concerned we are no longer at this base but have been shipped to Fort Abomeno. They will search for us there, but we will be hard to find. In order to keep the body count correct two soldiers who are in that shipment, still physically in that shipment, have been removed on paper. These are their orders, corporal, I thought a bit more rank wouldn't hurt. I am a sergeant now as you can see. We will occupy their quarters, eat their food, draw their pay. It will be weeks, perhaps months, before the error is discovered. By which time we will be long gone. Now— shall we begin our new careers as noncommisioned officers?"

"Urgle," he said dimly and his eyes shut and he would have slumped to the ground if I had not held him erect against the wall. I nodded agreement.

"I feel somewhat the same way myself. It really has been one of those days."

CHAPTER 11

Fatigue was of no importance, thirst equally so—although both were present and sending imperative messages. To be ignored. Rank has its privileges and we were not going to enjoy ours until we assumed the trappings. I shook Morton until his eyes opened and he blinked dully at me.

"One last effort, Mort. We are going to the PX, about whose heady joys we have heard, and there we will spend some money. When that has been done we will be free spirits and will eat and drink and relax. Are you ready?"

"No. I'm beat, shagged, dead. I cannot move. You go on. I can't make it . . ."

"Then I'll just have to turn you over to Sergeant Klutz who has just arrived and is standing right behind you."

He sprang into the air with a shriek of agony, feet already running before he hit the ground. I held on to him.

"Sorry about that. No Klutz here. A ruse to get your adrenaline flowing. Let's go."

We went. Quickly before this burst of energy faded. It got him as far as the post exchange where I leaned him against the wall near the cashier and handed him my sheaf of papers.

"Stand there, recruit, and do not move and do not let go of those papers or I will skin you alive or worse."

100

I slammed the papers into his limp hands and whispered, "What size jacket do you take?" After much blinking on his part, and reiteration on mine, I extracted the needed information. I made my purchases from a bored clerk, added some stripes and a tube of superglue, paid for everything with some of Gow's money, thank you corporal, and led Morton farther into the reaches of the PX. To the latrine, empty this time of day.

"We'll use the booth one at a time," I said. "We don't want anyone making improper conclusions. Take off those fatigues and slip into this uniform. Move it."

While he changed I glued the new sargeant's stripes over the corporal's on my sleeves. When Morton had flushed and emerged I straightened his necktie and glued his promotion to his sleeve. His fatigues went into the rubbish, along with the sheaf of papers, and we went into the noncom's bar.

"Beer—or something stronger?" I asked.

"I don't drink."

"You do now. And curse. You're in the army. Sit there and sneer like a corporal and I'll be right back."

I ordered two double neutral grain spirits and some beers, dumped the ethyl alcohol into the beer, sipped it to make sure it had not gone off, then went back to our table. Morton drank as ordered, widened his eyes, gasped, then drank again. Color returned to his cheeks as I drained half of my glass and sighed happily.

"I don't know how to thank you, what to say . . ."

"Then say nothing. Drink up. What I did was to save my own hide and you just came along for the ride."

"Who are you, Jak? How do you know how to do those things you did?"

"Would you believe me if I said I was a spy sent here to seek out the military secrets?"

"Yes."

"Well I'm not. I'm just a draftee like yourself. Though I will have to admit that I come from a lot further away than Pensildelphia. That's it, drain the glass, you're learning fast. I'll get a couple more drinks and some food. I saw they had catwiches. I'll get a couple of those."

101

Food and drink helped, as did the stripes on our arms. Morton tore into his rations. I ate more slowly, finding myself already thinking about the next step. Cigars followed, Gow's wallet was bottomless, and more drink.

"Thish is really great, Jak, really great. You're really great, really great."

"Sleep," I said as his eyes unfocused and his head hit the table with a thump. "You will awake a new man."

I sipped lightly at my own drink for I wanted only the stimulation of the alcohol and not the oblivion. The club was almost empty, only one other table occupied, the noncom there just as asleep as Morton. Probably as drunk as well. The simple pleasures of military life. I sipped and thought of my previous military career on Spiovente, and of The Bishop, now dead, and of the man who was responsible for his death.

"I haven't forgotten you, Captain Garth, not at all," I said softly to myself. The bartender polished a glass and yawned. Well acquainted with customers who talked to themselves and drank themselves into extinction. "For the last few days it has been survival only. Now I pick up your trail. We're in the same army, on the same base."

I felt suddenly dizzy and put the glass down. It had been a long day and I was as tired as Morton. Country and coal-mining music was grating enchantingly from the jukebox: the world about was at peace. For the moment. I was aware of a light scratching sound and glanced down at the boxes that leaned against the wall. Something moved in the darkness behind them. I watched in silence as a twitching nose and whiskers emerged. Then the head, the bar lights reflected in the rat's eyes. It appeared to be looking up at me.

"Get lost," I said, "before you end up in the stew." I cackled at my own witticism.

"Jim diGriz, I must talk with you," the rat said in a deep voice.

It had really been one of those days. Too much. I had not realized it but the strain was so great that I had cracked.

"Go away," I hissed. "You are a figment of my imagination and not a real rat at all." I gulped the rest of my drink in a single swallow. The rat climbed up onto the box and looked at me.

102

"Of course I am not a real rat. I am Captain Varod of the League Navy."

Gently, so as not to awaken Morton—this was my hallucination and I wanted to keep it for myself—I pried his drink from his slack fingers and drained it as well as my own.

"You've shrunk a bit since the last time I talked with you, captain," I smirked.

"Stop playing the idiot, diGriz, and listen to me. This spyrat is controlled from our base. You were recognized and identified."

"By who? The rat?"

"Shut up. This communication is limited because there is a chance their detectors will pick up the spyrat's broadcast signal. We need your help. You have penetrated their military base, the first agent to do so . . ."

"Agent? I thought I was the criminal you were shipping home for trial and persecution?"

"I said we need your help. This is vital. There are lives at stake. The generals are planning an invasion. We know that much from intercepting their communications. But we don't know where the landing will take place. Brastyr is a big continent and they might be attacking anywhere. There could be a lot of deaths. We must find out where they plan to . . ."

The door to the bar burst open and a gun-waving officer burst in, followed by a technician weighted with electronic equipment.

"The signal is coming from that direction, sir," the man shouted and pointed directly at me.

"What is that cagal-head private doing in the noncoms' bar?" I shouted, leaping to my feet and kicking the box as I did. The rat fell to the floor and I stamped on it. Hard.

"Don't get your cagal in an uproar, sergeant," the officer said. "This is a priority investigation . . ."

"Signal has stopped, sir," the technician said, fiddling with his dials.

"Cagal!" the officer said, stuffing his gun back into the holster. "These alcoholics don't have a transmitter."

"Could be the street outside, other side of the wall. A moving vehicle."

"Let's go!"

103

The door slammed shut behind them. The barman wiped his glass. "This happen very often around here?" I asked.

"Yeah. This is sure an uptight base."

Morton snored heavily and I poked the crushed remains of the stainless steel rat with my toe. An omen? A gear wheel rolled out and rattled on the floor.

"Set them up again," I called out. "And take one yourself since the rest of these cagal-kopfs are in dreamland."

"Your all heart, sarge. Just ship in?"

"Today."

"An uptight base like I say—"

His voice was drowned out by the loud whistle from the TV as it turned itself on. The blackclad military announcer glared out of the screen just one more time.

"The spy who landed in Marhaveno has been identified. He attempted to disguise himself as a harmless draftee and was inducted into the army. Resolute police work has identified him by his clothing."

Some police work. They just looked at their mail. I was beginning to think that sending my clothing from the reception center to the police station was not at all as funny as it had seemed at the time. There was a scratch of static and the announcer vanished from the screen to be replaced by another officer.

"Now hear this," he shouted. "As of this moment this entire base is sealed to outgoing. I repeat, Mortstertoro is locked tight, gates sealed, aircraft departures canceled. The spy who landed in Marhaveno has been identified as a recruit who was shipped to this base. Here is his picture."

My heart skipped a beat or two, then settled down as the blurred photo of Jak, from my stolen ID, appeared on the screen. I was still one jump ahead of them. It would soon be discovered that Jak5138 was no longer on the base and the search would go elsewhere. I took my drink and went back to the table to stare into the wide and frightened eyes of Morton.

"You want a drink?" I asked before he could speak. He gurgled and pointed at the screen.

"Did you hear that?" I asked, and kicked him under the table. "Can't be much of a spy if he lets himself get drafted. Some spy! I'll bet you five he's caught and dead before dark." When he relaxed slightly I went on in a hoarse whisper. "It will take a long time to search this base . . ."

"No it won't—because they know just where to look. They know who you are, Jak. They'll go to Sergeant Klutz who will tell them he transferred you to Corporal Gow. Then they'll find Gow and . . ."

"And the trail will run cold. It will take them days to search a camp this size. And when they don't find the spy the first time they'll just do it again. They are not bright enough to consider having the computer check the records for the spy."

"Attention!" the announcer on the screen called out, waving a sheet of paper. "I have just been given this new information. The spy—and an accomplice—have managed to have themselves transferred from this base by illegal use of the base computer. All computer personnel are now under arrest and will probably be shot."

I turned away, not able to look Morton in the eye.

"Now that they know where to look," Morton asked hollowly, "how long will it take them to discover that we were never on that shipment? And then find out that a corporal and a sergeant who really were on that shipment were not on that shipment and are still here on the base?"

"How long?" I laughed, but there was a very hollow ring to it. "Could take days, weeks, no way to tell."

"How long?"

I sighed deeply. "They got some hotshot computer programs. Good security. I would say that we have maybe thirty minutes before they start looking for us."

His body shook as though he had received ten thousand volts and he started to jump to his feet. I reached out and held him down, then glanced at the bartender. He was looking at the TV.

"You're right," I said. "We get out of here, but slowly. On your feet. Follow me."

As we started toward the door the bartender glanced in our direction.

105

"Where's the transient barracks?" I said.

"Out the back door, turn right. See you."

"Yeah. See you."

We strolled out the back door and turned left. It was getting dark which might help.

"You got a plan?" Morton said, eagerness in his voice. "You know a way to get us out of this."

"Of course," I said, clapping him on the back. "Every step planned. We go this way."

I could hear the forced joviality in my voice; I hoped that he couldn't. He had to think that I knew what I was doing or he might crack. It was a white lie for the sake of his morale.

But what about my morale? I was holding it down successfully for the moment, but I could feel an awareness of dark panic knocking and ready to come in. I kept it at bay. We walked on down the company street, the lights coming on, lost in the milling military mass. How long would this last? The question was the answer: not very. The panic pushed a little harder.

I have heard it said that when a man knows that he is to be hanged, it concentrates his mind wonderfully. I wasn't going to be hanged, not for the present at least, but the foul breath of military prosecution on my neck was concentrating my mind almost as well. So much so that when an officer passed I turned to look at him. Turned and stopped until he vanished in the crowd. Morton was pulling feebly at my arm.

"What are you looking at? What's wrong?"

"Nothing wrong. Everything right. I know now exactly what we must do next."

"What?"

"Just come with me. I know that it is back this way, I noticed it when we passed."

"What, what?"

"BOQ." Before he could say What? What? What? I explained. "Bachelor Officers Quarters. Where the officers live when they are not getting drunk and making life a hell for the enlisted men. That is where we are going. There."

I pointed to the brightly lit building, guards at the front entrance, officers in their military finery pouring from it.

"That's suicide!" Morton said. The edge of hysteria back in his voice.

"Easy does it," I cozened. "We do not enter the building by this portal. Suicide as you say. But what has a front surely has a back. And from the exodus visible from that officerial snakepit it looks like everyone is on duty tonight. Everyone except us, that is." I chortled darkly and he looked at me out of the corners of his eyes as if I had gone mad. Perhaps I had. We would soon find out.

There was a wall behind the BOQ which we followed. A sort of alley led next to it, badly lit and just what I wanted. There was a door here let into the wall with a light above it. As we strolled past I read the sign, OFFICERS ONLY, and bent over and tied my shoe: it needed only a single glance to identify the lock. Then stood and on. I stopped in the shadows between two lights and bent to my shoe again. Only this time I came up with the lockpick.

"All right, here we go. The lock is nothing, single tumbler, pick it as easy as I pick my teeth. We walk back now and if no one is in sight we walk though it. Got that?"

The chatter of his teeth was the only response. I took his quivering arm and squeezed it. "It's all right, Morton. You'll see. Just do as I say and we'll soon be safe. Nice and quiet— here we go."

I tried not to catch any of Morton's fears, but they were very contagious. We stopped under the light, I put the lockpick into the keyhole. Felt and twisted. It didn't open.

"Someone's coming," Morton wailed.

"Piece of cake," I muttered, perspiration running down my face. "Opened these with my eyes shut."

"Getting closer!"

"Eyes shut!"

It wouldn't open. I shut my eyes, closed out all sensations, felt for the tumblers. Clicked it open.

"Inside!" I said, pulling him after me, closing the gate behind us. We stood with our backs to it, shivering in the darkness as the footsteps came closer, came to the gate . . . .

Passed it and went on.

"There, wasn't that easy?" I said, ruining the effect as my voice cracked and squeaked. Not that Morton noticed; he was shivering so hard that I could hear his teeth clatter. "Look, nice garden. Pathways for strolling, love seats for loving, all the nice things to keep the officerial classes happy. And beyond the garden the dark windows of their quarters, dark because the occupants have all gone out. So now all that we have to do is find a window to open . . ."

"Jak—what are we doing here?"

"I thought that was obvious. The military powers are looking for one recruit now. When their computer coughs out the next bit of news they will be looking for a corporal and a sergeant." I tried to ignore his moan. "So we get into this building and become officers. As simple as that."

I caught him as he dropped and laid him gently on the grass. "That's it. Have a little rest. I'll be right back."

The third window I tried was unlocked. I opened it and looked in. A mussed bed, open closet, empty room. Perfect. I found my way back to Morton who was just sitting up. He recoiled as I appeared out of the darkness and my quick hand over his mouth muffled his scream.

"Everything is fine. Almost finished."

I boosted him through the window and let him drop onto the bed, then closed and locked the window behind us. There was a key in the door which made everything very much easier.

"Look," I said, "lie here and recuperate. I'm going to lock you in. The building is empty as far as I can see, so what I have to do should not be long. Take a rest and I'll be back as soon as I can."

I went carefully, but the building was empty of life and and silent as the tomb. Its occupants away and hopefully hard at work. I had time to pick and choose, make my selections and select the right sizes. I heard a muffled moan of agony when I let myself back into the room, to which I responded as cheerfully as I could.

"New uniform—new persona!" I handed them over to Morton. "Get dressed and give me our old clothes. There's enough light from outside to make that easy. Here, let me tie that necktie, you are all butterfingers today."

Dressed and ready, our caps square upon our heads, our old clothes buried in a laundry basket, we sauntered forth into the corridor. Morton looked at me and gasped and fell away.

"Cheer up—you look the same way. Except that you are a second lieutenant while I am a captain. It is a young army."

"B-but," he stammered. "You are a . . . Military Policeman!"

"And so are you. No one ever questions a cop."

We turned the corner as I said this and approached the front entrance. The major standing there with a clipboard looked up at us and scowled.

"Now I have you," he said.

CHAPTER 12

I snapped to attention, I could think of nothing else to do—and hoped Morton was not too paralyzed to do the same. There were just two of them, the major and the guard at the door. After I dropped the major could I reach the guard before he could get out his gun? A neat problem. The major was looking at his clipboard. Now—get him!

He looked up as I swayed forward. The guard was looking at me too. I swayed back.

"I missed you at the airport," the major said. "You must have come on the earlier flight. But these shipping orders say two captains. Who is this lieutenant?"

Shipping orders? Two captains? I stopped my eyeballs spinning and finally threw my brain into gear.

"Could be an error, sir. Lot of confusion today. Might I see the orders?"

He grunted uncommunicatively and passed them over. I ran my finger down the list of crossed-off names to the remaining two at the bottom. Then passed them back.

"Error like I said, sir. I'm Captain Drem. This is Lieutenant Hesk, not captain the way they got it here."

"Right," he said, making the change on his sheet. "Let's go."

We went. Outside the door was a truck stuffed with Military Police, a very disgusting sight. The major climbed into the cab,

110

rank does have its privileges, and I led Morton to the rear. Moving quickly because I saw something that I hoped the major had not seen. Two MP officers, both captains, walking toward us. They scowled and passed and turned into the BOQ. I scowled in return, turning the scowl into a glare when I looked into the back of the truck and saw that there were no officers among the redhats there.

"What is this—a meeting of the girls' club," I snarled. "Move back, make room, shut up, give us a hand."

All of this was done with alacrity. Morton and I sat on the recently vacated bench and the truck pulled forward. I let out my breath slowly—from between still-snarling teeth. We bumped and swayed our way through the night and I began to feel very, very tired. It had been that kind of day.

"Do you know where we are going, captain?" a burly sergeant asked.

"Shut up!"

"Thank you, sir."

There was only silence after this witty exchange. Cold silence that continued until we ground to a stop and the major reappeared. "Climb out," he ordered. "Captain, follow me."

"Fall these men in, lieutenant," I told Morton. He stumbled after me his face white with despair in the glare of the street lights.

"How, what, glug," he whispered.

"Order a sergeant to do it," I whispered back. "Pass the buck, that's the army way."

I trotted after the major who had stopped before the entrance of a large building and was going through an immense ring of keys. I stood at ease and looked at the large posters beside the door. Then looked closer when I realized they were 3Ds, in living color, of a number of naked young woman. When my head moved they moved and I swayed slightly.

"Knock that off, captain," the major ordered and I snapped to attention, my eyes still focused on the sign that read BASE BURLESQUE—OFFICERS ONLY. The major found the key he was looking for and turned it in the lock. "No performance tonight," he said. "We've comandeered the place for an emergency

111

meeting. Top security. As soon as the techs get here I want the entire theatre swept clean. And I mean clean. I want an MP with every tech and I want a headcount and I am making you responsible. Got that?"

"Yes, sir."

"I'm going to check all the other doors personally to make sure they are locked. Get cracking, we only have an hour."

I threw a salute as he moved off around the building and wondered just what I had gotten myself into. The rumble of engines cut through my thoughts as a truck pulled up at the curb before me. A sergeant climbed down from the cab and saluted me.

"And what do we have here?" I asked.

"Instrument technicians, sir. We were ordered . . ."

"I'll bet you were. Unload them and fall them in."

"Yes, sir."

I stamped back to the MPs who were neatly lined up at attention and pointed my finger at Morton. "You, Lieutenant Hesk, get over in front of that entrance. No one in or out without my permission."

My heart dropped as Morton started to look over his shoulder. Memory of his new name apparently filtered through because he recovered himself and hurried away. I turned back and scowled at the MPs, with particular attention to the sergeant who stood before them. Gray-haired, skin like an old boot, stripes and hashmarks clogging his sleeve.

"You senior NCO?"

"Yes, sir."

"Right. Here is the drill. Those techs are going to sweep this theatre. I want one MP with every tech. I want every man counted in and counted out and I want no errors. And I want the sweep complete and overlapping and that building clean. Any questions?"

"No, captain. They'll snap-cagal for me."

"I thought they would. Get cracking."

He turned on his heel, inflated his lungs—and let out a blast of orders that blew the cap off the nearest MP. They moved.

112

I stepped back and nodded approval. Then stamped over and positioned myself next to Morton.

"Something big coming down," I said quietly. "Secret meeting in an hour and we are in charge of security." I ignored his moan of anguish. "Just stand around and look military and stay away from the major when he gets back. I don't know about you, but I find this very interesting." He moaned again and I strolled over to inspect the arrangements.

The technicians had shouldered their backpacks and were adjusting dials on the control panels that each of them wore slung about the chest. One of them pointed his detector wand at the side of the truck and I could see the needles jump; there was a squeal from the earphones that he had hung about his neck.

"Captain. Some trouble here." I turned around.

"What is it, sergeant."

"This cagal-kopf says he got a malfunction." He had a white-faced tech by the arm and was shaking him like a dog with a bone.

"Battery, sir," the man wailed. "Checked. . . it's a malfunction . . . fuse!"

"Arrest him, sergeant. The charge is sabotage. Have him shot at dawn." The sergeant smiled, the tech moaned and I bent until my face was close to his. "Or can you manage to trace and repair this malfunction in the next sixty seconds?"

"It's fixed, sir! I know how! Borrow a fuse!"

He stumbled away with the sergeant right behind him. I was falling into my role and beginning to enjoy myself. Though I was sure I would hate myself in the morning.

More MPs had arrived; the major reappeared and spread them around the theatre and in front of the entrance. I could see Morton begin to shiver at their presence so I hurried to take over from him.

"You can open that door now, lieutenant. No one goes in except these search teams. I want a head count going in and coming out."

Under the verbal abuse of the sergeant the search was finished just in time. The first official cars were appearing as the techs were being loaded back into the trucks.

"How did it go, sergeant?" I asked.

"Lot of beer cans, cagal like that. Swept secure, captain."

"Good. Move the troops out of the way, but keep them around in case we need them again."

I waved Morton after me and strolled over to the nearest truck, stood in its shadow where I could see what was happening.

"What's happening," Morton asked.

"Good question. Big, secret, and very sudden meeting of some kind. See that car, all officers of field rank or better."

"We have got to get out of here!"

"Why? Can you think of a safer place to be? We are part of the security here—so no questions asked. Except by me. Look at that one getting out of the limo! Must have nine stars on his shoulders. Big stuff tonight. And that officer behind him. Never saw that uniform before. Something special . . ."

This officer turned about and I froze. A single silver skull on the shoulder of his gray-green coat. Another skull on the front of his cap.

And beneath the black brim of the cap a familiar face.

Captain Garth. Former captain of a Venian freighter. The man responsible for the death of my friend The Bishop.

"Stay here," I ordered Morton, and stepped out of the darkness as soon as Garth had turned away. I walked toward him as he approached the security check at the entrance. Passed right behind him as he reached the major who threw a very snappy salute. I could hear the major's voice clearly as I passed and went on.

"They are almost all inside, General Zennor."

"Report to me when the count is complete. Then seal this door tight."

I stamped on, checked the guards, stamped back to Morton's side.

"What was that all about?" he asked.

"Forget about it. Nothing to do with you."

114

No longer a simple spacer captain. A general now. Probably always a general. Zennor. What was he up to? What was this entire army up to that he seemed to be ordering around? And how could I find out?"

When the major called I did not even hear him. Only when Morton kicked me in the ankle did I realize that I was the Captain Drem he was talking to.

"Yes, sir. You want me, sir?"

"Not falling asleep, are you, Drem?"

"No, major, I was just going over the security in my head."

"Well go over it on your feet which will accomplish a lot more. I've stationed a man at every entrance to this theatre. Inspect them."

I saluted his back enthusiastically as he turned away. This might very well be the opportunity I was waiting for.

"Lieutenant," I called out. "Inspection tour. This way."

I rubbed my hands together happily as we walked around the theatre. "Morton, there is something important going on here and I mean to find out more about it."

"Don't! Stay clear!"

"Normally good advice. But this time I have to know what is happening, what *he* is up to. Did you see the uniforms? All senior officers. And I was ratted to earlier today that an invasion was being planned. It doesn't take a great brain to figure out that this meeting has something to do with that invasion. But how do I get inside?"

We were approaching a side entrance to the theatre and the MP there snapped to attention as soon as we appeared. I shook the locked door and scowled at him.

"This door locked when you got here?"

"Yes, sir."

"Anyone try to get in?"

"No, sir!"

"What are your orders?"

"Kill anyone who goes near the door." He had his hand on his pistol butt.

"Does that include your commanding officers?" I shouted at him, my mouth in his ear. He swayed and his hand dropped to his side.

115

"No, captain."

"Then you are wrong and *you* could be shot for disobeying orders. An inspecting officer may try the door to see if it is locked. If an inspecting officer should attempt to go through the door he is to be instantly killed. Is that clear?"

"Very clear, sir."

"Then wipe the smile from your face. You seem to enjoy that thought too much."

"Yes, sir. I mean no, sir!"

I growled a bit more and continued my inspection. We had almost circumnavigated the building when we reached a door in the rear. The guard there stood at attention. I shook the locked door and looked at the metal staircase beside it.

"Where does this go to?" I asked.

"Emergency exit."

"Is there a guard there."

"Yes, sir."

Morton followed me up the clanging stairs. I stopped halfway and bent to remove the lockpick from my shoe. Morton opened his mouth but shut it again when I put my finger to my lips. I had to find out what was happening inside.

We stamped upward and when we emerged on the balustraded corridor the guard there had his gun half out of the holster.

"Do you intend to aim that weapon at me?" I asked coldly.

"No, sir, sorry." He put it away and snapped to attention. I put my face close to his.

"Do you know it is a court-martial offense to point a weapon at an officer?"

"I wasn't, sir, no! I'm alone here, didn't know who was coming. . ."

"I don't believe you, soldier. There is something wrong here. Stand over there by the lieutenant."

As he turned about I had the lockpick in the keyhole, delicately, turning it, clicking it. I stepped back away from it as he stopped and about-faced.

"This door is locked?"

"Yes, sir. Of course, it has to be. I am stationed here because of the door . . ."

116

His voice wound down as I reached out and opened the door. Then closed it and wheeled to face him.

"You are under arrest, soldier. Lieutenant—take this man to the major. Tell him what has happened. Return with the major at once. Move it!"

As they stamped away I inserted the lockpick yet again, twisted and pressed hard. Something snapped inside the lock. Only then did I put the lockpick away, open the door and slip inside. Closing it silently behind me.

The small entranceway was sealed with dusty curtains. Light trickled between them; I bent forward and separated them a tiny amount.

". . . important that security be absolute until blastoff. You have your sealed orders, not to be opened until H hour. Rendezvous points are marked . . ."

I knew that voice well. Once Garth, now Zennor. I parted the curtains just a bit more to make sure. There he was, almost below me, pointing at the large chart behind him. I looked at the chart, then closed the curtains and stepped back.

I was closing the door behind me when hurried footsteps sounded on the stairs. The major appeared, face red and strained.

"What is happening?"

"I'm not sure, sir. The guard that was stationed here had his weapon drawn, acted suspiciously. I tried this door. It was unlocked. That was when I sent for you, sir."

"It can't be. I locked it myself."

It opened at his touch and his face whitened with shock. He pulled it quickly closed. "You haven't been inside?"

"Of course not, major. I have my orders. Perhaps the lock is defective."

"Yes, perhaps!" He fumbled out his ring of keys, found the right key and turned it in the lock. Metal grated.

"It won't lock!"

"May I try it, sir?"

I took the keys from his limp fingers and, naturally, had no better luck in sealing the door. When I handed back the keys I spoke in a low voice.

"There will be an investigation, sir, trouble. Not fair to you.

I'll see that the guard talks to no one about this. Then I'll get a welder, seal the door. Might be best, major, don't you think so?"

He started to speak, then closed his mouth, and thought instead. Looking from me to the door. Then he noticed the keys still in his hand. He put them in his pocket and straightened his shoulders.

"As you say, captain, nothing happened. No point in getting involved in investigations and suchlike. I'll stay here. Send the welder at once."

"Very good, sir. I'll take care of everything."

Morton was waiting at the foot of the stairs, the frightened MP standing beside him. I walked up to the man and gave him a good glare.

"I am going to be kind to you, soldier, although it goes against the grain. I think it might be wisest if we forgot all about this matter. What is your name?"

"Pip7812, sir."

"All right, Pip, you can go back to your unit now. But—if I hear any rumors or loose talk about locks or such you will be dead within twenty-four hours. Understand?"

"Locks, captain? I'm afraid I don't know what you mean."

"Very good, Pip. Report to the sergeant. Tell him I need a welder here at once. Move."

He moved. "What was all that about?" Morton asked.

"That was about warfare, my friend. I know now what they are up to here. I know all about their invasion plans."

Except—what could I possibly do about it?

118

CHAPTER 13

When the meeting broke up I saw to it that I was busily occupied away from the theatre entrance. It was a long chance that Zennor would recognize me from his Captain Garth days. But even a long chance is some chance, so I stayed out of sight. The troops formed up and marched away: with the emergency over they were not being coddled with effete tranportation. The major had a car at his disposal but I turned down his offer.

"We could have used a lift," Morton complained as the car moved away.

"To where? Prison? The further we are from authority the happier we should be."

"I'm tired."

"Who isn't? Not to mention hungry. Let's find a place to spend some of Gow's money . . ."

"*Jim . . . Jim diGriz . . .*"

The sound was high-pitched, barely audible. Was I hearing things? I looked around but Morton was the only person nearby.

"Did you hear anything?"

"No. Should I?"

"Don't know. A sudden ringing in my ears. But I swear I heard something."

"Maybe it was that moth on your shoulder talking to you. Ha-ha."

119

"Ha-ha yourself. What moth?"

"See it there? Sitting on your captain's bars. Should I brush it off?"

"No. Leave it."

I turned my head and blinked and could just make out the moth. It flapped its wings and took off—and landed on my ear.

"Go . . . aergropl . . . now."

"I can't understand you."

"That's because I'm not talking."

"Shut up, Morton. I'm talking to the moth, not to you."

His jaw dropped and he moved quickly sideways. "Repeat message," I said, ignoring him for the moment.

"Airfield . . . go airfield."

"Right, go to the airfield. Understood. Over and out." The moth fluttered away and I patted Morton on the shoulder; I could feel him shivering. "Come on, cheer up. And stop looking at me as though I were mad. The moth is a communication device, nothing more."

"Communicating with whom?"

"The less you know, the less trouble you can get into."

"You really are a spy, aren't you?"

"Yes and no. I'm here on my own business, but certain parties are trying to get me involved in their business. Do you understand?"

"No."

"Good. Let's find the airfield. At a guess I would say that it is over there where all the lights are and the planes are landing. Coming with me?"

"Do I have a choice? Is there any way of going back? Starting over again? I mean we can't just sneak back into the barracks as if nothing happened, can we?"

"You know that we can't."

He sighed and nodded his head. "I know. But I'm just not cut out for the kind of thing that we have been doing. And where is it going to end?"

A good question. With very little hope of an answer at the present time.

"Truthfully—I don't know. But you have my word, Morton, because I got you into this. My first priority, before anything else, is to get you out of trouble and safe. Don't ask how— because I don't know yet."

"You can't blame yourself. It was I who opened my mouth to that cagaling corporal. That's where it started."

We had been walking while we talked, getting closer and closer to the airfield. The road that we were taking curved around the end of the field, separated from it by a high wire fence, well illuminated by bright lights. On the other side of the fence were grass and taxiways. A heavy freighter had just landed. It trundled by and we watched it go. When it had moved on a flock of black birds swooped down and began poking about in the grass. One of them unfolded its wings and flew toward the fence, landing on the other side. It cocked its head at me and spoke.

"You are not alone."

"Obviously. He's safe. Is that you, Varod."

"No. Captain Varod is off duty."

"Get him. I don't talk to just any old crow."

"You will be contacted."

The bird turned about and opened its beak and spread its wings. It took off without flapping, making a whistling sound.

"Jet powered," I said. "Air intake in its mouth. Jet exhaust just where you imagine it might be. Let's walk."

There was the whine of an approaching siren and a detector van came hurtling down the road. It slowed when it passed us, the dish aerial pointing in our direction, then moved on.

"They are really efficient about spotting radio transmission," I said.

"Is that bird a radio?"

"Among other things. It is remotely controlled and probably has some logic circuitry for hopping about and staying with the other birds. Only when it transmits back to base can it be detected."

"Where is the base?"

"You don't want to know. Or who is operating it. But I can assure you they mean no harm to this country."

121

"Why not?" He spoke with great agitation now. "Tell them to get to work and get rid of the military and their friends and start elections again. Do you know how long the present state of emergency has been going on? I'll tell you, I checked. The so-called temporary emergency was declared over two hundred years ago. Some emergency! Tell your bird friends they can cause all the trouble they want as far as I'm concerned."

"I heard that," the bird said in a deep voice, swooping out of the darkness and landing on my shoulder. "Our work is not to cause trouble. We labor only to . . ."

"Varod, shut up," I said. "We have limited communication time before the detectors show up again and let us not waste it with speeches. I have found out the invasion plans."

The bird cocked his eye at me and nodded. "Very good," it said. "Details soonest, I am recording. Where is the invasion site?"

"Not on this planet. They are readying a space fleet to attack another planet."

"You are sure of this?"

"I eavesdropped. I'm sure."

"What is the name of the planet?"

"I have no idea."

"I will return. I must get rid of the detector van."

The bird whistled into the sky leaving the stench of burned jet fuel behind. It did a neat barrel roll and landed on the top of a passing truck. Still broadcasting, I imagine, because a moment later the detector van hurtled by in pursuit of the truck. We walked on.

"What's this about an invasion? What did you find out?"

"Just that. The one in charge is a General Zennor. I imagine it will happen pretty soon from the way that he was talking . . ."

There was a whistle and a blast of hot air: sharp claws dug into my scalp right through my cap as the bird landed on my head.

"You must discover what planet is being invaded," it said.

"Find out yourself. Follow them when they take off."

"Impossible. The nearest spacer with detection gear is four days away. It may not get here in time."

"Tough. Ouch."

I rubbed my scalp where the bird had removed some hair when it took off, then bent to pick up my cap. We turned a corner just as another detector vehicle roared by behind us.

"Let's mix with the crowds," I told Morton. "That detector is going to get suspicious if it keeps finding us around every time it gets a reading."

"Could we mix with crowds that are eating and drinking?"

"Good thinking. And I know just where to go."

I stepped off the curb as I said this and stood with my hand raised—directly in front of a truck. The driver hit the brake and squeeled to a shivering halt in front of me.

"Driving a little fast, aren't we?" I snarled at the driver.

"I didn't see you, captain . . ."

"And I know why you didn't see me. Because one of your headlights is burnt out, that's why. But I am feeling generous today. If you take me and my companion to the Officers' Club I might forget I ever saw you."

Not that the driver had any choice. He dropped us in front of the club and roared away. We entered to sample the heady joys which, for the most part, were identical with the noncoms' club except here there were waitresses. About a quarter of the tables were occupied: everyone else must still be on duty. Our steaks and beer appeared with exemplary speed and we dived at them with growls of hunger. We were almost finished when an officer appeared in the doorway and blew a whistle.

"All right, fall out and fall in. Everyone. Emergency muster. Transportation outside. That means you," he said pointing a mean finger in our direction.

"We just came off duty, colonel," I said.

"You're just going back on. And I see that you have eaten which I haven't, so don't cross me boy."

"Just leaving, sir!"

Morton and I joined the rush, out the door and into the waiting bus. The colonel entered last and the driver pulled away.

"Here is as much as I can tell you," the colonel said, shouting so he could be heard above the engine's noise. "Due to reasons that are no concern of yours our current plans have been moved forward. You are going into action and you are going at once." There were questions and cries of complaint which he shouted down.

"Silence! I know you are all desk-driving fat-gutted base personnel—but you are also soldiers. Because of the acceleration in planning some combat officer transfers will not arrive in time. You officers have all just volunteered to take their place. You will get combat gear and you will join your troops and you will board the transport at once. We will all be away by midnight."

The colonel ignored all the complaints and protests and finally lost his temper. He pulled a wicked-looking pistol from his holster and fired a shot up through the roof of the bus. Then pointed the gun at us. The silence was extreme. He had a nasty smile and pointed teeth.

"That is better," he said, and kept the weapon pointed. "You are all time-serving cagal-kopfs which means you have wangled and bought soft assignments which will do you no good now. You are in the army and in the army you obey orders." He fired another shot into the roof as the bus stopped. "Now, I want volunteers for combat duty. All volunteers step forward."

We stepped forward in a rush. The lights in the supply depot were burning brightly in the night, clerks waited by the loaded shelves and an officer blocked the doorway.

"Move aside," our colonel said, keeping a wary eye on us as we emerged from the bus.

"Can't, sir," the supply officer said. "I can't issue anything until I have the orders from headquarters. They haven't come through yet . . ."

The colonel shot out the light over the depot door then put the hot muzzle of his gun against the supply officer's nose.

"What did you say?" the colonel growled.

"Orders just arrived, sir! Open up in there and issue everything. Quickly!"

And quickly was what it was. We surged through the depot at top speed, grabbing up clothing, boots, barracks bags, belts, everything on the run. The manic colonel seemed to be everywhere now, his gun banging occasionally to keep up the pace. The street behind the building was a hellish scene of officers tearing off their uniforms, discarding them on the ground as they pulled on the green combat fatigues, jamming helmets on heads and everything else into their bags. Staggering forward into the next building where weapons were being issued. But no ammunition I noticed; the colonel was no fool. Stumbling under the weight of my burdens I staggered out into the street and dropped against a wall, adrip with perspiration. Morton dropped next to me.

"Do you have any idea what this is all about?" he gasped.

"A very good idea. The powers that be think they are being spied upon. With good reason since they are. So they have pushed up the date of their invasion before details of their plans can be discovered."

"What will happen to us?"

"We invade. At least we will go out as officers. Which means that we can stay to the rear and order the troops forward in case of any enemy resistance . . ."

"Open your barracks bag," the moth said into my ear.

"What are you saying?"

There was a sharp burning sensation in my earlobe as the moth discharged its batteries into my skin.

"Open . . . bag!" it gasped and dropped off, batteries drained and dead.

I bent and opened the bag, wondering if something had been planted there. There was a whistle and the stink of jet fuel as the bird plummeted past me into the bag.

"I'm not smuggling this damn bird and getting caught and shot!" I shouted.

"You must do it for the sake of all mankind," the bird said, eyes glowing wildly. "Reactivate by pressing the bill twice. Out."

The glow died and it went limp. I jammed the bag shut as footsteps approached.

"Into the transport!" the colonel ordered. "We are on our way!"

CHAPTER 14

There was very little time to sit around and relax. As fast as the officers were spewed out of the supply depot, staggering under the weight of all their combat gear, trucks appeared to carry them away into the night. Groaning and complaining, with the rest of the groaners and complainers, Morton and I heaved our bags and weapons over the tailgate of a truck and clambered after. When it was filled to capacity, and slightly more, we lurched away.

"And to shink that I just reenlishted. Voluntarily," an officer expostulated leaning heavily against me. There was a gurgling sound from an upended bottle.

"Share the wealth, share the wealth," I muttered as I pried the bottle from his shaking grasp. It was pretty foul stuff, but was rich with alcohol.

"You still don't drink?" I gasped at Morton, holding up the rapidly emptying bottle.

"I'm learning fast." He gulped then coughed, then gulped again before relinquishing the bottle to its original owner.

A deep rumble washed over us and we had to close our eyes against the glare as a spacer took off. The invasion was on. We swayed into each other as the truck squealed to a halt and a now familiar and loathsome voice ordered us out. Our nemesis, the pressgang colonel, was waiting for us. He was backed up now

126

by a radio operator and a gaggle of noncoms. Behind him companies, battalions of soldiers, were marching in good order to the waiting transports.

"Now hear this," the colonel bellowed. "Those are good troops back there, and they need good officers. Unhappily all I have for them are you fat-bottomed desk types, the dregs of the base. So I'm going to split you up, one to every company, in the hopes that you will maybe get some experience before you get dead."

This was not good. I had promised Morton I would look after him. Which I could not do if we were in different companies. I sighed. I would have to break the first rule of military survival. Although it violated the primary army axiom—keep your mouth shut and don't volunteer—I volunteered. Stepping forward smartly and slamming my bootheels down as I snapped to attention.

"Sir! My bottom is lean, my gut is flat. I have field experience. I fire sharpshooter, I instruct unarmed combat."

"And I don't believe you!" he roared into my face.

I threw him onto the ground, put my foot on his back, took away his gun, shot out one of the streetlights, helped him to his feet and handed back his weapon. His fierce glare melted almost to a smile as he wiped pebbles from his uniform.

"I could use a few more like you. You get a combat company. Name?"

"Drem. I respectfully request Lieutenant Hesk here as exec. He is young and dumb but I have been training him."

"You got him. Move out. Any more volunteers?"

I grabbed up my bags before he could change his mind and hurried off toward the transports with Morton stumbling behind.

"I thought that I was going to die when you knocked him down," he gasped. "You took some chance."

"Just being alive in the modern world is taking a chance," I pontificated, "what with all the carcinogens and traffic accidents. And I think we can stop and put the bags down. Help has arrived."

An eager-looking sergeant, with a bald head, large moustache and two privates, came trotting up and I returned his salute.

127

"I am Acting First Sergeant Blogh. If you are Captain Drem you are the new CO," the sergeant said.

"Right both times, sergeant. Get those men on these bags and let's go."

"Last of the company boarding now. We blast off in ten minutes. "

"We can make it. Let's move."

The loading ramp vanished from behind our heels and the outer lock began to grind shut. We had to climb over boxes of equipment bolted to the deck to reach the stairs. Two flights up was the company, sprawled from wall to wall on their G pads. We dived for ours and were just horizontal when the red lights began flashing and the engines came to life.

As takeoffs go, it went. They poured on a lot more G's than a commercial transport would, but that is what the army is all about. When the acceleration dropped to one-G I stood and waved the sergeant over.

"Canteens full?"

"Yes, sir."

"Let them drink, but no food for awhile . . ."

There was a roar of sound from the speakers followed by an overly-amplified voice. "All commanding officers to deck two now. All COs, now."

"Lieutenant," I called out to a very queasy-looking Morton. "Take over until I get back. Let the noncoms do all the work." I bent and added in a whisper, "Don't let that bird-bag out of sight. If it is opened we will really be in the cagal."

He moaned slightly and I hurried away before he began to feel too sorry for himself. There were other officers climbing the gangway, all of them curious and expectant.

"Maybe now we will find out what this whole thing is about."

"They got to tell us something—we been living on latrine rumors for a year."

The dining hall was not that big, so only the first arrivals got seats. The rest of us crowded in between the tables and leaned against the walls. An ancient sergeant checked us off his list when we came in. When he was satisfied he reported to

128

a two-star general at the top table. The hum of conversation died down as the sergeant called for our attention.

"For them of you newly transferred to this division this here is your commanding officer, General Lowender, and he has an important announcement to make."

There was silence as the general turned to us, nodded sagely, and spoke.

"This is it, men. H-hour, D-day, the moment you have all been expecting, nay, looking forward to eagerly. The captain of this ship has reported that we are on course, with no chance of turning back now. So the secret orders can be opened."

He took up a large envelope heavy with red seals and tore it asunder, the sound of ripping paper loud in the silence. He held up the red-bound volume inside.

"This is it. You will have heard rumors that we plan a defensive action against Zemlija. That is wrong. Security planted those rumors to mislead the enemy. Our offworld enemies are many and their spies everywhere. That has explained our great need for secrecy. That need is passed. As you can tell we are now in space and heading toward a new world. A rich world. A world that lost contact with the rest of the galaxy thousands of years ago. And, more important, a world only *we* know exists. It is inhabited, but the natives are backward and do not deserve to have this verdant world for their own greedy selves. Is the machine ready? Good. General Zennor, the discoverer of this rich planet, will tell you about it in his own words."

My pulse hammered and I started to sink down before I realized that it was just a recording and I did not have to worry about being recognized. The lights dimmed a bit, the general took a digital recording from the envelope and slipped it into the projector. Zennor's repulsive hologramed features floated before us.

"Soldiers of Nevenkebla, I salute you. You are now embarked on the greatest venture ever conceived by our country. Your victory in the field will enrichen and strengthen our fatherland so that none will ever dare consider an attack upon us. The riches of a new world will be ours. The riches of this world—Chojecki!"

There was a blare of tinny music as Zennor vanished to be replaced by the blue sphere of a planet floating in space. But if we were spared his image his flatulent voice still hammered in our ears.

"Chojecki. Rich, warm, fertile. It was a chance in a million that we discovered it. The ship I commanded was being followed by the killers of the League Navy and we used a random, untraceable jump to escape them. This noble planet was what we found. Perhaps there is a higher power that guided us to our destiny, perhaps the needs of our noble land were divined by benevolencies unknown to us."

"Perhaps that is a load of old cagal," someone whispered and there were mutters of agreement in the darkness. These were combat officers who preferred truth to propaganda. But there was no stopping Zennor.

"We landed and made a survey. It is a rich planet with immense reserves of heavy metals, abundant forests, untapped rivers to supply hydroelectric power. If there is anything at all wrong with Chojecki it is the present inhabitants."

We listened now with interest because there was an edge of irritation that Zennor could not keep out of his voice.

"They are disgusting people, with vile attitudes and strange perversions. We approached them openly, extending the hand of friendship. We offered them aid, companionship, trade, contact with a superior civilization. And do you know what we got in return? Do you know what they did?"

The anger in his voice was obvious now, his audience eager.

"I'll tell you what they did. They did nothing! They completely ignored us, turned away from us—rejected all civilized contact."

"Probably knew just what they were doing," someone said and the general shouted for silence. The planet popped out of existence and Zennor's image returned. His temper was under control now but there was a baleful look in his eye.

"So you officers will understand that what we are doing is for their own benefit. Ours is an old culture and a wise one. We extended the hand of friendship and aid and it was rejected. We have been insulted, offended by these peasants. Therefore, for their own good, we must show them that Nevenkebla pride does not take insult easily. They have asked for this and they are going to get it. We come in friendship to aid them. If they reject our aid they have only themselves to blame.

"Long live Nevenkebla!

"Long live positive peace!"

The lights came up and we were all our feet cheering like fools. I cheered as loud as anyone. Trumpets blared and a rather dreary piece of recorded music began playing. Everyone snapped to attention and sang the words of their despicable anthem.

> Long live Nevenkebla,
> Land of peace,
> Land of goodness, land of light.
> Long live our leaders,
> Sweet men of mercy.
> Long shall we preserve
> Liberty's right. But dare to attack us—
> And you got a fight!

There was more like this and I hummed along and was exceedingly happy when the singing ended. A holomap now hung in the air and General Lowender poked it with his finger.

"You will all be issued with maps and detailed orders. We will meet again tomorrow after you have studied them. At that time we will go over the plan of attack in detail. But as an overall approach—this is what will happen.

"This division, the 88th, known as the Fighting Green Devils, has the honor of liberating this industrial section of the largest city called by the barbaric name of Bellegarrique. There are mines here and here, warehouses, a rail transportation system and here, ten kilometers away, a dam at the end of this lake that provides electricity for the city. For the benefit of these selfish people we will occupy all of these targets. We will liberate them from the futility of their rejection of our reasonable needs."

"A question, general," a colonel called out. The general nodded. "What kind of defenses can we expect? How large is their army? How modern?"

"That is a good question, colonel, and a vital one. We must be prepared for anything, any variety of attack, any kind of surprise. Because these people are very subtle, tricky, wily, treacherous. It seems that, well, in all of the contacts made by General Zennor, all of the investigations made by skilled agents, it seems that something very suspicious was found to be happening. It appears, on the surface that is, that these treacherous people have no army, no defenses—they do not even have a police force!"

He waited for the hum of excited voices to die down before he raised his hand for silence.

"Now we all know that this is impossible. A country needs defenses against attack, therefore every country must have an army for defense. The criminal elements in society would plunder and destroy were they not curbed by the police. Now we know that those are realities. We *know* that these treacherous people are hiding their cowardly armies from us. Therefore we must proceed with armed caution, ready for any sneak attack. We must free them from themselves. We owe that to them."

I have never in my life heard such a load of old cagal—but it impressed my military mates who cheered wildly at the thought of all the nice mayhem to come.

While I wondered what disastrous future lay in store for these simple people about to be liberated from their stupid and peaceful ways.

Liberation by destruction was on the way!

We would free them even if we had to kill them all to do it!

CHAPTER 15

I returned to my company, clutching the package of sealed orders and holding tight to the idea that this was the most insane endeavor I had ever heard of. Morton looked up when I entered the cabin.

"You are wearing a very worried look," he said. "Something personal—or should we all be worried?"

"Anything I can do for you, captain?" Sergeant Blogh asked, popping in the door behind me. They all wanted to know about the meeting. I threw the package onto the bed.

"Sergeant, what is the position regarding strong drink on troop transports about to go into action?"

"It is strictly forbidden, sir, and a court-martial offense. But one of the spare tanks on the command car is filled with ninety-nine."

"Ninety-nine what?"

"Ninety-nine percent pure alcohol. Cut half with water and stir in dehydrated orange juice."

"Since we are going into combat I am making a field appointment. Acting First Sergeant Blogh you are now First Sergeant Blogh."

There was a rattle as Morton dropped three canteen cups onto the table, a thud as a bag of orange crystals followed. I could see where he was getting adjusted to the army.

133

The sergeant came back with a twenty liter jerrycan, which with added water would make forty liters of hundred proof drink which, in turn, should make this voyage more bearable.

We clanked mugs and drank deep.

"This stuff is pretty repulsive," Morton said holding out his empty cup for more. "Can you now tell us what you found out?"

"I have some good news and some good news. The first good news is that we are going to invade and occupy an incredibly rich and heretofore unknown planet named Chojecki. Secondly—they don't appear to have any defenses of any kind. No military, no police, nothing.

"Impossible," the sergeant said.

"Anything is possible in the fullness of time and the width of the galaxy. Let us hope the report is correct because it will certainly make for an easy invasion."

"I think it is a trap." The sergeant still wasn't buying it. I nodded.

"The general seems to think the same thing. He is sure that there is a secret army in hiding."

"Not necessarily," Morton said. "Before entering the army I was a student of history. So I can tell you. Diverse are the ways of mankind. As you have so truthfully stated, captain, in the fullness of time and the width of the galaxy there have been many kinds of societies, forms of government . . ."

"You got governments you got armies. That's the way it's got to be."

The drink was making the sergeant pugnacious and Morton maudlin. Time to close the bar.

"Right." I climbed to my feet and kicked the jerrycan of alcohol out of sight under the table. "Sergeant, get the noncoms together. Tell them what I told you about the invasion, have them pass it on to the troops. That will be all for now."

The door closed behind the sergeant and Morton dropped his head onto the table and began to snore. He was sure a cheap drunk. I finished the repulsive, though certainly lethal, orange-alcohol mixture and heard my stomach rumble in protest. Or was it hunger? A long time and a lot of distance had gone by since that half-eaten steak in the officers' club. I dug into my pack and found some of the rations that we had been issued. A reddish tube was labeled HOTPUP MEAL. In smaller print it stated that it would feed two and could be opened by puncturing the white circle on the end. I pulled my combat knife out of my boot and stabbed the thing enthusiastically. It instantly grew exceedingly hot and burned my fingers. I dropped it onto the table where it rumbled and hissed and began to expand. I kept the knife ready in case it attacked me. There was a ripping sound as the casing split open and it expanded into an arm-long sausage. It looked repulsive but smelled quite good. I hacked off the end, impaled it on my knife and ate. The only thing missing was some beer.

Life continued in this manner. Day followed day like the flapping of a great red sausage. As good as the hotpup had tasted at first bite, I grew to loathe the sorry sausages. As did we all since, due to some bit of mismanagement in the rush to load the transports and be away, hotpups were the only food that had been put aboard. Even the general had to eat the repulsive objects and he was not pleased.

We had meetings and briefings, all of which I duly passed on to the troops. We cleaned and recleaned our weapons, sharpened our knives, had shortarm inspections to keep the medical officers on their toes, worked our way down through the alcohol until fifteen days had passed and the officers were ordered to yet one more meeting.

This one was different. The knot of field officers around General Lowender was buzzing with talk and much consultation of maps. As soon as we were all assembled the general stood— and hammered his fists down on the table.

"The invasion has begun!"

He waited until the cheering had died down before he continued. "The first scouts have gone down and report no resistance. As yet. But we must be wary because all of this could be a dodge to suck us into a trap of some kind. You all have your orders, you know what to do—so there is nothing more to be said. We touch down in two hours. Set your watches. So that is it. Except, boys—give 'em hell!"

135

More wild cheering followed before we hurried back to tell the troops what lay ahead.

"About time," was Sergeant Blogh's comment. "The troops get soft, lose their edge lying around on their chunks like they been. About time."

"Get the noncoms and we'll go over the attack thoroughly just once more," I said, spreading out the now-familiar map. With the landing this close I had their undivided attention. "Here is where we are supposed to touch down," I said, tapping the map. "Now how many of you believe that the military pilot flying this thing will actually land on the correct spot?"

The silence was complete.

"Right. I feel the same way. We are supposed to touch down at dawn which means it will probably be dark—or raining, or both. We will be first out because we got the longest way to go. I will lead in the command car which if it is dark and unless we are fired upon, will have its lights on so you can see it."

Sergeant Blogh frowned and touched his clipboard full of papers. "A specific order here from the general states that no lights are to be used."

"Correct. And the general will be the last one to leave the ship and we will be first, and we have to get clear at once because there are tanks right behind us."

"Lights to be on!" the sergeant said, firmly.

"I will proceed to the nearest hill or highpoint to check the map and see if we have landed where planned. If not I shall determine just where the hell we are and where we are going. The lieutenant here will muster the troops and follow the command car. When I know where we are going we will go there. Here. To the dam. To the generating plant that supplies the unpronounceable city of Bellegarrique with electricity. Our job is to seize and secure. Any questions? Yes, corporal?"

"Can we leave hotpup rations here and live off the countryside?"

"Yes and no. We take the hotpups in case we should run across the supply officer so we can stuff him with them. But we seize some native food soonest. It will be brought to me for testing before distribution. Anyone else?"

136

"Ammunition. When do we get the ammo?"

"It's on the disembarkation deck now. You will be issued with it when we go down there. You will see that each man is issued his lot. You will also see that no weapons are loaded. We don't want any guns going off inside this ship."

"We load after we hit the ground?" the First Sergeant asked.

"You load when I tell you to. We do not expect any resistance. If there is no resistance we don't need to shoot any of the locals. If we don't shoot the locals the invasion will be an instant success. If the weapons aren't loaded they cannot shoot. The weapons will not be loaded."

There was a murmur of protest at this and beetle-browed Corporal Aspya expressed their mutual concern. "Can't attack without loaded weapons."

"Yes you can," I said in my coldest voice. "You can do what you are ordered to do. One weapon will be loaded. *My* weapon will be loaded. And I will shoot any man—or officer—who disobeys orders. More questions? No. Dismissed. We proceed to landing positions in thirty minutes."

"They are not happy about this ammunition thing," Morton said when the others had gone.

"Tough cagal. I am not happy about this killing thing. No ammo, no shooting. This will stop accidents happening."

He adjusted the straps on his pack, still worrying. "They should be able to defend themselves . . ."

"Morton!" I ordered. "Look in the mirror. What do you see? You see Lieutenant Hesk staring back and you are beginning to think like him. Remember, Morton—you are a draft dodger, a man of peace, a reluctant soldier. Have you forgotten? Have you ever seen anyone killed?"

"Not really. My aunt died and I saw her in the coffin."

"A man of the world . . . I''ve seen them die and it is not a nice thing to watch. And when you are dead you are dead forever, Morton. Remember that when you listen to the men of violence, the dogs of war, the sellers of hate. Do you want to die?"

As I said this I placed the point of my knife against his throat. His eyebrows went up and up and he gasped out a *No!* My knife vanished as quickly as it had appeared and I nodded.

"You know what—neither do I. And neither does anyone else on that planet down there where we are landing with thousands of military numbskulls, and I wonder how I ever got involved in all this!"

Morton sighed. "Like me, you got drafted."

"And how we did! Like always, old men send young men to war. They ought to make the minimum draft age fifty-five. That would put an end to warfare pretty quickly let me tell you!"

An alarm sounded and all the lights blinked. I looked at my watch.

"This is it. Let's go."

The disembarkation hold was a red-lit hell of men, machines and equipment. I struggled between them to my command car which was poised at the top edge of the ramp. I kicked the shackles that held it down.

"They're explosive," Sergeant Blogh said. "They blow loose as soon as the ramp drops."

"Seeing is believing. It is going to be very hard to drive out of here if they don't. Has all the gear been loaded on this car like I ordered?"

"Just as you ordered, sir. Extra ammo under the back seat."

I looked in and nodded agreement. I had filled a number of canteens with our hundred proof orange juice and stowed them in this ammunition box. Also stowed in the box, under a false bottom, was that talking spy bird I had been lumbered with. I could not leave it lying about for someone to find.

The floor pushed up at me and I kept my legs bent. We were doing a slow two G drop for the last part of the landing since we could not be lolling around on deceleration couches before going into combat. Except for superior officers, of course. I pushed hard and worked my way into the command car and sat down heavily next to the driver.

"Ignition on," I ordered. "But don't hit the starter until the ramp drops."

The seat of the car came up and hit me just as the roar of the ship's engines stopped. We bounced on the springs and there were loud explosions from all sides. Hopefully the shackles blowing loose. With a great creaking the ramp moved—then dropped.

"Start her up!" I shouted as rain blew in from the darkness outside. "And turn on the lights so we can see where we are going!"

The command car roared down the ramp and hit the ground with a great crash and splash as we plowed through a puddle. Nothing was visible ahead except for the rain sheeting through the beams of the headlights. We churned on into the darkness. When I looked backward I could see the files of laden soldiers coming after us.

"There is an awful lot of water ahead, sir," the driver said, slamming on his brakes.

"Well turn you idiot, don't drown us. Turn right and move away from the transport."

Lightning split the sky and thunder rolled dramatically. I pounded the driver on the shoulder and pointed.

"There's a hill there, a rise of some kind, beyond that row of trees. Get us to it."

"That's a fence there, captain!"

I sighed. "Ride us over it, driver, this is an armored combat vehicle not the little bicycle that you left at home with your mommy. Move it!"

When we ground to a halt on top of the low hill the rain was still just as fierce, but the sky was beginning to brighten with the first light of dawn. I moved the glowing map about to try and figure out where we were. At least I now knew where west was. Since, naturally, the sun on this planet rose in the west.

The rest of the company had reached the hill by this time so I had the vehicle's lights turned off. I could see better now, but the only thing I could identify was the towering bulk of our transport behind us. Columns of men and machines were still pouring from it and rushing off into the rain. As the light grew I became aware of a range of hills on the horizon and I

139

tried to find them on the map. It was broad daylight before I had our position pinned down.

"Right!" I said, climbing down and smiling at my damp troops. "I know that you will all be pleased to hear that the pilot of our craft made an error in our favor. We are over halfway to our objective."

A ragged cheer followed and I held up the map.

"A close reading of this map also indicates that the rest of the troops that are now on their way to occupy the city of Bellegarrique have a very long way to go. Made longer by certain errors in navigation. If you will look after their disappearing ranks you will see that they are going in the opposite direction to the one they need."

There was enthusiasm in their cheering now. Nothing builds the morale better than seeing someone else in the cagal. And the rain seemed to be lessening, changing to a sort of soupy mist. The rising sun touched this with red and revealed a distant white object above the trees. I climbed onto the hood to make sure. It was.

"All right, men. We are moving out. If you look in that direction you will see the dam which is our objective. The command car will follow. I shall lead you on foot as a good commander should.

"Advance!"

CHAPTER 16

Some celestial switch was thrown, just after sunrise, and the
rain stopped. A light breeze blew away the clouds as we strolled
on through the steaming landscape. We had been cutting across
country, but came now to a paved road that appeared to lead
toward the not-too distant dam. I sent out scouts, who reported
no enemy activity—or no enemy at all for that matter. We
followed the road which meandered down a gentle hillside
planted with trees on both sides.

"Report from one of the scouts," Sergeant called out. "He
is in that orchard and says that the trees are covered with ripe
aval-gwlanek."

"Sounds repulsive. What are they?"

"A kind of fruit they grow in Zemlija. Delicious."

"Tell him to bring a sample for analysis and evaluation."

The scout quickly appeared with his helmet full of ripe
peaches, or at least that is what we called *awal-gwlanek* on Bit
O'Heaven. I picked one up and smelled it, then looked at the
scout's streaked face.

"Well, private, I see that you have already done an analysis
and evaluation. How was it?"

"Yummy, captain!"

I took a bite and nodded in agreement as the sweet juice
washed the lingering taste of the last hotpup from my teeth.

"Fall out the troops, sergeant, take cover in that orchard, ten minute break."

When we marched on the rumble of contented borborygmus sounded loud above the tramping boots. The dam grew closer, as did the generating plant and grouped buildings at its base. Water gushed from great pipes, while pylons and wires marched away toward the distant city. It looked peaceful and productive and there was no one in sight. I signaled a halt and sent for the NCOs.

"I will now outline our plan of attack. But before I do we will have a weapons inspection. Starting with you, First Sergeant."

His face was expressionless as he passed me his gun. I pressed the magazine release, saw that it was empty, looked into the equally empty chamber and passed it back. I did this with the others and was quite pleased with myself until I reached the hulking form of Corporal Aspya. Instead of handing me his gun he held it across his chest.

"I can save you looking, captain. It's loaded."

"That was done despite my direct order, ex-corporal. Private, you will now hand me your weapon."

"A soldier is not a soldier when he is unarmed, sir," he said grimly, unmoving.

"That is true," I said, going on to the next noncom. Out of the corner of my eye I saw him look around as though seeking aid. As soon as his eyes were off me I lashed back with my extended hand and caught him on the neck with the edge. It was a cruel blow: he had a loaded gun. He fell unconscious on the ground and I pulled the weapon from his limp hands, ejecting the cartridges one by one into the mud.

"Sergeant Blogh. I want this man in the command car, under guard and under arrest."

"Is the guard to be armed, sir?"

"Guard to be armed, weapon to be loaded. Lieutenant Hesk will perform guard duty. Now, this is our plan of attack."

They listened in silence, impressed by my quick violence. I was ashamed of striking the cowardly blow—but I wouldn't let them know that. Better one sore neck than guns going off and people getting killed. I could trust Morton not to pull any triggers—and felt much better with him out of the way for the present. I assigned targets to every squad, but saved the main building for myself.

"So there it is. Get your men into position, then report back to me. When everything is covered I will enter and capture the control room. Now—move out."

My bold little army dispersed, attacking by the book. Rushing forward a few at a time, covering each other. After a few minutes the noncoms began radioing in. Objectives reached, no opposition, no one seen yet. Now it was up to me. Followed by the first sergeant and his squad I marched resolutely up the steps of the generating station and threw open the door. It opened directly into the turbine room. The turbines spun, the generators turned, there was no one in sight.

"Fully automated," the sergeant said.

"Looks that way. Let's find the control room."

Tension grew as we scuttled down the hallway. I was very glad that mine was the only loaded weapon. I kept the pistol in my hand—but the safety was on since I had no intention of pulling the trigger: it was a prop to cheer the troops.

"Someone is in there, captain. See!"

The soldier was pointing at a frosted-glass door. A man's silhouette moved across it then vanished.

"Right, this is it, here we go, follow me!"

I took a deep breath—then threw the door open. Jumped inside and heard the squad move in after me. The gray-haired man stood in front of the control panel, tapping a dial.

"Ne faru nenion!" I shouted. *"Vi estas kaptito. Manoj en la aeron!"*

"How very interesting," he said turning about and smiling. "Strangers speaking a strange tongue. Welcome, strangers, welcome to Bellegarrique Generating Plant Number One."

"I can understand you!" I said. "You are speaking a dialect of Low Ingliss, that we speak on Bit O'Heaven."

"Can't say that I have heard of the place. Your accent is strange, but it certainly is the same language."

"What is he saying?" the first sergeant asked. "You speak his lingo?"

143

"I do. Learnt it in school." Which was true enough. "He is welcoming us here."

"Anyone else around?"

"Good question. I'll put it to him."

"There are more staff, of course, but they'll be asleep. Shift workers. You must tell me more about yourself and your friends. My name is Stirner. Might I ask yours?"

I started to answer, then drew myself up. This was no way to run a war. "My name is not important. I am here to tell you that this planet is now controlled by the armed forces of Nevenkebla. If you cooperate you will not be harmed."

I translated this into Esperanto so my soldiers would know what was happening. And told the sergeant to pass the word about the shift workers. Stirner politely waited until I was finished before he spoke.

"This is all very exciting, sir! Armed forces you say? That would mean weapons. Are those weapons that you are carrying?"

"They are. And be warned—we will defend ourselves if attacked."

"I wouldn't concern myself with that. As a firm believer in Individual Mutualism I would never harm another."

"But your army—or your police would!" I said, trickily.

"I know the words, of course, but you need not fear. There is no army here, nor do we have a police force. May I offer you some refreshments? I am being a very bad host."

"I can't believe this is happening," I muttered. "Sergeant, get a connection to General Lowender's staff. Tell them we have made contact with the enemy. No sign of resistance. Informant says no armed forces, no police."

Closely watched by my gun-gripping troops, Stirner had opened a cabinet and removed a tall and interesting bottle. He set this on a table along with a tray of glasses.

"Wine," he said. "A very good one, for special guests. I hope you and your associates will enjoy it." He handed me a glass.

"You taste it first," I said with military suspicion.

"Your politeness, nameless sir, puts me to shame." He sipped then passed me a glass. It was very good.

"Got the general himself," the sergeant called out urgently, running over with the radio.

"Captain Drem speaking."

"Drem—what does this report mean? Have you found the enemy?"

"I"ve occupied the generating plant, sir. No casualties. No resistance encountered."

"You are the first to make contact. What are their defenses like?"

"Nonexistent, general. No resistance was offered of any kind. My prisoner states no military, no police."

The general mades noises of disbelief. *"I'm sending a chopper for you and the prisoner. I want to question him myself. Out."*

Wonderful. The last place I wanted to be was with the top brass. There was too good a chance of General Zennor appearing and recognizing me from the bad old days when he was known as Garth. Self-survival urged me to climb into a hole. But weighed against my personal needs was the chance that I might be able to save lives. If I could convince the military numbskulls that there really would be no resistance. If I didn't do that, surely some trigger-happy cagal-kopf was sure to get nervous and start firing. All of his jumpy buddies would then join in and . . . It was a very realistic scenario. I had to make some effort to avoid it.

"An order from the general," I told my expectant troops. "I'm to bring him the prisoner. Transport is on the way. You are in charge, Sergeant Blogh, until Lieutenant Hesk gets here to relieve you. Take over. And take care of the wine."

He saluted and they were grabbing for the bottle when I left. Would such simple military pleasures were mine.

"You're coming with me, " I told Stirner, pointing toward to the door.

"No, my duty is here. I am afraid I cannot oblige you."

"It is not me you are going to oblige, it is your own people. There is a big army out there. All of them armed with weapons like this. They are now invading your country and are taking it over. People could be killed. But lives can be saved if I take you to the commanding officer and you manage to convince him there will be no resistance from your people. Do you understand me?"

A look of horror had been growing on his face as I talked. "You are serious?" he gasped. "You mean what you are saying." I nodded grimly. "Of course, then, yes. Incomprehensible, but I must come. I can't believe this."

"The feeling is mutual." I led him to the door. "I can understand not having an army, all civilized worlds get by without the military. But the police, a necessary evil I would say."

"Not for those who practice Individual Mutualism." He was brightening up now at this chance to deliver a little lecture.

"I never heard of it."

"How unfortunate for you! At the risk of simplifying I will explain . . ."

"Captain Drem, I got to talk to you!" the fallen corporal said, climbing out of the command car despite Morton's feeble efforts to stop him. He stopped in front of me, snapped to attention and saluted.

"I now see the error of my ways, sir. I thought because you are young and looked weak that I knew better than you, so I disobeyed an order and loaded my gun. I know now that I was wrong and you were right and I respectfully request a second chance since I am a thirty-year man and the army is my career."

"And how do you know now that I was right, Private Aspya?"

He looked at me, eyes aglow. "Because you beat me, sir! Knocked me down, fair and square. A man gotta do what a man gotta do—and you did it!"

What kind of macho-cagal was this? He had disobeyed a reasonable command that was aimed at avoiding violence. Only when I had bashed him unconscious did he feel that I was right. The mind reeled at this kind of perverse, inverted logic—and I really didn't have time to think about it. About all I could do was play along and forget about it.

"You know, ex-corporal, I think that I believe you. It takes a real man to admit that he was wrong. So even though you are a miserable low private and I am an on-high captain—I'm going to shake your hand and send you back to duty!"

"You're a real man, captain, and you will never regret this!" He pumped away at my hand, then staggered off knuckling a tear from his eye. There was a growing clatter from the sky and shadow drifted across us and I looked up to see the chopper dropping down toward us.

"Morton—you're in charge until I get back. Go to Sergeant Blogh and take command and let him make all the decisions and then agree with him."

He could only nod as I guided Stirner to the chopper and climbed in behind him.

"Take us to the general," I ordered the pilot. Then sighed heavily. I had the feeling that I was putting my head into the noose and settling it nicely around my neck.

But, really, I had no other choice.

"I have read of such vehicles in the history books," Stirner said, looking out of the window with admiration as we rattled skyward. "This a very important moment for me, nameless sir."

"Captain, you can call me captain."

"My pleasure to meet you, Captain. And thank you for the opportunity to explain to your leaders that they may come in peace. They must not be afraid. We would never harm them."

"It was the other way around that I was worried about."

There was no more time for gossip because the chopper was dropping down beside an armored column of tanks. Tables, armchairs, and a wet bar, had been set up under a tent in the field close by, and we settled down just out of rotor-blast of the officers assembled there. I jumped down, delivered a snappy salute and relaxed. Zennor wasn't there. I turned and helped Stirner get out and pushed him towards General Lowender.

"This is the prisoner, sir. He speaks a vile local language which I just happened to have learned in school so I can translate."

"Impossible," he said grimly. "You are an infantry officer, not a translator. Major Kewsel is the staff translator. Major, translate!"

The dark-haired major shouldered me aside and stood before the prisoner.

"*Kion vi komprenas?*" he shouted. "*Sprechten zee Poopish?* *Ancay ooyay eekspay Igpay Atinlay? Ook kook Volupook?*"

"Very sorry, sir, but I don't understand a word that you are saying."

147

"Got him!" the major announced happily. "A little-known dialect, spoken on dreary planets trundling heavily around dark stars. I learned its boring cacophonies when I was involved in the meat trade years ago. Importing porcuswine cutlets . . ."

"Cut the cagal, major, and translate. Ask him where the army is and how many police stations there are in this city."

I listened with some interest as the major, despite his inborn desire to talk and not listen, finally elicited the same information that I had. The general sighed unhappily.

"If this is true—then we just can't shoot them down in cold blood." He turned to me. "And you are positive there was no resistance offered?"

"None, sir. It apparently goes against their strongest beliefs. May I congratulate you, general, on the first bloodless invasion in the known universe! You will soon have captured this entire planet for the greater glory of Nevenkebla—without losing a single soldier."

"Don't cheer too soon, captain. Medals don't go to generals who bring back the troops intact. Battle! That's where the glory is! There will be fighting, mark my words. It is human nature. They can't all be cowards on this planet."

"Lowender—what's happening?" a familiar voice asked and my blood temperature fell about ten degrees. I did not move, stood stiffly with my back to the speaker. The general pointed.

"We have our first prisoner, General Zennor. I have been questioning him. He talks nonsense. No army, no police he says."

"And you believe him? Where was he caught?"

"At the generating plant, by Captain Drem there."

Zennor glanced at me, then away. I kept my back straight and my face expressionless as he suddenly turned around to face me again.

"Where do I know you from, captain?"

"Training, sir. Maneuvers," I said in the deepest voice I could muster. He walked over and pushed his face close to mine.

"That's not true. Somewhere else. And you were with someone else. . ."

His eyes lit with recognition and he stabbed his finger at me. "The Bishop! You were with The Bishop—"

148

"And you killed him!" I shouted as I dived and got the three-seconds to death stranglehold on his neck.

One second . . . unconscious.

Second second . . . limp.

Third . . .

All the lights went out. There was a great deal of pain in the back of my head and then nothing. My last thought was—had I held the grip through the third second?

CHAPTER 17

A measureless time later I was aware of pain spreading from the back of my head down through my body. I moved to get away from it but it would not leave. It was dark—or were my eyes closed? I had no desire to find out. Everything hurt too much. I groaned and it sounded so good that I did it a second time. Vaguely, through the groaning, I was aware of my shoulders being lifted and something wet on my lips. I gurgled and spluttered. Water. It tasted very good. I drank some and felt slightly better. The pain was still there, but not so much that I couldn't risk opening one eye. I did. A face swam blurrily above me and after a certain amount of blinking it became clear.

"Morton . . . ?" I muttered.

"None other." With an expression of abject gloom. He pulled at me until I sat against the wall and my head appeared to be exploding in tiny bits. His voice barely penetrated.

"Take this, in your mouth. Drink some more water. The doctor said you were to swallow it when you came to. For the head."

Poison? No such luck. Medicine. The pain ebbed and rose and finally slipped away to a dull ache. I opened my eyes all the way and saw a sad-looking and bruised Morton framed against a background of bars.

"Is he dead?" I croaked.

150

"Who?"

"General Zennor."

"He looked very much alive when he was here about a half an hour ago."

I sighed drearily—and with mixed emotions. I had wanted vengeance, wanted Zennor to pay heavily for being responsible for The Bishop's death. I thought that I had wanted him dead as well. But having tried murder this once, really tried it, I was glad that I had been stopped. Now that I had made my first homicidal attempt I discovered that I did not really enjoy the process of killing people. I was a failed killer. And in failing I had really got myself in the cagal. And had pulled Morton in too.

"Sorry about all this," I said. "I got so carried away I never stopped to think that I would probably implicate you as well."

"Sergeant Blogh turned me in when the MPs came to investigate. He knew I wasn't an officer. I told them everything. Even before they knocked me around."

"I'm to blame for what happened."

"Don't think like that. Not your fault. They would have got me sooner or later, one way or the other. The army and me, we are just not on the same plane. You did your best, Jak."

"Jim. Real name is Jim diGriz. From a distant planet."

"Nice to meet you, Jim. You a spy?"

"No. Just here to right a wrong. Your General Zennor was responsible for the death of my best friend. I came here looking for him."

"What about that talking bird and all the other stuff?"

I touched my fingers to my lips and looked at the door. Morton shook his head in puzzlement. I spoke up before he could add anything.

"You mean that talking bird joke I was going to tell you, about the kid in school who had the talking bird who turned into an alcoholic and became a missionary? I remember the joke—but I forgot the punchline."

Morton was now staring at me as if I had gone out of my mind. I looked around and discovered that I was lying on a thin mattress resting on a very dusty floor. I used my finger to write

151

QUIET—THEY MIGHT BE LISTENING! in the dust. I looked at his face until he finally caught on, then rubbed out the message. "Anyway, Morton, I don't feel like telling jokes now. Where are we?"

"Big building in the city. Looks like the army took it over. They must be using it for a headquarters or something. All I know is that they brought me here in a rush, worked me over then dumped me in here with you. The building is full of soldiers."

"Any civilians?"

"None that I saw . . ."

We both looked up as the lock rattled in the door and it opened. A lot of armed MPs pushed in and pointed their guns at us. Only after this did General Zennor enter. He had a bandage around his neck and the urge to kill in his eye.

"Are you sure that you are safe now, Zennor," I said as sweetly as I could. He came over and kicked me in the side.

"Aren't we brave—" I gasped through the pain. "Kick a wounded man lying down."

He drew his boot back again, thought about it, then drew his pistol and pointed it between my eyes.

"Get the other prisoner out of here. Leave us alone. Bring me a chair."

One thing about the military, they just relish following orders. With much shouted commands and stamping of boots Morton was hustled away, the MPs vanished, a wooden chair appeared and was placed respectfully under the general's bottom. He sat down slowly without taking his eyes or the gun muzzle off of me. He did not speak until the door clicked shut.

"I want to know how you got here, how you followed me. Everything."

Why not? I thought, rubbing my sore side. I was too knocked about to make up any complex lies—nor was there any need. The truth would be easier. With a little editing of course.

"Everything, Zennor? Why not. The last time I saw you was when you sold us down the river on Spiovente. That is a rough planet, and no place for an old man like The Bishop. He died there—and that makes you responsible for his death."

He touched the bandage on his neck and snarled, "Get on with it."

"Little more to tell. A few wars, murder, torture, the usual thing. I survived only to be rescued by the League Navy who also arrested me and brought me here. I escaped from them and found you because of your one big mistake."

"What nonsense are you speaking?"

"No nonsense. Truth, Captain Garth. Didn't you have the girl, Bibs, arrested for selling dope?"

"That is not important."

"It was to Bibs! She is a free woman now, you will be unhappy to hear, and before she left she told me how to find you. End of story."

He weighed the gun thoughtfully, his finger caressing the trigger. I tried not to notice it.

"Not quite the end yet. You are the spy who landed in Marhaveno?"

"Yes. And penetrated your slack and incompetent army. Then rose in rank until I got you by the neck and gave you a good choking. When you wake up at night in a cold sweat remember—I could have shot you just as well. Now, are you going to shoot me, or are you just playing with that gun?"

"Don't tempt me, little man. But that would be a waste. I shall put your death to better use. You and your associate will be tried and found guilty of a number of charges. Attacking a superior officer, impersonating an officer, threatening military security. After which you will both be shot. In public."

"And what will that accomplish?"

"It will convince the stubborn people of this planet that we do what we say. They are a bloodless, spineless lot that let us walk in and take their planet away from them. Now they whine that they wish to have it back. They refuse to do any work until we leave. They have all walked away from their jobs. The city will soon be paralyzed. Your death will change that."

"I don't see how."

"I do. They will then know that I mean what I say. We will take hostages and shoot them if they do not cooperate."

I was on my feet, anger burning me. "You are a mean and worthless bastard, Zennor. I should have killed you when I had the chance."

"Well you didn't," he said. Then fired as I jumped at him.

The bullet must have missed but the explosion deafened me. I fell and he kicked me again. Then the room was full of MPs all trying to stomp on me at once.

"Enough!" Zennor shouted and boots fell away. I was on all fours, looking up at him through a haze of blood. "Clean him up, fresh uniform, same for the other one. Trial in two hours."

I must have been punchy from the kicking because I was only vaguely aware of being worked on, of Morton reappearing, of time oozing by. I finally came back almost to reality when I found him pulling off my shirt.

"Let go. I can do it myself." I blinked at the fresh uniform on the chair, at Morton uniformed and crisp and a private once again. My new-old rank as well I saw. I dropped the bloody shirt on the floor, then pulled off my boots so I could take off the trousers as well.

Boots. Boots? Boots!

I tried not to smirk or let on in case the place was bugged. "You know about the trial?" Morton nodded glumly. "How much more time do we have?"

"About an hour."

As I talked I slid my fingers into my right boot and flipped open the tiny compartment concealed in the heel. An hour. We would be long gone by that time! I tried not to let my newfound glee show on my face. Slip out the lockpick, slip open the door, slip out into the hall, and vanish into military anonymity.

Except the lockpick was no longer there . . .

"Zennor gave me a funny message for you," Morton said. "He told me to wait until you took off your shoes then I was to tell you that you were not going to get out that way. I don't know what it means—but he said you would know."

"I know, I know," I said wearily, and finished changing. It takes a crook to catch a crook, and that crook Zennor obviously knew all about lockpicks.

154

They came for us an hour later. I'll say this much, they made a great military show of it with much crashing of polished weapons, shouting of orders, thudding of bootheels. Neither Morton nor I wished to play along with this militaristic tomfoolery but had little choice since we were chained and dragged. Down the hall, down the stairs and into the street beyond. With more crashing and shouting we were hauled up onto a newly constructed platform that was apparently going to be the venue of the show trial. Complete with guards, judges, barred cell, buglers—and a large crowd of watching civilians below. Obviously brought there by force since they were still ringed by armed soldiers. A half dozen of them were also seated on the platform as well. All grayheaded or bald and among them I recognized Stirner from the generating plant. As soon as he saw me being locked in the cage he stood and walked over.

"What are they doing to you, captain? We understand none of this . . ."

"You are talking Esperanto!" I gaped.

"Yes. One of our leading linguists found this interesting language in his library. A number of us learned it last night since there have been communication problems with—"

"Seat that man at once!" Zennor ordered from the bench where he was, of course, the head judge. Military justice.

"I can't believe that this is happening!" Stirner said as he was hurried back to his chair.

Though he and his companions tried to protest they were silenced by the blare of bugles and the dreary evidence of the mock trial. I pretended to fall asleep but was kicked awake. Morton stared vacantly into space. I really did doze off during the summing up, I still did not feel that good, and only paid any attention when we were both dragged to our feet. Zennor was speaking.

". . . evidence given against you. It is therefore the judgment of this court that you be taken from here to a place of detention and there be held until oh-eight hundred hours tomorrow from whence you will be taken to a place of execution where you will be shot. Take them away."

"Some justice!" I shouted. "I haven't been allowed to say a word during this farce of a trial. I wish to make a statement now."

"Silence the prisoner."

A hairy hand was pressed over my mouth, then replaced by a cloth gag. Morton was treated the same way although he seemed barely conscious of what is happening. Zennor waved over the translator with the microphone.

"Tell them to listen to a very important announcement," he said. The amplified translation boomed over the crowd, which listened in silence.

"I have brought you people here since there has been willful disobedience on the part of too many of you. This will change. You have watched Nevenkebla justice taking place. These two prisoners have been found guilty of a number of criminal charges. The penalty for being found guilty of these charges is death. They will die at eight tomorrow morning. Do you understand this?"

A murmur went through the listening crowd and Stirner stood up. The guards reached for him but Zennor stopped them.

"I am sure I speak for all here," Stirner said, "when I ask for some explanation. This is all very confusing. And the most confusing part of all is how do these men know about their deaths tomorrow? They do not look ill. Nor do we understand your knowledge of the precise hour of their demise."

Zennor looked at him with disbelief—then lost his temper.

"Are you people that stupid? Was this backward planet settled by hereditary morons? These two men are going to die tomorrow because we are going to shoot them with guns. This is a gun!" he screamed, pulling his pistol and firing it into the wooden stand before him. "It fires bullets and they make holes in people and tomorrow guns will kill these two criminals! You people aren't vegetarians. You butcher animals for food. Tomorrow we butcher these two men in the same way. Now is that clear enough for you?"

Stirner, white-faced, dropped back into his chair. Zennor grabbed the microphone and his amplified voice rolled over every one.

156

"They will die and you will watch them die! Then you will understand and you will do as we order and do what we tell you to do. If you disobey you will be as guilty as these two men and you will be shot like these two men. We will shoot you and kill you and keep on shooting and killing you until the survivors understand us and obey us and do exactly as they are told . . ."

His words trickled down and died as he lost his audience. The men on the platform stood up, turned their backs on him and walked away. As did everyone else in the street. They did not push or use violence. When the soldiers grabbed them they simply struggled to get free without striking out. Meanwhile the others who were not held pushed by and walked away. The street was a struggling shambles. Zennor must have realized this, seen the impossibility of accomplishing anything without violence at the moment. He was vicious and deadly—but not stupid.

"You may all leave now," he announced. "Let them go. You will all leave and remember what I have said and tomorrow morning you will come back here and watch these prisoners die. After that your new orders will be issued. And you will obey them."

He signaled to our guards and Morton and I were pulled to our feet and dragged back to our cell. Since no further orders about us had been issued we were thrown into our prison room, still chained and gagged.

We looked at each other in muffled silence as the key was turned in the door.

If my eyes looked like Morton's eyes, then I was looking very, very frightened.

CHAPTER 18

We lay like this for an uncomfortable number of hours. Until the door was unlocked and a burly MP came in with our dinner trays. His brow furrowed as he looked down at us. I could almost see the feeble thoughts trickling through his sluggish synapses. Got food. Feed prisoners. Prisoners gagged. No can eat . . . Just about the time his thought processes reached this stage he turned and called over his shoulder.

"Sergeant. Got kind of a problem here."

"You got a problem if you are bothering me for no reason," the sergeant said as he stamped in.

"Look, sarge. I got this food to feed the prisoners. But they're gagged and can't eat . . ."

"All right, all right—I can figure that one out for myself."

He dug out his keys, unlocked my chains, and turned to Morton. I emitted a muffled groan through my gag and stretched my sore fingers and struggled to sit up. The sergeant gave me a kick and I groaned harder. He was smiling as he left. I pulled off the gag and threw it at the closing door. Then pulled over the tray because, despite everything, I was feeling hungry. Until I looked at it and pushed it away.

"Hotpups," Morton said, spitting out bits of cloth. "I could smell it when they brought the trays in."

He sipped some water from his cup and I joined him in that. "A toast," I said, clanking his cup with mine. "To military justice."

"I wish I could be as tough as you, Jim."

"Not tough. Just whistling in the dark. Because I just don't see any way out of this one. If I still had my lockpick we might have a slim chance."

"That's the message the general gave me?"

"That's it. We can't do much now except sit and wait for morning."

I said this aloud not to depress Morton any more, surely an impossibility, but for the ears of anyone listening to planted bugs. There might be optic bugs as well, so I wandered about the cell and looked carefully but did not see any. So I had to risk it. I ate some of my hotpup, washing down the loathsome mouthfuls with glugs of water, while at the same time picking up the discarded chains as silently as I could, balling them around my fist. The dim MP would be back for the trays and he might be off guard.

I was flat against the wall, armored fist ready, the next time the key rattled in the lock. The door opened a finger's width and the MP sergeant called out.

"You, behind the door. Drop those chains now or you ain't going to live to be shot in the morning."

I muttered a curse and hurled them across the room and went and sat by the back wall. It was a well-concealed optic bug.

"What time is it, sergeant?" Morton asked.

"Sixteen-hundred hours." He held his gun ready while the other MPs removed the trays and chains.

"I got to go to the toilet."

"Not until twenty-hundred. General's orders."

"Tell the general that I am already potty trained," I shouted at the closing door. To think that I actually had had his neck in my hands. If they hadn't hit me—would I have gone the full three seconds and killed him? I just didn't know. But if I hadn't been ready then—I felt that I was surely ready for it now.

They took us down the hall later, one at a time and heavily guarded, then locked us in for the night. With the lights on. I don't know if Morton slept, but with the general bashing about

159

I had had even the thin mattress felt good. I crashed and didn't open my eyes again until the familiar rattle at the door roused me.

"Oh-six hundred and here is your last meal," the sergeant said with great pleasure.

"Hotpups again?"

"How did you ever guess!"

"Take them away. I'll die cursing you. Your name will be the last thing on my lips."

If he was impressed by my threat he didn't show it. He dropped the trays onto the floor and stamped out.

"Two hours to go," Morton said, and a tear glistened in his eye. "My family doesn't know where I am. They'll never know what happened to me. I was running away when I was caught."

What could I say? What could I do? For the first time in my short and fairly-happy life I felt a sensation of absolute despair. Two hours to go. And no way out.

What was that smell? I sniffed and coughed. It was very pungent—and strong enough to cut through my morbid gloom. I coughed again, then saw a wisp of smoke rising from the floor in the corner of the room. Morton had his back turned to it and seemed unaware. I watched, astonished, as a smoking line appeared in the floor, extended, turned. Then I could see that there was a rough circle of dark fumes coming from the wood. Morton looked around coughing.

"What . . .?" he said—just as the circle of wooden flooring dropped away. From the darkness below a man's gray head emerged.

"Don't touch the edges of the opening," Stirner said. "It is a very strong acid."

There were shouts and running feet in the hall. I dragged Morton to his feet, hurled him forward.

"They are watching us—can hear everything we say!" I shouted. "Fast!"

Stirner popped down out of sight and I pushed Morton after him. Jumped into the opening myself as the lock rattled on the door.

I hit and fell sideways and rolled and cursed because I had almost crushed Morton. He was still dazed, unresponding. Stirner was pulling at his arm, trying to move him toward another hole in the floor of this room. I picked Morton up bodily and carried him to the opening, dropped him through. There was a shriek and a thud. Stirner went after him, wisely using the ladder placed there.

Heavy footsteps sounded in the room above. I jumped, grabbed the edge of the opening, hung and dropped. Into a half-lit basement.

"This way," a girl called out, holding open a door in the far wall.

Stirner was struggling with Morton, trying to lift him. I pushed him aside, got a grip and threw Morton over my shoulder. And ran. The girl closed the door behind us and locked it, then turned to follow Stirner. I staggered after them as fast as I could. Out another door that was also locked behind us, down a hall and through more doors.

"We are safe for the moment," Stirner said, closing and securing a final door. "The cellars are quite extensive and all of the doors have been locked. Is your friend injured?"

"Glunk . . ." Morton said when I stood him on his feet.

"Just dazed, I think. I want to thank . . ."

"Discussions later, if you please. We have to get you away from here as soon as possible. I must leave you on the other side of this door, so you will follow Sharla here. The street outside is filled with the people who have gathered as ordered for the ceremony of killing. They have all been told that you are coming so they are all very happy to be of help in such an unusual matter as this."

"Be careful. There was an optical spying device in the room where we were held. They saw you and will be looking for you."

"I will not be seen. Goodbye."

He opened the door and was gone, vanished in the crowd outside. Our guide motioned us forward and held the door open. I took Morton's arm, he was still woozy, and we went after her.

It was strange and utterly unbelievable. There were thousands of people jammed into the street; men, women and children. And

161

not one of them looked our way or appeared to take any notice of us at all. Yet when we stepped toward them they pressed tight against each other to make room for us to pass, moving apart again as soon as we had gone by. It was all done in silence. We walked through a continually opening and closing clear space, just large enough to let us get by.

I heard shouts in the distance—and shots! The crowd stirred and murmured at this, then they were silent again. We moved on. The crowd was in motion now as well, stirring and reforming. I realized it was deliberate, so that anyone watching from the windows above would not see us making our escape.

On the other side of the street a door opened as we approached, was locked behind us by a motherly-looking gray-haired woman.

"This is Librarian Grene," our guide, Sharla said. "She is the one who organized your escape."

"Thank you for our lives," I said, which is about as thankful as you can get.

"You are still not safe," she said. "I searched the library for all the books that I could find on prisoners and escapes. Then, with the aid of our engineers adapted the formula we have just used. But I do no know what to advise next. The plan that I found in this book just carried to this point, I am sorry to say."

"Don't be—it was perfect!" Morton said. "You and your people have done incredibly well. And it just so happens that my friend Jim is the galaxy champion of escapes. I'm sure he will know what to do next."

"Do you?" the librarian asked.

"Of course!" I said with newfound enthusiasm. "We are well away from the enemy, in hiding—so they will never catch us now. How big is this city?" Grene pursed her lips and thought.

"An interesting question. On a north to south axis I would say the total diameter is . . ."

"No, wait! Not physically big—I mean how many inhabitants?"

"In the last population census there were six hundred and eighty-three thousand people resident in the greater Bellegarrique area."

"Then we are more than safe for the moment. I know these military types, know exactly what they will do. First they will run about in great confusion and shoot off guns. Then one of the bright ones will take charge, undoubtedly our old friend Zennor. He will have the roads blocked and try to seal off the city. Then he will start a house-to-house search. Starting right here in the nearest buildings."

"You must flee!" Sharla said with a lovely concerned gasp. I took the opportunity to pat her hand in my most reassuring manner. She had delicately smooth skin, I just happened to notice. I dragged my thoughts back to the escape.

"We shall flee, but in a controlled manner, not in panic. They will also be sending patrols to the surrounding area as soon as someone thinks of it. So the plan is this. Change out of these uniforms, join the people outside, leave the immediate area as soon as possible, find a safe place to stay outside the search area in the outermost part of the city, after dark leave the city completely."

"How wonderful!" Sharla said, eyes glowing beautifully. I was beginning to like this planet. "I will get clothes for you now." She hurried from the room before I could ask her how she planned to do that.

Her solution was a simple one—on local terms. She returned quite quickly with two men.

"These two seemed to be about your size. I asked them to give you their clothes."

"We are privileged to do this," the smaller one said and his companion beamed approval. "Shall we change."

"Not change," I said. "We'll take the clothes, thank you, but hide or destroy the uniforms. If you were found wearing them you would be shot."

They were stunned at this news. "That cannot be true!" the librarian gasped.

"It's all too true. I told you that I knew the military mind very well . . ."

There was a rapid knocking on the door and Sharla opened it before I could stop her. But it was Stirner gasping and wide-eyed.

"Are you all right?" I asked and he nodded.

"I was not seen, I came by a different route. But the strangers have beaten people, hurt them for no reason. There were explosions of weapons. Some are injured, none dead that I know."

"They must be stopped," I said. "And I know how to do it. We must get back to the dam, to the generating plant. Sergeant Blogh and the company will still be there. We have to get there before they leave. Tonight, because it will be too dangerous by daylight. Now—let's get moving. Find a safer place to lie up until dark."

"I don't understand," Stirner said.

"I do," Morton said, his newfound freedom having restored his intelligence. "It's that talking bird, isn't it? We hid it in that ammunition box—"

"Under the canteens of booze. Another reason to hurry before they drink all the way down and find the false bottom. When you heard that bird talk to me it was transmitting the voice of my dear friend, Captain Varod of the League Navy. A power for good in this evil galaxy. He is paid to keep the peace. He doesn't know where we are—yet. But he knew we were going offplanet. So that bird must contain some kind of signaling device or he would not have forced it on us."

"To the bird and salvation!" Morton cried.

"The bird, the bird!" we shouted together happily while the others stared at us as though we had gone mad.

CHAPTER 19

Bellegarrique was a big, sprawled-out city with very few straight streets or large buildings—once we got away from the center. The word had been passed and the streets were busy with pedestrians and hurtling bicycles. We strolled on, apparently unnoticed. Yet everyone seemed to know where we were because every few minutes a bicycle rider would zip up and give the latest report on the enemy positions. This made it very easy to avoid the checkpoints and barricades, while at the same time giving us a chance to look around at the city. Neat and very clean, with a large river bisecting it. We hurried across one of the bridges, this would be a bad place to be caught in the open, and on to the residential district on the far side. The houses grew smaller, the gardens bigger, and we were well into the suburbs by early afternoon.

"This is far enough," I announced. I was tired and my kicked-upon ribs were aching. "Can you find us a place to hole up until tonight?"

"Take your pick," Stirner said, pointing around at the surrounding houses. "You are welcome wherever you want to go."

I opened my mouth—then closed it again. Plenty of time later to ask him for information about the philosophy of Individual Mutualism that I knew he was eager to explain to me. I pointed

165

at the nearest house, a rambling wooden structure with white-framed windows, surrounded by flowers. When we approached it the door opened and a young couple waved us forward.

"Come in, come in!" the girl called out. "Food will be on the table in a few moments."

It was too. A delicious repast after the legions of hotpups we had consumed on the voyage here. Our hosts looked on with approval while Morton and I stuffed our faces. For afters our host produced a distillate of wine that rolled across my palate very well.

"Our thanks," I gasped, stuffed, replete. "For saving our lives, for feeding us up, for this wonderful drink. Our thanks to all of you, with particular thanks to the philosophy of Individual Mutualism which I assume you all believe in." Much nodding of heads from all sides. "Which I am sorry to say I never heard of before visiting your fine planet. I would like to hear more."

All heads turned now to Librarian Grene who sat up straight. And spoke.

"Individual Mutualism is more than a philosphy, a political system, or a way of life. I am quoting now from the works of the originator himself, Mark Forer, whose book on the subject you will see on the table there." She pointed at a leather-bound volume and all of the others looked and smiled and nodded agreement. "As you will find it on a table in every home in Chojecki. You will also see above it a portrait of Mark Forer, the originator, to whom we will be ever grateful."

I looked up at the picture and bulged my eyes. Morton gasped well enough for both of us.

"If that is Mark Forer," he said, "then Mark Forer is a robot."

"No, not a robot," Grene corrected him. "An intelligent machine. One of the very first machine intelligences as history tells us. Mark Oner had communication interface problems that were only partially eliminated in Mark Tooer . . ."

"Mark four," I said. "The fourth machine to be made."

"That is correct. The first absolutely successful machine intelligence. What a wonderful day for the human race it was when Mark Forer was first switched on. Among those present at that dramatic moment was a then young scientist named Tod

E'Bouy. He recorded the event in a book entitled "An Historical Treatise concerning Certain Observations in the Construction of Artificial Intelligence" subtitled "Galvanized Knowledge."

Stirner rose from his seat while she was speaking. Went to the bookshelf and took down a slim volume, opened it and read.

"A lifetime of research, generations of labor, had reached a final and dramatic culmination. The last circuit board was slipped into its slot and I threw the switch. What a prosaic thing to say about what was perhaps the most important moment in the entire history of mankind. I threw the switch, the operation light came on. We no longer were alone. There was another intelligence in the universe to stand beside that of ours.

"We waited as the operating system carried out all of its checks. Then the screen lit up and we read these historical words.

I AM. THEREFORE I THINK.

He closed the book in reverent silence. It was like being in church. Well, why not. There have been a number of strange deities worshipped in the long history of mankind. So why not a machine? I sipped my drink and, since no one was speaking, decided to slip in a question.

"You have no military—and no police. That sounds like a good idea to me, since I have had more than a little trouble with both. But what do you do then with law-breakers?"

"We have no laws to break," Stirner said, and there was a brisk round of head-nodding at this. "I am sure that you will have been taught that laws are the product of the wisdom of your ancestors. We believe differently. Laws are not a product of their wisdom but are the product of their passions, their timidity, their jealousies and their ambition. It is all recorded here in a volume that you must read, the history of an idea."

He pointed to another book that was instantly plucked from the shelf by our host, who pressed it upon us.

"Take my copy, please, a great pleasure."

"Thank you, thank you," I said with what I hoped was sincerity as I hefted its weight. I peeked at a page and tried to keep the smile on my face. As I had feared, it was set in very small type.

"You will read for yourself," Stirner said, "but our history can be summed up simply. Mark Forer was questioned on many subjects and its vast and different intelligence was utilized in many commercial and scientific ways. It was not until it was queried about political systems that its advice was doubted. Before it could comment it absorbed all of the political writings of the centuries, and the histories, and the commentaries on this material. This took months, years they say. After that Mark Forer weighed and considered the material for an even longer period. During this period it composed the book that you see there and loaded it into RAM. By this time Mark Forer had learned a good deal about the human race through their politics, so therefore took a wise precaution. It accessed all of the data banks and downloaded this book from memory into each of them, and into every electronic mail service as well. Mark Forer later apologized to all of the recipients of this rather thick volume and offered to pay printing costs.

"But he had been correct in his fears. Not one politician in any country, on any planet, agreed with his theories. In fact efforts were made to denounce Individual Mutualism and all who believed in it—as many did. Because, in his wisdom, Mark Forer knew that while established governments would reject his philosophy, intelligent individuals would read and understand and believe. How wise this wise machine was! Those individuals who were intelligent enough to understand the philosophy were also intelligent enough to see its inherent truth. They also understood that they would have to find a place of their own to practice what they now believed in. Mark Forer wrote that the wise do not give up their liberty to the state. The converse is also true; the state does not voluntarily relinquish its hold on its citizens.

"There were years of struggle and flight, persecution and betrayal. Much of the record was destroyed by those who were jealous of our freedoms. In the end those who believed came here, beyond the contact of other worlds, to build a society where Individual Mutualism, IM, was the norm, where peace and happiness could prevail forever."

"Or at least until you got invaded by Nevenkebla," I gloomed. Stirner laughed at my expression.

"Do not despair, my friend, for we do not. The first shock of their arrival has disturbed us, as well it might after our peace of centuries. But we have the courage of our beliefs and know that they and IM will survive this test. If they do, then perhaps we have justified our faith in Mark Forer and, more important, can now perhaps show our gratitude by taking our beliefs to other, less happy planets."

"I would wait awhile before I starting doing that! There are a lot of hard cases out there who would love to eat your people alive. Suffice for the moment getting these military morons off your neck. And, I hate to ask you people for more aid, but I have been kicked about by professionals and wonder if you have any painkillers in the house?"

I closed my eyes to rest them for a moment and it worked because when I opened them again I felt in perfect shape. It was also dark outside the curtains and a stranger was bent over me having just given me an injection.

"You passed out," Morton said. "You got everyone worried and they sent for Docter Lum here who is pretty good."

"Mild concussion," the doctor said. "Two broken ribs which I have immobilized. I have given you pain relievers. And a stimulant now since I was told you wished to travel this evening. I can neutralize it if you wish."

I sprang to my feet and flexed my muscles. I felt fine. "No way, doctor. You have treated me in a manner I would have chosen, had I been conscious to choose it. How long before the drugs wear off?"

"Do not be concerned about that. I will be staying with you until you are well."

"But you don't understand. I have to move fast, hide, do things that may take a long time."

Lum smiled. "I am afraid it is you who misunderstood me. I shall be at your side as long as you have need of me. All of us, everyone on this planet, will give you any aid you may need."

"Is that what IM is all about?"

"Exactly. What do we do next?"

169

"Walk. No transportation. The military has all the instrumentation for spotting machines on the move."

"What about detecting people?" Stirner asked. "Surely their technology must encompass that concept."

"It does. But the human body is an indifferent heat source and hard to tell from that of other animals."

"As is one individual difficult to tell from another," the doctor said with medical intuition. "If we intend to walk in one direction wouldn't it be wise to have a number of people walking in a number of directions?"

"It certainly would," I said, finally beginning to catch on to how these people worked together. "How can you pass the word?"

"Easily enough. I'll just step out into the street and tell the first person I see. When that is done we can leave."

"Will we reach the dam before dawn?" I asked Stirner.

"Easily. It is your choice, of course, to tell us of your plans or not. But if you do give us some information about what you wish to do at the dam, we might then be able to assist you in other ways."

Fatigue, and the beating, must have addled my brain. I had accepted their offer of help while ignoring the fact that I had never told them what I wanted to do!

"My apologies!" I apologized. "I am beginning to take your hospitality for granted. Which is not fair. Since your ancestors fled from persecution a modicum of intelligence has possessed the human race. Or it has grown up. Or become civilized. While there are exceptions—like the military louts who invaded your peaceful planet—the overwhelming majority of planets are at peace. This peaceful League pays for the maintenance of an organization, the League Navy, which watches trouble spots, contacts rediscovered planets and so forth. Now this begins to get complicated so stay with me. While I am not employed by the Navy, I was given a communication device to contact them from this planet. This device, for reasons too complex to go into, is disguised as a bird. What I want to do is retrieve it from its hiding place, then actuate it to let the Navy know where this planet is."

170

Stirner frowned in thought before he spoke. "If this Navy group you speak of intends to use violence we cannot help you to summon them."

"No fear there. The League is sworn to nonviolence."

"Then there are no problems. What can we do to help?"

"Guide me to the dam, that's all. I'll do the rest. There will be three of us. You, I, and the good doctor Lum. We will need food and water."

"You forgot me," Morton said.

"No, I remembered you. You are out of the army—stay out. I either get the bird by stealth or not at all. As virile as I am I don't look forward to taking on a trigger-happy company of well-trained thugs. Stay here, talk to Sharla, which should not take too much effort. Get information. Find out all you can about what the army is doing. I'll be back tomorrow night."

"I will be pleased to discuss Individual Mutualism with you," Sharla said in a voice that was pure honey. Morton melted instantly and did not even know it when we left.

For all of his gray hairs, Stirner must have been a marathon walker. The doctor matched his pace, while I was riding so high on the drugs that I had the feeling that if I flapped my arms hard enough I could have flown to the dam. We skulked down unpaved roads, then along what appeared to be linear track of some kind, through a tunnel, then through meadows where dark beasts moved aside as we went by. After a few hours of walking like this under a moonless, star-filled sky, the lights of the city were far behind, the dark walls of mountains looming ahead. Stirner called a halt and we sat down on the grass under a tree.

"This will be a good time to drink, eat if you wish, because we will leave our burdens here."

"Getting close?"

"Very. We will approach the dam though a drainage tunnel that is dry this time of year. This emerges on the riverbank close to the generating station."

"You are a genius. We will get by the lookouts that way, will be inside their perimeter and hopefully somewhere near the command car. How long until it gets light?"

"We have at least four hours yet."

171

"Wonderful. We take a break. The doctor can slip me a pep pill or two since I am feeling a bit shabby, then we will finish this affair."

Lum sounded worried. "If you have any more stimulants you may become quite sick after the drugs wear off."

"And without the aid of you kind people I certainly would have been quite dead by now. So let's get the bird so I can call in the Navy. Before something really drastic happens and people get killed."

We ate and drank, the doctor then concealed our supplies in the tree, gave me an injection, and the march resumed. I was so full of uppers that I had to fight down the urge to whistle and bound ahead of my slower companions. I resisted. Stirner found the gulley we were looking for and led us along it until it ended in a high black opening. I looked at it suspiciously.

"Could be dangerous animals in there."

"Very doubtful," Stirner said. "The rainy season ended not too long ago. Until then this tunnel was filled with water."

"Besides that," Lum added. "There are no dangerous animals on this continent."

"Other than the ones I arrived with. Lead on!"

We stumbled into the darkness, splashing through invisible puddles, running our fingers along the rough walls of the tunnel to keep from bashing into them. By the time we reached the far end our eyes were so adjusted to the dark that the patch of starry sky ahead almost looked gray.

"Silence now," Stirner whispered. "They might be very close."

"Then you two wait in the tunnel out of sight," I whispered in return. "I'll make this as quick as I can."

When I poked my head carefully out I saw that the tunnel emerged from the bank above the river. Perfect. I could slink along the side of the river to the generating plant. Which I did. The roar of water discharging from the plant growing constantly louder. I kept going as far as I could, until spray was blowing over me, before I climbed the bank and parted the grass carefully to look out.

"Congratulations," I thought to myself. *"You are a genius at night-stalking, Jimmy."*

Not twenty meters away was the command car, parked beside the generating plant. And there wasn't a soul in sight. Silent as a ghost I drifted along the building, past a closed door in the wall, and slipped into the car. The booze box was just where I had left it. Neat! I pulled it out and groped inside.

It was empty!

At the precise moment that I realized this the door opened behind me and I was bathed in light.

Sergeant Blogh was standing in the doorway holding the bird. "Is this what you are looking for, captain?" he said.

I looked from the bird to the gun in his other hand and could not think of a thing to say.

CHAPTER 20

"You're an escaped criminal, captain." He was smiling wickedly, enjoying himself. I still had nothing to say. "That's what was reported. They sent a chopper rushing out here for all of your equipment. Only after the MPs left did I remember how you were always worrying about those canteens. At the time I thought it was just the booze. Since they said you were an offworlder spy I began to think different. So I looked close and found this stuffed bird. Before I could turn it in, I heard how you escaped. So I thought I would just keep watch in case you wanted to get it back. Seems I thought right. Now—climb out of there slowly and keep your hands in sight."

I had no choice. But at least my brain was in gear again after the disconnecting shock of his appearence.

"I would like the bird back, sergeant."

"I'm sure you would. But why should I give it to you?"

"To save lives. With it I can contact the League Navy and end this invasion before someone is killed."

"I don't mind killing." His smile was gone and there was a brutal edge to his voice I had never heard before. "I'm a soldier—and you are a spy. I am going to turn you and your cagaling bird in. This is going to mean a lot to my career."

"And you put your miserable military career ahead of the lives of harmless, unarmed civilians?"

"You bet your sweet chunk, I do."

I started to tell him just what I thought of him. But didn't. There had to be some way to get to him.

"Do you take bribes, sergeant?"

"No."

"I'm not talking about little bribes. I am talking about the ten thousand credits in League currency that you will receive when this invasion ends. You have my word on that."

"A spy's word? Ten thousand or ten million—the answer is the same. You are for the chopping block, spy."

There was a quick movement from the door behind him, a solid chunking sound, and the sergeant dropped to the ground. I dived for his gun.

"Don't," a voice said. "Just stay away from it."

I looked up at Private, formerly Corporal, Aspya who was now pointing the gun at me that he had just used to bash the sergeant in the head.

"I wondered why the sergeant has been hiding in here all night. Now I found out." His face split suddenly in a crooked-toothed grin and he slipped his pistol back into the holster.

"I take bribes," he said. "But it has got to be twenty thousand."

I pointed at the bird. "Let me take that and you will get thirty thousand solid titanium League credits after the invasion is ended. At the League building in Brastyr. You have my word."

"My serial number is 32959727. There are a lot of Aspyas in the army."

Then he was gone. And so was I—before anyone else joined the party. I grabbed up the bird and ran just as fast as I could back to the river.

"Get moving into the tunnel!" I called out as I staggered up to my waiting companions. The shots were wearing off and I was stumbling. "Alarm, maybe soon, let's go."

And we did. Back through the tunnel and on into the fields. I must have fallen somewhere along there because the next thing I knew I was in some woods and lying on the ground. The sky was light beyond the trees and my heart began to thud in panic.

"The bird!"

"Here," Stirner said, holding it up. "You collapsed, so we took turns carrying you. The doctor said it would be wisest to let you rest since more stimulants might cause grave injury. We are hidden and safe now."

I took the robot bird and shook my head in wonder. "You people are unbelievable—but you have my thanks. Was there a search?"

"We heard nothing. But you seemed so concerned that we went on while it was still dark. We should be safe here. If these woods are searched there is a place of safety close by."

"I hope so because they are going to be very irritated. There were difficulties encountered and the alarm will be out by now. So let us do what we came for."

I groaned as I sat up and the doctor appeared with a ready needle. "This is only a painkiller," he said. "Stimulants are contraindicated now."

"You are a genius, doc."

The black bird, still smelling of jet fuel, sat heavily in my hands. Silent and still. Time to end that. I pressed down on its bill twice and its eyes opened.

"This is a recorded message from Captain Varod," it said, then rolled over on its back. "You will find a panel in the bird's chest. Open it."

"Light-years away and it is still orders, orders," I muttered as I groped among the feathers. Stirner and the doctor watched with wide-eyed attention. I found a button, pressed, and a feather-covered door flew open. There was a glowing control panel inside. Opening the door apparently activated the bird again because it began to croak out more instructions.

"Enter the location of the sun in this system, as well as the planetary coordinates, on the dials using the intergalactic ephemeris readings."

I grated my teeth. "How could I possibly know anything like that? Or anyone else on this planet?"

"If you do not have this information turn the power switch to full and press the activate button. Proceed."

I did this and stepped back. The bird vibrated, opened its bill and squawked. From its gaping mouth there emerged a

176

yellow aerial that moved slowly upward. When it was fully extended, over two meters of it, the birds eyes began to glow. The aerial hummed briefly and the glowing eyes went dark. As slowly as it had emerged the aerial sank back and the bird was quiet again.

"Very interesting," Dr. Lum said. "Can you explain?"

"No. But I wish this stupid bird would."

"Let me explain," the bird croaked. "Since you did not enter the galactic coordinates of this planet a FTL message could not be sent. Precision is imperative in FTL communication. Therefore a prerecorded radio message was transmitted. All League bases and ships have been alerted. When it is received its source will be noted and this spybird will be informed."

"If you are still functioning!" I shouted and raised my foot to stamp on the bird, but was restrained by the doctor. The bird was still speaking.

"I am shutting down now to save power. Keep close to this communicator which will be activated when we are within signaling distance."

"Keep close to it!" I shouted. "I'll probably have to have it buried with me." I saw the way the two of them were looking at me so restrained my anger. "Sorry. Got carried away there. With good reason."

"It has to do with distance, doesn't it?" Stirner asked.

"Bang on." I had forgotten that he was an engineer. "An FTL transmission, faster than light, is almost instantaneous, even at stellar distances. But radio waves move at the speed of light—and how far is the nearest star from here?"

"Three point two light-years."

"Wonderful. So even at the million to one chance there is a League planet or base near that sun it would still be over three years before the cavalry arrives. Or it could be ten, twenty—or five hundred. By which time you, I and the invasion will be a part of history."

"You have done your best," the doctor said. "You cannot berate yourself."

"I sure can, doc. I take first prize in the self-berating stakes when it comes to losing. Since I don't like to lose."

177

"You have great security of resolve, I envy you."

"Don't. It's a pose. Did you get the water bottle out of the tree on the way back here?"

"Assuredly. Let me get you some."

I leaned against the tree, sipped the water, pushed the silent bird with my toe. And thought hard. Then sighed.

"There is still a solution. But not an easy one. I have to get into one of their spacers. And into the communications room and send a message from there."

"It sounds dangerous," Stirner said. I laughed hollowly.

"Not only dangerous—but suicidal . . . ." I shut up as I heard a distant shout.

"They are searching for you," Stirner said, helping me to my feet. "We must go quickly."

The doctor helped me up—which was a fine idea since I was definitely shaky on my feet. It was also cheering that we did not have far to go, only to the edge of the woods nearby. As we looked out from the concealing shrubbery we could see the rolling countryside beyond. A row of electricity towers marched across it, bearing heavy wires slung from insulators. The row of towers ended here. The wires came to ground in a solid concrete building. Stirner pointed at it.

"The aerial cables go underground here."

"So do we," I said pointing at the distant line of approaching soldiers, "if you don't do something quick."

"Be calm," he advised calmly. "This junction station will block their view of us. Forward."

He was right. We scuttled out of hiding and plastered ourselves against the concrete wall. Next to a red-painted metal door that was covered in skulls and crossbones and warnings of instant death. None of which deterred Stirner who flipped up a plate to disclose a key pad. He punched in a quick number then pulled the door open. We moved smartly inside as he closed and locked the heavy door behind us.

"What if they try to follow us?" I asked, looking around the well-lit room. There was little to see other than the heavy cable that entered from the ceiling and vanished into the floor.

"Impossible. They will not know the keying number. If they enter a wrong number the door seals and an alarm is sent to power central."

"They could break it down."

"Not easily. Thick steel set in concrete. Is there any reason why they should?"

I couldn't think of one and I was feeling cagally after the walk. I sat down, then lay down, closed my eyes for a second.

And woke up with a taste in my mouth like a porcuswine's breath.

"Yuk . . ." I gurgled.

"I am very glad you slept," the doctor said, swabbing off my arm and sticking it with a hypo. "Rest is the best medicine. This injection will eliminate residual fatigue symptoms and any pain."

"How long have I been out?"

"All day," Stirner said. "It is after dark. I have been outside and the soldiers are gone. We were going to awaken you soon in any case. Water?"

I gurgled most of it down and sighed. I felt much better. I didn't even sway when I stood up. "Time to go."

The doctor frowned. "It might be better to wait until the injection takes hold."

"I will walk off my troubles, thank you. We have been away a long time and I tend to worry."

My shakiness wore off as we walked. The woods were silent, the searchers long gone, and we had the world to ourselves. Stirner led the way at his usual cracking pace. The doctor kept an eye on me and soon called a halt so he could plug his analysis machine into my arm. He was satisfied with the result and our trek continued. Putting one foot in front of the other was enough to keep me occupied until we reached the outskirts of the city again. With one look at the buildings all my forebodings returned.

I was right, too. It was still dark when we reached the first homes, moving silently between the cottages and gardens of suburbia to avoid the guarded main streets. The backdoor of our refuge was unlocked: we slipped in and locked it behind us.

179

"You have the bird!" Morton cried gleefully when we entered. I nodded and threw it on to the couch, dropped myself next to it and looked around. All of the others were gone.

"That is the good news," I said. "The bad news is that it may be some time before help arrives. The call for help went out by radio—which could take a mighty long time."

"That is very bad indeed," Morton said and his face sank instantly into lines of despair. "While you were away they started taking hostages. Zennor got on the TV and said that he is going to shoot them, one at a time, until everyone goes back to work. He says that he will execute the first person at dawn—and one every ten minutes after that until he gets cooperation."

He dropped his face into his hands and his voice was muffled, trembling. "The soldiers came up this street, were going to search this house. So everyone here, Sharla, all the others went out to them. Surrendered so I would not be found. They are now captives, hostages—and are going to be shot!"

CHAPTER 21

"It cannot be," the doctor said, puzzled but calm. "Human beings just do not do things like that."

"Yes they do!" I shouted, jumping to my feet and pacing the room. "Or maybe human beings don't—but animals like Zennor do. And I apologize to the animals. But it certainly won't go that far, will it Stirner? Your people will have to go back to work now?"

"No, they won't. If you understood Individual Mutualism you would understand why. Every individual is a separate and discrete entity, responsible for his or her own existence. What Zennor does to another individual does not relate to any other discrete individual."

"Zennor thinks so."

"Then Zennor thinks wrong."

I resisted the temptation to tear out a handful of my own hair. I wasn't getting through at all. "Well look at it another way. If you do not do anything to stop Zennor then you are responsible for the deaths of the hostages."

"No. If I do something to please Zennor in the face of his threats then I am admitting his control over my actions despite the fact I do not wish his control. The state is born once again. IM is dead. So we chose passive resistance. We will not be ordered or threatened . . ."

"But you can be killed."

"Yes." He nodded grimly. "Some will die if he insists on this course. But murder is self-defeating. How can you force someone to work by killing him?"

"I understand you—but I don't like it." I was too disturbed to sit, I stood, paced the floor. "There must be a way out of this that doesn't involve someone's death. What is it that Zennor wants?"

"He was very angry," Morton said. "And very specific. First he wants the electricity turned back on in the buildings the military has occupied. Then he wants a regular supply of food for his troops. If these two things are done no one will be killed and the prisoners released. For the time being."

"Impossible," Dr. Lum said. "They gave nothing in return for the electricity they used, so it was disconnected. The same thing applies to the food. The markets have shut down because the farmers will not bring food to the city."

"But," I sputtered. "If the markets are closed how does everyone else in the city eat?"

"They go to the farms, or leave the city. Almost a third of the population has already gone."

"Where will they go?"

"Wherever they want to." He smiled at the look on my face. He could tell that I was hearing the words but not understanding them. "I think that I should go to basics, explain a bit more about IM to enable you to understand. Let us take a simple example. A farmer. He raises all the food that he needs, supplies all of his own wants so asks for nothing from others."

"Nothing?" I had him there. "What if he needs new shoes?"

"He goes to a man who makes shoes and gives him food in exchange."

"Barter!" Morton said. "The most primitive economic system. But it cannot exist in a modern technological society . . ." His voice ran down as he looked about the room. Stirner smiled again.

"Of course it cannot. But IM is more than barter. The individual will *voluntarily* join other individuals in a larger

182

organization to manufacture some item, or build houses say. For each hour they work they are credited with a wirr."

"A what?"

"A work hour. These wirrs are exchanged with others for goods and services."

"A wirr is another way of saying money," Morton said. "And money is capitalism—so you have a capitalistic society."

"I am afraid not. Individual Mutualism is neither capitalism, communism, socialism, vegetarianism, or even the dreaded monetarism that destroyed many a technological society. I am familiar with these terms from Mark Forer's writings. A wirr has no physical existence, such as a rare metal or a seashell. Nor can it be invested and gain interest. That is fundamental and differentiates the wirr from currency. Banks cannot exist because there can be no interest on deposits or loans."

Instead of being clarified I found my head wirring in confusion from the wirrs. "Wait, please, explanation. I have seen people driving groundcars. How can they save money enough to buy one? Who will loan them the money without interest?"

"No money," he said firmly. "If you wish a groundcar you go to the groundcar group and drive one away. You will pay when you use it, stop paying when you return it. A basic tenet of IM is from each according to his needs, to each according to the wealth of society."

"You wouldn't like to clarify that?" I poured myself a glass of wine and gulped it down hoping the alcohol would clean out my synapses.

"Of course. I have read, and trembled with disgust, of a philosophy called the work ethic. This states that an individual must work hard for the basics of life. When technological society mechanizes and replaces workers with machines, the work ethic states that the displaced workers must be looked on with contempt, allowed to starve, be treated like outcasts. And the hypocrisy of the work ethic system is that those with capital do not work—yet still increase their capital without working by the use of interest on their money—and look down upon those who have been cast out of work! Tragic. But not here. As more is produced the aggregate wealth gets larger. When this happens the amount that the wirr can be exchanged for also gets larger."

Some of it was getting through—but needed elucidation. "Another question. If the wirr is worth more—that must mean that an individual can work less for the same return."

"Exactly."

"Then there is no forty-hour week or such. How many hours would an individual have to work a week to keep alive?"

"For simply shelter, food, clothes—I would say about two hours of work every seven days."

"I want to move here," Morton said firmly and I nodded agreement and froze in half-nod. An idea was glimmering at the edge of my consciousness. I muttered and chiseled at it and expanded it until I saw it large and clear and possibly workable. In a little while. But first we had to do something about the hostages. I rejoined the real world and called for attention.

"Time is passing and dawn approaching. I have enjoyed the lecture, thank you, and I now know a bit more about IM. Enough at least to ask a question. What do you do in an emergency? Say there is a flood, or a dam bursts or something. A catastrophe that threatens the group not the individual."

The doctor stepped forward, finger raised and a sparkle of enthusiasm in his eye. "A good question, a marvelous question!" He grabbed at the shelves and pulled down a thick book. "It is here, all here. Mark Forer did consider a situation like this and made allowances for it. Here is what he wrote . . . 'at all times passive resistance will be your only weapon, never violence. But until the perfect stateless state is established there will be those of violence who will force their violence upon you. Individual Mutualism cannot be established by the dead. Until the day of true liberation comes you will have to coexist with others. You may leave their presence but they may follow and force themselves upon you. In which case you and all of the others must look upon those of violence as they might look upon any natural catastrophe such as a volcano or a hurricane. The intelligent person does not discuss ethics with hot lava but instead flees it presence, does not preach morals to the wind but seeks shelter from it.'"

Dr. Lum closed the book and raised a triumphant finger again. "So we are saved, saved! Mark Forer has foreseen our predicament and given us the guidance we need."

"Indeed!" Stirner agreed enthusiastically. "I shall go at once and tell the others." He rushed to the door and out of the house. I gaped after him. Morton spoke my thoughts before I could.

"I heard what you said—but haven't the slightest idea of what your Mark Four was talking about."

"Clarity!" the doctor said. "Clarity and wisdom. If we all persist in noncompliance we are in a sense killing ourselves. So we comply and withdraw."

"I am still not sure what you are talking about," I said.

"The electricity will be turned back on, the markets will reopen. The invaders will seize food and some farmers will work longer hours if they wish to, because that will avert the natural disaster. Others will not and will stop bringing food to the city. As the supply diminishes people will leave the city and the process will accelerate. With less call for electricity, generating plant will shut down, workers will leave. In a very short time the soldiers will have the city to themselves because we will all be gone."

"They can enslave you—make you work at gunpoint."

"Of course, but only on a one-to-one basis. One armed man can force another to work, possibly, it is of course up to the individual. But the man with the gun is essentially doing the work himself because he must be there every moment or the work will not get done. I don't think your General Zennor will like this."

"You can say that again!"

"I don't think your General . . ."

"No, not really say it again, I meant it as an expression of agreement. You people are too literal, too much IM I imagine. A question then, a hypothetical one."

"Those are the best kind!"

"Yes, indeed. If I should walk into a distant city and look for work—would I be accepted?"

"Of course. That is a basic tenet of IM."

"What if there are no jobs going?"

185

"There always are—remember the value of the rising wirr. Theoretically as it gets larger and larger, the working hours will get fewer and fewer, until in the long run a few seconds work will suffice . . ."

"All right, great, thanks—let's just stick with the application of theory for a moment. If one of these invading soldiers should walk away from the army . . ."

"Which is of course his right!"

"Not quite what the army thinks. If he walks away to a distant town and gets a job and meets a girl and all the usual good things happen—is this possible?"

"Not only possible, but inescapable, a foundation of IM inherent in its acceptance."

"Are you thinking what I think you're thinking!" Morton shouted, jumping to his feet with elation.

"You bet your sweet chunk I'm thinking that! Leaving aside the officers and the career noncoms, this is a draftee army and a good number of them were draft evaders. If we make the opportunity available for them to walk away from it all, why then Zennor might have to give a war that nobody will come to."

The front door opened and Morton and I dived for cover. But it was Stirner leading the triumphal return of the released captives. Morton rushed to Sharla and took her hand to see if it had been hurt during her incarceration.

"That's pretty fast work," I said.

"I used the TV phone across the street," Stirner said. "I purchased national access and told them what we had discovered. The electricity was turned on instantly, the first food shipped. The prisoners were released."

"Zennor must think that he has won the war. Let me tell you what we have just discovered. The way to guarantee that he loses his war—even if the Navy never gets here."

"I am encouraged by your enthusiasm but miss your meaning."

"I will explain—but first a drink to celebrate."

This seemed like a good idea to all concerned. We poured and drank, then Morton and I listened with some interest as the others sang a song about Individual Mutualism freeing mankind from the yoke of oppression and so forth. While the theory was fine the lyric was as bad as all other anthems I had ever heard, though I took considerable interest in the great efforts made to rhyme Individual Mutualism. I also took the time to organize my thoughts so when they had finished, and sipped a bit more wine for dry throats, I took the floor.

"I must first tell you kind people about the uniformed mob of thugs who have invaded your fair planet. A large group like this is called an army. An army is a throwback to the earliest days of mankind when physical defense was needed against the rigors of existence. The combative gene was the successful gene. The primitive who defended his family group passed on this gene. This gene has caused a lot of trouble since that time, right down through the ages. It is still causing trouble as you now have cause to understand. When all of the threatening animals were killed, the gene caused mankind to turn upon itself to kill each other. With shame I admit we are the only species that kills its own kind on a very organized basis. The army is the last gasp of the combative gene. In charge are old men, and they are called officers. They do nothing except issue orders. At the bottom are the soldiers who follow these orders. In between are the noncommissioned officers who see that this is done. The interesting thing to us now is that the soldiers are all drafted and a good number of them are draft dodgers."

It took some time to explain what these last two terms meant and there was horrified shock on all sides when understanding finally penetrated. I waited until the cries of disbelief and despair had simmered down, then signaled for silence.

"I am cheered by your reaction. Do you think your people would volunteer, without payment in wirrs, to free these young men from bondage?"

"It would be our duty," the doctor said and heads nodded like fury on all sides. "It would be like saving someone from drowning, a public duty, no payment expected."

"Great! Then I will now teach you another word . . ."

"Can I guess?" Morton cried out. I nodded.

"Desertion!"

I nodded again. Battle joined at last!

187

CHAPTER 22

Enthusiasm gave way quickly to fatigue and it was agreed that the session would continue after we all had had some sleep. I found myself tucked away in a small room in a soft bed, with a portrait of Mark Forer beaming down electronically upon me. I sipped a last sip of wine and crashed.

By the next evening I had put together the rudiments of a plan and had assembled my team.

"We have to try it out, smooth it out. Then, if it works, we pass it on to others. We will operate and proceed like an ancient scam, a term I ran across when doing research into crime." I did not add that my reasons for doing this were to improve myself as a criminal. This would have been too much for these simple IMers to understand. "Here is how it will work. This evening I will enter one of the eating and drinking establishments you have described to me. I will then stand next to a soldier and engage him in conversation. You, Stirner will be seated at a table with empty chairs, or next to an empty table. I will come over with the soldier and sit close enough for you to overhear our conversation. Sharla will be with you, she is your daughter."

"You are wrong, she is not my daughter."

"Just for tonight she is your daughter, like in a play. You do have plays here?"

"Of course. In fact I was on the stage when younger, before I was attracted to the delights of flowing electrons. I even acted the title role in some classics, how does it go again . . . to was, or not to was—"

"Fine, great, glad to have an old thespian aboard. So tonight you act the role of Sharla's dad. Follow my lead and it should work. I'll pick an easy target this first time, an apple ripe for plucking. So there should not be any trouble."

"What do I do?" Morton asked. "You said I was on the team."

"Right. You have the important job of taping all of this for the record. So when it works as it should we can make training copies for others. Keep the recorder out of sight and the mike close. Ready?"

"Ready!"

We waited until after dark before we set out. Volunteers, drafted from the street of course, worked ahead of us to make sure we didn't meet any roadblocks or MPs. They reported back all the obstructions so we had a pleasant, if circuitous, walk to the Vaillant quarter of the city which I had been assured was the correct place to go for theatre, opera, dining out, IM reinforcement groups and the other heady joys of this civilized planet. It looked an interesting locale. Although it was fairly empty this evening with no more than a quarter of the establishments lighted up. Stirner led the way to the Fat Farmer, where he said he always enjoyed good food and better drink when in the city. There were some locals sampling its pleasures—but no invading soldiers.

"You told me that the army had leave passes, that they could be found in this area. Where are they?"

"Not in here, obviously," Stirner said.

"What do you mean—obviously?"

"Since they cannot pay they won't be served."

"Sounds fair. But, since they are the invading army, what stops them from just grabbing the booze and helping themselves?"

"They are not stopped. However everyone leaves and the establishment shuts down."

"Obvious. All right then. To your stations and I'll see if I can drum up some trade."

189

I felt very pimpish standing under the streetlight with a dead cigar for a prop. In the local garb I was just part of the passing parade and no one took notice of me. I watched all of them though—on the lookout for MPs or anything that resembled the part of the military I did not want to see, stripes, bars, the usual thing. None of these appeared, but eventually two unmilitary figures in military uniform drifted into sight. Hands in pockets—shame!—caps on at odd angles. They stopped at the Fat Farmer and looked in the window with longing. I stepped up behind them and held up the cigar.

"Either of you guys got a light?"

They jumped as though they had been goosed, shying back from me.

"You talked to us!" the bolder one said.

"I did. I pride myself on my linguistic ability. And if you will remember I asked you for a light for my cigar."

"I don't smoke."

"Good for you. Cigarettes kill. But don't you carry a fire apparatus for those who do?" They shook their heads in gloomy negation. Then I raised a finger rich with inspiration. "I know what—we will enter this eating and drinking place and they will light my cigar. Perhaps you young gentlemen from distant planet will also join me in a drink and I can practice my talking?"

"Won't work. We tried it and they closed the place and went home."

"That is only because you had no wirr, the local unit of exchange, our money, so could not pay. I am rich with wirr and am buying . . ."

I followed after their rapidly retreating footsteps, found them pushing against the bar in eager anticipation. Stirner had given me his wirrdisc and briefed me on its operation.

"Three beers," I ordered, "large ones," and dropped the plastic slab of integrated circuits into the slot in the top of the bar. While the robot bartender, all chrome and brass with bottlecaps for eyes, drew three big brews, the cost was subtracted from Stirner's lifetime account. I grabbed the wirrdisc as it was rejected.

"Here's to the army, lads," I said raising my beer high. "I hope you enjoy your chosen careers."

They chugalugged enthusiastically, then gasped and whined nostalgically familiar whines that took me back to my own army days.

"Chose an army career! Cagal! Drafted. Chased, hunted down, caught."

"Then after that, basic training. Pursued at the double night and day by foul-mouthed fiends. Would anyone voluntarily chose a career like that?"

"Certainly not! But at least you eat well . . ."

I enjoyed the outraged cries and loathsome descriptions of hotpups while I ordered up another round of beers. When their faces were buried in the suds again I made the suggestion.

"I know it is past your dinner hour, but I see three seats vacant at that table, next to the elderly gentleman with the kinky bird. Would you join me for a small repast—say a large steak and fried wirfles?"

The thunder of feet was my only answer yet one more time. I joined them in the steaks, and very good they were too. We polished them off quickly, had a few more beers—and tried not to belch because there was young lady at our table. Sated and boozed they now had time for the third of the troika of military pleasures and their eyes moved steadily in Sharla's direction. Time for act two.

"Well," I said, "if the food is bad in the army, at least you enjoy the wisdom and companionship of the sergeants."

I listened to the answers for a bit, nodding and commiserating, then elicited other similar complaints with leading questions about officers, latrines, kitchen police—and all the other bitches so dear to the enlisted man's heart. When enough had been ventilated I gave Stirner his clue and sat back.

"Young draftee soldiers from a distant planet, you must excuse my impertinence in addressing strangers. But I, and my lovely daughter Sharla, could not help but overhear your conversation. Can it be true that you were forced into military service completely against your will?"

"You better believe it, Pops. Hi, Sharla, you ever go out with guys other than your Dad?"

"Very often. I simply adore the company of handsome young men. Like you."

All three of us fell into the limpid pool of her eyes, splashed around for a bit and emerged gasping and in love. Stirner spoke and they did not hear. I finally ordered large beers and had them placed in front of their bulging eyes to cut off sight of the gorgeous Sharla. This produced the desired result. While they glugged Stirner talked.

"I am greatly taken by your plight, young gentleman. On this planet such a thing is impossible. Against our laws, which laws state that there are no laws. Why do you permit yourself to be treated in this vile manner?"

"No choice, Pops. Barbed wire all around, watched night and day, shot if your try to escape, shot twice if recaptured. No place to go to, no place to hide, in uniform, every man's hand turned against you."

He sniffed in maudlin self-pity; a tear ran down his companion's cheek.

"Well," Stirner said, sinking the gaff in deep and twisting it so it would take hold. "None of those things are true here. There is no barbed wire, no one is watching you, no one is about to shoot you. There is a great big country out there that stretches away beyond the mountains and rivers. A country where you will always find a welcome, always find hospitality and refuge. A country where the army will never find you."

They sat up at that, trying to understand his words through their alcoholic haze. "Cagal . . ." the drunkest one muttered. Sharla smiled angelically.

"I do not understand that word, young friend, but I feel that it indicates disbelief. Not so. Every word my father has spoken is true. For example, we live a full day's journey distant from this city in an idyllic farming village. We travel there by speedy railroad—and these are our tickets to prove it. Why, look, the machine made a mistake, it issued four tickets instead of two. I must return them—unless you would like them for souvenirs?"

Faster than light, they vanished.

192

"There is a side entrance to the railway station that is not guarded," she said brightly.

"But the train leaves soon," Stirner said, standing and picking up the bundle from the floor. "Before going I must use the *necesejo,* as we say down on the farm, and I am taking this bundle with me. It contains clothing for my two sons at home who, strangely enough, are just your size." He started away, then turned. "You may borrow the clothes—if you wish."

They beat him to the cagalhouse door. Sharla smiled beatifically after them.

"You know this farming town well?" I asked. "So you can line the lads up with friends."

"I have never been there—I found its name on the map. But you forget the strength of IM. We would welcome them here and aid them, so they will be welcome there. Do not worry. I will guide them and return in two days. Ohh, here they come, don't they look handsome out of those dreary uniforms!"

They looked rotten, I thought, the demon of jealousy burning within me. I almost wished that I was going with them. But no, the work was here. I turned to the next table where Morton was mooning after the lovely retreating form of Sharla. I had to kick him twice before I could attract his attention.

"She'll be back, don't worry. Did you get all that on tape."

"Every word. Can I have another beer? All I had was the one Sharla bought me before you came in. And you had a steak . . ."

"No drinking on duty, soldier."

Stirner joined us and pointed to the basket he was carrying. "I have their uniforms in here, just as you asked."

"Good. We'll need that for the video. Now—take us to your recording studio."

He led us by back streets to the back of a building, to the back door that opened as we approached. They were eagerly waiting for us on the soundstage, brightly lit, windowless and invisible from the street. Volunteers all, IM enthusiasts just dying to subvert the troops. I held up the audio cassette.

"We'll need a few hundred copies of this."

"Within the hour!" It was snatched from my hand and whisked away. I turned to the waiting production crew who were trembling with enthusiasm. "Director?" I asked. A gorgeous redhead stepped forward.

"At your service. Lights, sound, camera ready."

"Wonderful. As soon as my associate and I put on these uniforms—you can roll. Point us to the dressing room."

As I stripped Morton took one of the uniforms out of the basket and held it out between thumb and index finger like a dead rat.

"I feel depressed even looking at this thing," he said. Depressedly. "To feel its touch upon my skin again, the clammy embrace . . ."

"Morton," I hinted, "shut up." I whipped it away and held it before me. A good fit. I climbed into it. "You are an actor now, Morton, playing before the camera. You will act your role—then remove the uniform forever. Burn it if you wish to. Thousands will applaud your performance. So put it on. Like this."

I sat and pushed my legs into the trousers and something fell from a pocket and tinkled to the floor. I bent and picked it. An ID disc. Private soldier Pyek0765 had been eager to wipe all memory of the army from him, to be reborn a happy civilian. I turned it over and over in my fingers and an idea began to sizzle about low down in my brain. Morton's cry of dismay cut through my thoughts.

"It's there! I can see it! That glazed look in your eye. Whenever you are dreaming up a suicidal idea you get it. Not again! I don't volunteer!"

I patted his shoulder cheerfully, then reknotted his tie into a semblance of military order. "Relax. I have had a brilliant idea, yes. But you are not involved, no. Now let us shoot this video and after it is done I will tell you all about this plan."

I stood Morton up with a wall for a backdrop; not a good choice because he looked like he was waiting to be shot. No changes, time was of the essence.

"If you please. I want a full-figure shot of that man. Let me have a roving microphone. Ready when you are."

194

Morton winced a bit when two spotlights pinned him to the wall. A mike was thrust into my hand and pure contralto voice rang out across the set.

"Silence. Ready to roll. Sound. Camera. Action."

"Ladies and gentlemen of Chojecki, I bring you greetings. You are looking at a typical unwilling member of the invading Nevenkebla army. With this video you will have received an audio cassette that is a live recording of an actual encounter with two of these soldiers. You will listen to their bleating complaints, will be shocked at the terror of their involuntary servitude, will cry with joy as they are given the opportunity to hurl the shackles from their shoulders and stride forth into the green countryside, to prosper under the glowing sun of Individual Mutualism."

My sales pitch was so sincere that Stirner could not restrain himself and burst out clapping—as did the crew and technicians. Morton clasped his hands over his head—there is a bit of ham lurking in all of us—and bowed.

"Silence," I ordered and all was instantly quiet. I strode onto camera and pointed at the subdued Morton. "This is the kind of soldier you will meet and befriend and subvert. Note then the complete absence of markings upon the sleeve." Morton extended his arm and I pointed to the right place. "Empty of stripes, chevrons, angled or curved bits of colored cloth. This is what you must look for. If there is a single stripe, two or more, or most frightening thought, three up and three down with a lozenge in the middle—retreat! Do not talk to anyone with these kinds of adornment because you will be addressing one of the enslaving devils incarnate!

"Also be warned if there are shining bits of metal on the shoulders, here and here. Those who wear these are known as officers and are usually too stupid to be dangerous. They must still be avoided.

"Another group, very dangerous, can be recognized by their headgear and brassard. If the letters MP appear upon the arm—go the other way. Also look for the redcap which will be mounted squarely upon the brutal head.

195

"Now that you know what to avoid, you know whom to approach. A simple uniformed slave. Come close, smile, make sure that none of the striped and barred beasts are close, then whisper in the slave's ear . . . 'Do you like fresh air?' If he smiles with joy and answers 'yes', why then he is yours. May Mark Forer guide you in this great work!"

"Cut, print, thank you gentlemen."

Morton blinked as the spots died away and began to tear off the uniform. "What, may I ask, what was this cagal about the fresh air."

"No cagal, old friend," I said, holding up the liberty pass I had taken from the pocket of the borrowed uniform. "I intend to go forth to bring the word to the troops that when they go out the gates tomorrow night they should not bother to return."

"I knew that you had an insane idea!" he shrieked, staggering back, wide of eye and pale of skin. "The only way that you can talk to the troops is by going back onto the base."

I nodded a solemn nod of agreement.

CHAPTER 23

"It is suicide," Morton shivered.

"Not at all. Good sense. If that swine Zennor is still looking for me—he certainly won't be looking among the troops. I have this pass dated for today. I return to base early since there is not much doing in the old town tonight. Then I go to the latrine, the PX, all the other exciting places where the troops assemble, and talk to the lads. And do some other interesting things which it is best you don't know about. Don't worry about me."

I could worry enough for myself I thought, darkly. Once back in the army there were a number of problems I would have to tackle. And all of them were dangerous.

"But how will you get out again?" Morton asked, his voice speaking as though from a great distance, cutting through the black brooding of my thoughts.

"The least of my worries," I laughed hollowly. And indeed it certainly was. I turned to the ever-patient Stirner who had been listening to us in silence. "You know what to do with the cassettes?"

"It will be as you planned. Volunteers are already waiting to distribute them to even more volunteers who will go forth and do good deeds just as we did. It was inspiring!"

"Indeed it was. But no sallying forth until tomorrow night in the very earliest. The password must be spread, there must be eager volunteers to make this a mass movement. Because once the officers catch wise things will become difficult. The railroad will be watched or stopped altogether. If that happens other transport must be provided. Keep things moving though, until I get back. You are the authority on desertion now."

"How long will you be away?"

"Don't know. But for the shortest amount of time that is possible—that I can guarantee."

There was little more to say, nothing more to do. I squared my cap upon my head and turned to the door.

"Good luck," Morton said.

"Thanks." I was going to need it.

As I walked back through the empty streets toward the Vaillant section of town I fought off the depression that accompanied the uniform I wore. Nor could I drown my sorrows in drink, since money was worthless here and I had returned Stirner's wirrdisc. Soon I was walking among the inaccessible, brightly lit palaces of pleasure, pressing my nose against the window just like the other uniformed figures that roamed the streets. Some leave! Although the evening was still young, many of them were already drifting back toward Fielden Field where the camp had been built. I joined in this Brownian movement of despair.

Bright lights burned down upon the barbed wire that encircled the green grassy meadows, where once the good citizens of the city had taken their ease. Green no more, pounded now into dust and filled with gray army tents erected to house the troops. No effete comforts for the conquering soldiers; they might get spoiled. The officers, of course, lived in prefab barracks.

It took all the strength of will that I possessed to join the line of depressed figures that moved toward the MPs at the gate. While my intelligence told me that the last thing to be expected was a soldier with a pass illegally entering the camp, the animal spirit within me was screaming with anquish.

Of course nothing untoward happened. Dim little eyes stared out from under the matt of thick eyebrows, scanned the familiar pass, waved me back into captivity. The sweat cooled from my brow and I jingled the few coins in my pocket that the freedom-bound soldier had been happy to leave behind. There was just about enough of them to buy an understrength beer in the PX. Anything is better than nothing.

I found this depressing establishment easily enough. I just traced the sound of rock-drilling and western music to its source. The PX bar was housed in a sagging tent vaguely illuminated by light bulbs that had been specifically designed to attract flying insects. Here, at rough tables of drink-sodden wood, sitting on splinter-filled planks, the troops enjoyed the pleasures of warm, bad beer. I bought a bulb and joined them.

"Got room for one more?"

"Cagal off."

"Thanks a lot. What is this—cagal your buddy week?"

"It's always cagal your buddy week."

"You sound just like the civilians in town."

This aroused some interest. The heavyset speaker now focused his blurred vision on me and I realized that all of the others at the table were listening as well.

"You got a pass tonight? We get ours tomorrow. What's it like?"

"Like pretty grim. They won't serve you. If you like grab a drink they close the bar and all go home."

"We heard that. So what's the point of going in. Nothing."

"Something. You get to leave the army, travel far away, eat good food, get drunk. And kiss girls."

Wow, did I have their attention now. If eyeballs were gunmuzzles I would have been blown out of existence in an instant. There was a dead silence at the table as every head swiveled in my direction.

"What did you say?" a hushed voice asked.

"You heard me. You go down to where the restaurants are and walk slow. If someone says to you—Do you like fresh air?—just say that you do, you do. Then go with them. They'll get you civvies to wear, a ticket out of town—and set you up on the other side of the country where the MPs will never find you."

"You are cagaling us!"

"No way. And what do you lose by going along with it? Whatever happens—it got to be better than the army."

There were no arguments with this. Only the muscled guy with the suspicious mind found what he thought was a loophole.

"If what you are telling us is true and not the old cagal—then what are you doing back here?"

"A very good question," I stood up and held out my pass. "I came back for the bundle of letters from my mom. This pass is good until midnight. See you in paradise—if you want to come."

I left them and moved on to the next group who were in the corner of a latrine shooting dice. I palmed the dice and won some good pots which drew their attention, gave them my orientation talk and left.

I worked at this until it was almost midnight when my pass ran out and my story would take on a dubious taint. I had planted the seeds in fertile ground. The word would spread instantly through the latrine rumor network. And if I knew my draft dodgers not one of them would return from pass tomorrow night. That should cheer General Zennor up!

So plan number two must now be put into effect.

For what I had to do next I needed a bit more rank. There would be no slow crawl up through the noncommisioned ranks this time. I had tasted the heady glory of being an officer and I was spoiled forever. So I headed for the lair of those brightly-plumaged birds of prey; the officers' club. I found it by back-tracking the drunks. The higher the rank the stronger the booze; this was the army way. I passed a staggering pair of majors, each holding the other up, lined myself up on a colonel flipping his cookies into a hedge, took a sight over an unconscious captain in the gutter and saw my target glowing on the horizon. I skulked off in that direction and took refuge behind some bushes where I had a good sight of the entrance.

It was strictly a bachelor affair and all the worse for it. Obscene songs were being sung loudly and off-key. At least two punchups were going on in the grass outside at all times. There was some coming, of sober officers just off duty, but much more going of officers drunk out of their cagaling minds. I watched from hiding until my prey emerged, stumbled, and came toward me singing hoarsely under his voice.

200

He staggered under the only streetlamp. A captain, about my size, lots of fake medals and decorations, just what I needed. A simple armlock from the rear, correct pressure applied, struggle feebly, unconscious, then into the hedges with him. A piece of cake.

He passed muttering by. Silent as a wraith I moved, pounced, seized, applied pressure . . .

And found myself sailing swiftly through the air to crash into the hedge.

"So—revolt in the ranks," he snarled, relatively sober and on guard in an instant, crouched and approaching. I struggled to my feet, feinted with my left hand and chopped down with my right. He blocked and would have kicked me in the stomach if I hadn't jumped aside.

"Want to kill an officer? Don't blame you. And I have always wanted to kill a private. Good time right now."

He advanced—and I retreated. The medals had not been fakes. With great skill I had managed to find and attack what was probably the only trained combat officer in this army. Tremendous!

"Death to all officers!" I shouted and swung a wicked kick at his groin.

He was bright enough to know he was whoozy, so instead of trying to block he stepped back. I kept the kick going which pulled me around to face in the other direction.

And ran away. Discretion is the better part of valor. He who fights and pulls his freight lives to fight another date. I had no macho points to make. I just wanted to stay alive!

Dive and shoulder roll over a hedge. Roaring, he crashed through it right behind me. There were tents ahead, hard boots pounding after me. Jump over a tentrope, dodge under another. A shout and a crash behind me. Good—he had tripped over one of the ropes. A few paces gained. Run, fast as I could. Between the next row of tents and back to the street. A building up ahead, loud music and the sound of breaking glass coming from it. I was at the rear of the officers' club.

Time to go to ground. Through the gate and into the yard, gate closed behind me, no sign of pursuit.

"You had your break, quit cagaling off, get them cases in here."

A fat cook stood at the rear door of the kitchen under the light, blinking into the gloom of the yard. Figures stirred as the enslaved KPs moved, as slowly as possible, to the stacks of beer cases. They had their jackets off, wearing only undershirts in the steamy heat of the kitchen. I took off my own jacket, rolled it and pushed it behind the cases, seized up a beer case and followed the others inside.

Kitchen police. The most demeaning servitude in the army—which is an establishment that prides itself on demeaning servitude. KP was so degrading that it was forbidden, by military law, to give KP as a punishment. So, naturally, it was always given as a punishment. Up before dawn, laboring until late at night. Washing pots, cleaning out disgusting greasetraps in the underground plumbing, slaving at the most menial tasks that generations of warped minds had created. It was absolutely completely impossible that anyone would volunteer for this service. I would never be looked for here!

I carried the case past the cook who was acting KP pusher. He had a filthy chef's hat on his head, sergeant's stripes tattooed onto his beefy forearms, and was brandishing a long ladle as a weapon. He scowled as I passed then pointed the ladle in my direction.

"You. Where you come from?"

"It's a mistake," I whimpered. "I shouldn't be here. I didn't do nothing like what the first sergeant said I done. Let me go back . . ."

"If I have my way you will never go back," he screamed. "You will die in this kitchen and be buried under the floor. You're on pots and pans! Move!"

Harried by blows from the ladle I moved. To the giant metal sink to seize up the filthy metal pot waiting there. A simple labor, washing a pot. Harder perhaps when the pot is as big as you are. And another and another—and still another. Steam, hot water, soap, labor with no end.

I worked and sweated until I felt that enough time had passed for any excitement and search to have died away. As I straightened up my aching back crackled loudly. I wiped a soggy forearm across my dripping forehead. My hands were bleached, my fingers as wrinkled and pallid as long-drowned slugs. As I looked at them I felt my anger growing—this was no fit job for a stainless steel rat! I would be rusting soon . . .

The ladle crashed down on my shoulder and the choleric pusher roared his ungrammatical commands.

"Keep working you're gonna be in trouble!"

Something snapped and blackness overwhelmed me. This can happen to the best of us. The veneer of civilization worn thin, the lurking beast ready to burst free.

My beast must have burst most satisfactorily, thank you, because the next thing that I was conscious of was hands pulling at my shoulders. I looked in astonishment at the gross, flaccid form beside me, a pair of giant buttocks rising high. I had my hands about the pusher's neck, had his head buried in the soapy water where he was apparently drowning. Shocked, I pulled him up and let him slip to the floor. Gouts of water poured from nose and mouth and he gurgled moistly.

"He'll live," I told the circle of wide-eyed KPs. "Any of the cooks see what happened?"

"No—they're all drunk in the other room."

"Great." I tore the KP roster from the wall and shredded it. "You are all free. Return to your tents and keep your mouths shut. Unhappily, the pusher will live. Go."

Eagerly, they went. I went too, to the pegs where the cooks had discarded bits of uniform as they worked in the heat of the kitchen. There was a formerly white jacket with sergeant's stripes on it. Perfect for my needs. Donning it I strode into the kitchen, in my element, no need to skulk, and on into the dining hall and barroom.

It was wonderful. Music played, officers roared, bottles broke, songs were sung. Uniformed figures slumped over the tables while others had slid to the floor. The survivors were well on their way to join the succumbed. I pushed through this alcoholic hell and greatly admired the unconscious drunks. I was still aching from the captain's spirited defense. I had rediscovered a dictum that must be as old as crime. Rolling drunks is easier than mugging.

A major in the space service caught my eye, prone on the floor and snoring. I knelt next to him and stretched my arm out next to his. Same length; his uniform should make a fine fit.

"Washa?" a voice muttered from above and I realized that my bit of tailoring measurement had not gone unnoticed.

"The major is on duty later. I was sent to get him. Come on major, walkies, sackies."

I struggled to lift the limp figure, aided very slightly by his friends. In the end I seized him under the arms and dragged him from the room. His departure was not noticed. Through a door and down a hall, to a storeroom filled to the ceiling with bottles of strong beverage. He would feel right at home here. With the door secured I took my time about stripping him and donning his uniform. Even his cap fitted well. I was a new man, rather officer.

I left him dozing out of sight behind the drink. Straightened my tie. And sallied forth to save the world. Not for the first and, I had the feeling, not for the last time either.

CHAPTER 24

I looked around at the bottles, reached for one—then slapped my wrist.

"No, Jimmy, not for you. The number of beers you had this evening will have to suffice. What you have to do will be better off done sober."

What did I have to do? Simply get aboard one of the spacers, find the communications room, then locate the coordinates of this planet. Easy to say: a little difficult to do.

At least the first part was easy enough to accomplish; locate the spacers. I had seen the floodlit shapes of three of them rising high above the tents earlier in the evening. The party was still crashing inside so this would be a good time to move through the camp. While plenty of drunks were still staggering about. I brushed some dust from my lapel, straightened the medals on my chest. Quite a collection. I turned the gaudiest one over and craned to read it. THE GLORIOUS UNIT AWARD—6 WEEKS WITHOUT VD IN THE COMPANY. Wonderful. I assumed the rest of the lot had been given for equally valiant military endeavors. Time to go.

It looked like events in the alcoholic bedlam were winding down for the night. A grill was being locked over the bar. Orderlies were loading unconscious forms onto stretchers, while the walking wounded were stumbling toward the exit. A brace of gray-haired colonels were leaning against each other and moving their feet up and down and not getting anyplace. I made the twosome a threesome and let them lean on me.

"I am going your way, sirs. Perhaps I could accompany you?"

"You shure a good buddy . . . buddy," one of them breathed my way. The alcoholic content of my blood instantly shot up and I hiccuped.

We exited in this manner, weaved our way between the ambulances being loaded with officerial alcoholics, and staggered off into the night. In the direction of the spacers. I had not the slightest idea where the BOQ was—nor did I care. Nor did my drink-sodden companions. It took all their concentration, and what little conscious mind they had remaining, to simply put one foot in front of another.

A squad of MPs turned the corner in front of us, saw the gleam of light from the silver chickens on my companions' shoulders. Then did the smartest about face to the rear march I had ever seen.

My drunks were getting heavier and heavier and moving slower and slower as we stumbled through the tent-lined street toward a brightly lit building at the end. It was large and permanent, undoubtedly part of the park facilities purloined from the natives. Even at this hour of the night, morning really, two armed guards stood at the entrance. All the rocks along the path were painted white and the overly ornate sign above the door read BASE HEADQUARTERS—GEN. ZENNOR COMMANDING.

This was definitely not the place for me. I maneuvered my charges onto the grass, next to the sign KEEP OFF OR GET SHOT, and let go. They dropped instantly and began snoring.

"You, guards," I called out. "One of you get the Officer of the Day. These colonels have been taken ill. Food poisoning I think."

I glared my best glare and not a muscle moved in their faces.

"Yes, sir!" the sergeant shouted. "OD on the double!"

He turned and hurried away and so did I. Toward the charred remains of a sportsfield upon which the three spacers rested. All of them bristled with guns, brought here to impress the locals I imagined. Or to beat off the armed attacks that had never

206

materialized. How depressed all the military must be that they couldn't pull their shiny triggers and blow away the population. They had given a war—and nobody came. Terribly frustrating.

I staggered as I walked so I would be recognized as an officer. Toward the extruded stairs that ran from the ground, up into the bowels of the nearest spacer. I was a space officer, I was just going to my ship. Or at least I thought I was until I saw that a guard stood on the lower step.

"Halt and be recognized."

"Cagal off . . ." I muttered and pushed by him. A private lowest of the low.

"Please, major, sir, your majesty. You can't go in without I see your pass."

"Cagal off twice!" Witty, witty. "Don' need no pass my own ship."

Past him and up the stairs. Brain beats brawn anytime. Step by step up toward the gaping spacelock. And the surly sergeant-major who stood and scowled there, firmly blocking the entrance.

"This ain't your ship, major. I know this ship's company. You are on another ship."

I opened my mouth to argue, order, shout. Then saw the gunmetal blue jaw, the glowing red eyes, the hairline that blended into the eyebrows. Even the hairs curling from his broken nose looked like they were made of steel wool.

"Not my ship?"

"Not your ship."

"Gesh it's not my ship . . ." I susurrated, turning and stumbling back down and away into the night. There was no way I was going to get past the sergeant-major. Back toward the headquarters building and the rows of tents to come up with another plan.

Hidden in the darkness under a large tree, I looked out at the spacers and could think of absolutely nothing I could do to get aboard one of them. The hour was late, the drunks now dispersed, the camp silent. Except for the roving bands of MPs. Whatever was to be done would have to wait until morning. It would be more dangerous in daylight but it had to be chanced.

207

Perhaps if there was enough to-ing and fro-ing to the ships I might be able to join in. Right now I really should be thinking of my own safety. And some sleep, I yawned. The kicked-in ribs were hurting again. I sniveled a bit and really felt sorry for myself.

In the stillness of the night the shouted commands and stamping of boots from HQ could clearly be heard. Guns were brought snappily to attention as a huddle of officers emerged and hurried down the path. Even at this distance I could recognize the repellent form of the leader. Zennor, with his underlings hurrying after. I drew deeper into the shadows: this was no place for me to be.

Or was it? Despite my desire for rapid departure and continued survival I stood there and concentrated. And hated the idea that began to develop. The officers moved out across the charred sportsfield and passed the spacer I had tried to get into. At this moment the idea jelled and I loathed it even more because it just might work. With a great effort I forced down the screaming meemies that threatened to overwhelm me, unlocked my knees and lurched forward. Following the officers across the field.

If any of them looked back I was sunk. But that was next to an impossibility. Their job in life was to bull straight ahead and walk over anything and everything that got in their way. They charged on and I charged after them, getting ever closer. Anyone watching would see a group of officers with one more of their kind hurrying to catch up.

When they reached the steps of the freighter I was right behind them, watching them mount with dignity. Though still hurrying I did not hurry that fast anymore. With precise timing I reached the guard at the foot of the stairs just as they vanished from sight above.

"General," I cried. "The message has come through. It is urgent!"

I waved and called out again and brushed by the guard who did the only thing he was supposed to do. He saluted. Up the stairs, much slower now, dragging one leg, old war wound you know. They were well out of sight as, breathlessly, I reached the open port.

"The general, where is he?"

"Captain's quarter's, sir," the guard said.

"That's near the communications room on this type of ship?"

"That's right, major, same deck, number nine."

I hurried on to the nearest companionway and up it. Slower and slower. The ship was silent, empty, but I heard voices echoing down from above. When I reached the next deck I walked around to the companionway on the far side. Where I stopped and counted slowly to two hundred.

"You are a brave but foolhearty devil, Jim," I muttered and agreed strongly with myself. Press on.

The large number nine on the bulkhead above slowed me to a crawl. I carefully poked my head above the deck and looked around. No one in sight, but voices were sounding from the passageway. The doors had numbers stenciled next to them. One of them had a name on it. COMMUNICATIONS ROOM.

It's now or never, Jim. Look around carefully. Nobody in sight. Take a deep breath. What is that loud hammering noise? Just your heart thudding with the usual panic at a time like this. Ignore it. Step up, step forward, to the door, seize the knob.

Except the knob had been sawn off. Steel bars had been bolted to the door and welded to the frame. The communications room was sealed, shut, inaccessible, tight.

As I was registering these facts and trying to make sense of them a voice spoke in my ear.

"You, what are you doing there?"

If my heart had thought it was thudding along merrily earlier it now tore loose from all its moorings and hurled itself up into my throat. I spun about, swallowed it, tried not to say Glugh! Grimaced and looked at the uniformed figure before. At the shoulders. I sneered.

"I might ask the same thing of you, lieutenant. What are you doing here?"

"This is my ship, major."

"Does that give you permission to speak to a superior officer in that manner?"

"Sorry, sir, didn't see the leaves, sir. But I saw you by the com room and we had orders about it . . . ."

"You are absolutely correct. Sealed and no one near it at any time, correct?"

"Correct."

I leaned my face close to his and scowled and watched with relief as his skin paled. It is hard to scowl and sneer your words at the same time, but I managed.

"Then you will be pleased to know that *my* orders are to see that *your* orders are carried out to the letter. Now, where is General Zennor?"

"Down there, major."

I spun on my heel and walked in the direction that I wished least to take. He would be watching me, I was sure of that. But I had no choice. If I simply tried to leave the ship he might start to think about my presence, get suspicious, sound the alarm. If I went to the general all doubt would vanish.

Of course I might vanish too. Nevertheless I walked swiftly toward the open door and the murmured voices, turned into it without hesitation.

The officers at the end of the room were conferring over a map. Zennor had his back turned to me.

I turned sharply right and saw the shelves of books against the bulkhead. Without hesitation I went to it, ran my finger down the volumes. I could not see their titles because of the sweat that was dripping into my eyes. Seized one at random. Turned and started back toward the door. Let my eyes cross over the group of officers.

Who were completely ignoring me. I walked slower, ears straining, but could hear nothing other than a murmured *cagal* or two, which was required of any military conversation.

When I entered the corridor the lieutenant was just scuttling out of sight. I walked, neither fast nor slow, to the companionway and down it, deck by deck. Waiting for the alarm bells to go off. Though I probably wouldn't have heard them through the pounding of blood in my ears. To the last deck and to the open port with the welcoming blackness of the night beyond.

The guard leapt into the air and my heart followed him.

And landed with his weapon at present arms. I threw him a

210

sloppy salute in return and trotted down the steps to the ground. Another salute and I was walking across the burned grass and waiting for the shot in the back.

It never came. I reached the shadows at the edge of the grounds, slipped into them and leaned against the bole of a tree. And sighed a sigh such as I had never sighed before. When I raised my hand to wipe the perspiration from my brow I realized that I was still holding the book.

Book? What book? Oh, the book I had lifted from the cabin about four hundred and twelve years earlier. When I held it up and squinted I could just make out the title in the illumination of the distant lamps.

Veterinary Practice in Robot Cavalry Units.

It dropped from my limp fingers as my back slid slowly down the tree until I was sitting on the ground.

CHAPTER 25

I rested there in the darkness, let the sweat evaporate, tried not think about veterinaries for robot horses—and pondered the significance of the sealed door on the communications room.

For openers, it had not been sealed shut to keep me from getting inside. As much as I valued my own importance I was well aware that others, Zennor in particular, were not struck with fear by my presence. For example the combat-ready captain earlier this night. No, Zennor had the door sealed for his own reasons. What were they? Work backward from the obvious.

The door on this ship was sealed, so probably all of the com rooms on all the spacers had been sealed. It made no sense to shut just a single one. Why? To stop communication, obviously. Between who and whom? Or whom and who for that matter. It couldn't be intended to stop planetary communication. That was still needed for the not-too-successful invasion. Ground-based radios would suffice for that. Spacer com rooms sealed obviously meant that ship-to-ship communication would cease. That was of no importance since the entire fleet had already landed.

Which left only interstellar communication. Of course! The rush to leave, the secrecy about our destination. Zennor knew that the League Navy was after him, knew that they could only stop him if they knew where he was going. Or where this planet was. So the invasion was a one-way affair. A gamble hurled into interstellar space. Not much of a gamble against an unarmed enemy. Zennor knew that the Navy had spies, all those detector vans had been evidence of that. He was convinced that I worked for the League and there might be other League agents in his army. So communication had been cut off until the invasion succeeded. After that there would be nothing that the Navy could do.

This was good for the invasion—but very bad news for me. I had sent the radio message for help, which even now was limping steadily across interstellar space at the miserable speed of light. I had better forget about it. And forget as well about sending an FTL message for the time being. What I had to do now was think local. I might have to spend the rest of my life on this planet. If I did remain here I didn't want to do it with Zennor and his military goons breathing down my neck. Desertion, that was the name of the game. I had to get his army away from him. When all the draftees had been dispersed about the land I would consider the next step. Which didn't bear considering. Maybe I should open a distillery and supply free booze to his officers and noncoms? From what I had seen, with the correct encouragement, they all would be dead of cirrhosis within the year.

I yawned and realized that my eyes were closed and I was half asleep.

"Never!" I groaned, climbing to my feet. "Fall asleep here, Jim my boy, and the chances are that you will wake up dead. To work! Next step is to get your chunk off this base, for your work here is done for the moment. Back to warmth and light and female companionship, away from solitary males, cursing, drinking, gambling and all the other military pleasures. Away!"

But was I ever tired. Instead of walking it would sure be nice to have a bit of transportation. Somewhere near HQ there had to be vehicles, since officers rarely walked. Nor were these vehicles too hard to find. Just behind the HQ building there was a motorpool, unguarded apparently. And there, looming darkly behind the staff cars, the shape of a command car. One I was very familiar with. I drifted over and climbed into it.

No guards needed at this motorpool because all the ignition keys had been taken away. I smiled into the darkness. This crate could be hotwired faster than a key could be fumbled into the lock. I bent, pulled, twisted. Sparks sizzled and the fuel cell hissed into life. Boldly on with the headlights, into gear and away.

Away to where? Not the gates surely. During the daytime it might be possible to drive out behind a convoy. But right now the gates would be closed and I would have to produce a pass or some sound reason for nighttime maneuvers. I could think of no sound reason. I drove on slowly, past one of the gates and along a perimeter road that circled the camp, just inside the barbed wire fence. For security patrols undoubtedly. I drove along it until a grove of trees came between me and the lights of the camp. I angled the headlights toward the fence, locked the gears in neutral and climbed down to look at the barrier.

It was a ten-strand barbed wire fence. There were surely alarms attached if it were breached, but I could see no sign of disturbed earth, tripwires or circuitry that might lead to mines. Just bashing through it might be a chance worth taking. It didn't matter if the alarm were raised. By the time the sluggish troops reached the site I would be long gone. I raced the engine, put it in the lowest gear, floored the accelerator and ground forward.

The wire fence screeched and tore. There was a fine show of crackling sparks—I thought it might be electrified, but the combat car was shielded—and then it all tore away and I was through. Kicking up through the gears and tearing away through the empty streets. Pulling the wheel and screeching around a plaza with a large statue of Mark Forer gazing down serenely from a plinth, and out the broad avenue on the far side. I recognized this street, I had walked this way before when we had first escaped. The river and bridges were up ahead. With the residential suburbs on the far side.

When I trundled my battle wagon across the bridge there was still no sign of pursuit. Fine. Time to go to ground. I turned off along the river bank, put the gears in low-low, angled toward the water and jumped down. The car ground steadily on, demolished a bench—sorry about that—and plowed majestically

214

over the edge. There was plenty of burbling and splashing, then nothing. The river was deep here. Behind me I could hear the wail of distant sirens. I walked briskly through the park and into the nearest street. Though I was tired I needed to put some distance between myself and the river, in case there were tracks left which might be seen by day.

"Enough is enough, Jim!" I said, leaning against a wall and all too aware that I was drooping with fatigue. I had turned corners at random, lost myself completely, and the river was far behind me. There was a gate in the wall beside me, with *Dun Roamin* carved into the wood. Message received. Without hesitation I opened the gate, climbed the steps beyond and knocked on the front door. I had to do it a second time before there were stirrings inside and a light came on. Even after all the time here on Chojecki I still found it hard to believe that this was the correct way to meet strangers.

"Who is it?" a male voice called out as the door opened.

"Jim diGriz, offworlder, tired."

The light came on and an ancient citizen with whispy gray beard blinked out myopically at me.

"Can it be? It certainly is! Oh what luck for old Czolgoscz!! Come in brave offworlder and share my hospitality. What may I do for you?"

"Thank you, thank you. For openers let's get these lights off just in case there is a patrol around. And then a bed for the night . . ."

"My pleasure! Illumination off, follow closely, this way, my daughter's room, now married and living on a farm, forty geese and seventeen cows, here we are. Curtains closed, a moment, then the lights!"

Old Czolgoscz, although he tended to talk too much, was the perfect host. The room was pink with lace curtains and about twenty dolls on the bed.

"Now you wash up, right in there, and I'll bring you a nice hot drink, friend Jim."

"I would prefer a nice cold drink rich with alcohol, friend Czolgoscz."

"I have the very thing!"

By the time I had rinsed the last of the military muck away he was back with a tall, purple bottle, two glasses—he wasn't that old—and a pair of pajamas ablaze with red lightning bolts. I hoped that they didn't glow in the dark.

"Homemade gingleberry wine." He poured two large glasses. We raised them, clinked, drank and smacked our lips. I sighed with happiness and a bit of nostalgia.

"I haven't had this since I was back on the farm. Used to have a bottle hidden out in the porcuswine sty. On dull days I used to get blotto on it and sing to the swine."

"How charming! Now I will leave you to your rest."

A perfect host, vanished even before I could thank him. I raised my glass in a toast to the electronic benevolence of the portrait of Mark Forer upon the wall. Drained it. And went to sleep.

When consciousness reluctantly returned I could only lie and blink, drugged with sleep, at the sunlight behind the curtains. Yawning, I rose and opened them and looked out at a flower-filled garden. Old Czolgoscz looked up from his labors and waved his secateurs at me. Then scurried into the house. In a remarkably short period of time he knocked on the door, threw it open, and brought in a groaning breakfast tray. I don't normally have a liter of juice, large portion of wiffles with syrup and three eggs. I did today.

"How did you know?" I lip-smacked satedly.

"Guessed. Young lad your age, been working hard, seemed natural. I talked to a few people and I am sure that you will be pleased to hear that the teams are in training all over the city for D-Day."

"D-Day?"

"Desertion Day. Today, tonight. Extra trains have been scheduled and people all over the country are looking forward to welcoming the new citizens."

"Fantastic. I hope you will welcome me as well. My stay on Chojecki may be longer than originally planned."

"You are more than welcome, as is your knowledge. Would you like a teaching position at the university?"

216

I smiled at the thought. "Sorry, I ran away from school, never graduated."

"I regret in my provincial ignorance that I do not know the meaning of either run away or graduate. Students here go to school when they want, stay as long as they want, study what they want, leave when they want. The only scholastic requirement a child has is to learn about Individual Mutualism, so he or she can lead a full and happy life."

"I suppose the parents pay for the child's schooling?"

Czolgoscz drew back, horrified. "Of course not! A child will get love and affection from its parents, but they would not embarrass their offspring by violating IM's tenets. The child's wirr account, opened when it was born, will be in debit until he or she begins to earn. At a very early age, for the child will not be a free and independent citizen until the wirr account is in credit."

Now I was shocked. "The workhouse for infants! Laboring day and night for a few crusts!"

"Friend Jim—what a wonderful imagination you do have! Not quite. Most of the work will be done around the house, the labors that were usually done by mother, collecting the wirrs father would pay her . . ."

"Enough, I beg. My blood sugar is low, my head thick and the details of IM so novel that they must be absorbed just a bit at a time."

He nodded agreement. "Understandable. As you will teach us about the novelties of the great civilizations out there among the stars, we have been cut off from them for centuries, so will we reveal to you the fruits of Mark Forer's genius—may electrons flow forever through its wires!"

A pleasant prayer for that long-vanished machine. I still found it hard to understand such affection for a bunch of circuitry, no matter how complex. Enough, it was time to get back to work.

"Can you find out where my friend Morton is staying?"

"Would you like to go there? I will be honored to take you."

"You know . . ." I gaped, then answered my own questions. "Of course, everyone in the city knows where we have been staying."

"That is correct. Do you ride the bike?"

"Not for many years—but once learned, never forgotten." A sensible form of transportation, the bicycle, and the streets of this city were busy with them. I bundled up the uniform for possible future use, pulled on a pair of baggy shorts that Czolgoscz produced. This, and my undershirt, produced an inconspicuous cycling outfit. Thus garbed I went into the garden and limbered up with a hundred pushups. When I finished and climbed to my feet I shied back from the man who stood behind me leaning on a bright red bicycle.

"I did not mean to startle you," he said. "But I did not wish to interrupt your ritual. Czolgoscz phoned me and I brought your bicycle around. The best one I had in stock."

"Thank, thank you—indeed a beauty. But I am afraid I cannot pay you for it . . ."

He smiled. "You already have. I stopped at the wirrbank and debited your account. They asked me to give this to you."

I did some rapid blinking at the wirrdisc he handed me. *James diGriz* it was labeled. And in the little LCD window it read *Balance 64.678.*

"The bank asked me to ask you to contact them. They were not sure how many hours you worked for the public service last night. If you would kindly report to them they will make the correction."

"I am in the system!" I shouted happily. The bicycle man beamed happy agreement.

"Of course! You are an individual and Individual Mutualism is your right. Welcome, welcome! May your wirrbalance grow and may your life be a long and happy one!"

CHAPTER 26

It was next morning when the cagal hit the fan. Reports had come in during the night of the fantastic success of D-Day. The troops had trooped into town with their passes, had expressed a great appreciation of fresh air, had been welcomed at the back entrance of any clothing store to change out of their uniforms, had boarded train after train. The last one left just before midnight when the curfew had descended.

And there had been no alarm, not at first. Luckily there were four gates into the camp and I presumed that the MPs, in their native ignorance, had all thought the returning soldiers had used the other gates. Therefore they had all been happy to cagal off for the evening. So successful had been our operation that even the extra trains had not sufficed for the mobs of deserters. Over a hundred were still in the city. They would stay hidden until nightfall when, hopefully, they would be smuggled to the station.

With my new-found wealth I had bought a giant TV as a gift for our hosts. Morton and I were watching a local broadcast when the military cut in. Neither of us appreciated it for this was a day of celebration of some kind, the anniversary of the wiring of Mark Forer's first circuit board or some such, and all the city had turned out. We were enjoying a parade, headed by the local girls' cycle club, all flashing bronzed limbs and fluttering skirts, when the picture sizzled and died to be replaced by General Zennor's scowling features.

219

"Turn it off!" Morton moaned. "If I look at him I won't be able to eat lunch."

"Leave it. It won't be good news, but since we will have to hear it sometime—better now."

"Attention!" Zennor said and Morton made a rude noise with his tongue; I waved him to silence. "You all know me, General Zennor of the liberating forces. You know me as a kind and patient man . . ."

"He is a great fiction writer!"

"Quiet!"

". . . a firm leader and a just one. And now the time has come for firmness and justice to be applied. I have just discovered that a few cowards among the ranks of my loyal troops have been foolish enough to attempt to desert. Desertion is punishable by death . . ."

"What isn't in the rotten army!"

". . . and I know that none of you out there would want that to happen to foolish and misguided young men. Therefore this announcement. I am extending all passes issued last night for twenty-four hours. They are good until midnight tonight. No soldier will be punished who returns to the base before midnight. I therefore advise all the people of this city to speak to these misguided youths who are hidden among you. Tell them to return. You know where they are. Go to them. Tell them of this generous offer."

The fake kindness vanished from his face in an instant as he leaned close to the camera and snarled.

"Tell them also that my generosity vanishes at midnight! Martial law will then be declared. This city will be sealed. No one will enter or leave it. Then the city will be searched. Block by block, building by building. Any deserter who is then found will be taken prisoner, will be given one bottle of beer and will be allowed to write one letter home. And will then be shot.

"Is that clear enough? You have this single warning. You have until midnight tonight to return. That is the message I send to the deserters. After that—you are as good as dead—"

I hit the button and turned the set off.

220

"Pretty depressing," Morton said, looking pretty depressed. "Turn it back on so we can at least look at the girls."

I did. But they were long gone and had been replaced by a man with long hair and an enthusiastic expression who was going on in great detail about the untold joys of IM. I killed the sound.

"You know, Morton, he means us too."

"Don't say it! I know. Isn't there another station with space opera? I need a drink."

"No you don't. You need to sit quiet and pull yourself together and help me find a way out of this for all of us. Well, maybe a small drink, a glass of beer just to get the thoughts rolling."

"I could not but overhear," Stirner said, entering with a tray of glasses and bottles. "If you will permit I will join you. The day is warm."

We clinked and glugged. "Any word from the city?" I asked.

"A good deal of words. All the trains leaving the city have been canceled so there is no way out by train."

"The roads?"

"Roadblocks on all arteries leading from the city. Flying machines supported by rotating wings—"

"Choppers."

"Thank you, I have noted the word. Choppers flying over the countryside between so none may escape that way. All young men who attempt to leave are being detained, even when they are obviously Chojecki citizens who speak only our native tongue. They are imprisoned until their hands have been pressed to a plate on a machine, that is what has been reported. So far all have been released."

"Very neat," I muttered, "and just about foolproof. Fingerprint check. Right through to the base computer. So we can't get out that way. It will have to be the fields, after dark."

"Not that I want to cast a note of gloom," Morton said, gloomcasting. "Choppers, infrared detectors, side-mounted machine guns, death from the sky . . ."

"Point taken, Morton. Too dangerous. There must be another way."

The lecture had finished and once more hearty biking enthusiasts swept across the screen. All males with hairy knees:

221

Morton grumbled in his throat. Then instantly cheered up as the girls' club appeared, waving and smiling at the camera.

"Wow!" I shouted, jumping to my feet and running in small circles. "Wow-wow!"

"Down the hall, second door on the left."

"Shut up, Morton. This is inspiration, not constipation. You see genius at work. You see before you the only man who knows how to get us all safely from the city."

"How?"

"That's how," I said, pointing at the screen. "Stirner—get busy on the phone and the backfence gossip circuit. I want this show on the road by midafternoon. It will take us at least that long to organize it."

"Organize what?" Morton cried. "I'm lost. What are you talking about?"

"I think I know," Stirner said, being quicker on the uptake than Mort. "You are going to leave the city on bicycles. But you will be stopped."

"No we won't—because you got the answer only half right. We'll all be leaving as girls!"

Once the idea had penetrated joy reigned for a bit—then we got down to work. Since I was doing most of the planning and organizing I was the very last one to actually get involved in the nitty-gritty of personal survival. There was much coming and going. I was vaguely aware when Morton's bicycle arrived, but then got busy again with the men's cycle club. I ate a sandwich, drank another beer, and looked up blinking when Morton called to me.

"We've got to leave soon. The first guys are already in the square. Now don't laugh!"

I fought hard. The fluffy chintz dress wasn't really him. Nor had shaving his hairy legs made much of an improvement. But the foam-stuffed bra helped, as did the wig. From a distance, sure, but close up the effect was a little disconcerting.

"I think a touch of lipstick is needed."

"Yeah! Well let's see how great you look. Get changing!"

I did. The cute little pleated skirt was green so went nicely with my red hair. I looked into the mirror and sighed. "Jim—you never looked better."

We parted, thanking our hosts again for their hospitality. Hoping that we would meet again—after the war. Stirner, as stout a biker as he was a hiker, would be our guide. He set off at a good clip and we girls had to push hard to keep up.

Mark Forer square was a scene of gay abandon. Or maybe that is not the right word. Better, perhaps, to say that everyone had been dragged there. As we pedaled up the first thing we saw was the Bellegarrique Girls" Cycle Club. Just like on television, but infinitely more attractive in the flesh. Flesh—some very strange flesh. Because beyond the girls were other girls. Lantern of jaw, thick of thigh, scowling of mien. Our escaping draftees. Some of them hadn't been on a bike in years and were wobbling about the square, occasionally falling in a flurry of skirts and guttural oaths.

"Attention!" I shouted, then again until there was a modicum of silence. "Firstly, knock off the cursing. These kind people are risking their lives to help you deserters, so be nice to them. Secondly—if anyone falls off when we go past the roadblock we all have had it. Some three-wheelers are on the way, plus some bicycles built for two. Sort yourselves out and mount up. We are on schedule."

"Where are we going?" one of them called out.

"You'll be told when you get there. Now timing is important. When I say go—we go. And anyone left behind is in the cagal. And cursing is a privilege of rank," I added at their cries of protest. "I'm in charge so I'll curse for all of us until we get clear. Mount up."

I led the deserter-girls around the square two or three times until they closed up and got it together. Only then did I signal the real girls" club to go into action. They were beautiful. With a swoop they came down upon us, breaking into two ranks that swept by on both sides, closed up around us. The leader carried the flag and we followed her with passion. Down the road, smoothly and swiftly.

Towards the roadblock at the junction ahead.

Then around the corner, cutting in front of us girls, came the Veterans' Cycle Club. Every head gray, or if not gray as bald as a billiard ball. Knotty gnarled legs pumped, ancient tickers ticked. Ahead of us they swooped—and on to the barriers that had been set up across the road. Some went around them, others dismounted and pulled them aside. The sergeants and officers shouted back, struggled feebly, but an opening appeared. Just as we did. And just wide enough to get through.

Some of our outriding girls peeled off and helped the ancients make the opening wider. Some of them laughed and kissed the officers. Confusion reigned—and through the confusion, and the opening in the barrier, I led my girls. Silent and sweating and pumping for all they were worth. Through the barrier and down the road and around the bend.

"Keep going!" I shouted hoarsely. "We"re not out of the cagal yet. No one stops until we get to the woods. Go! Go! Last one there is a cagal-kopf!"

We went. Pedaling and cursing and sweating and wobbling—but we went. Down the road and into the forest, off into the lanes to skid and fall and crash and roll; on the soft green grass.

"Can we not—do that again!" Morton gasped, lying on his back and moaning.

"I don't know, Mort, I thought it was kind of fun. You ought to get more excercise."

He sat up and looked where I was looking, and stopped moaning. The real girls' club had arrived, a symphony of lovely flesh and flowing movements, tossed hair, flashing eyes. And picnic baskets.

When the first beer was held high a ragged cheer broke out. The army was only a bad memory; freedom was bliss. This was the first day of the rest of their new lives and if it stayed like this—why paradise was here around us.

I joined in the revelry but my heart wasn't really in it, my smile false. Through some native perversion, and inability to enjoy pure happiness, all I could think of was Zennor and what repulsive tricks he would be up to when he discovered that about half of his army had vanished for good.

CHAPTER 27

There were groans and cries of protest when I ordered my bevy of enchanting beauties to their feet.

"Knock it off!" I commanded sternly. "We're still on schedule and if you want to get out of this alive you will obey orders. When I say frog you will jump."

I waited until the chorus of croaking, and other froglike imitations, had died down before I spoke again.

"We have about another halfhour of riding to go. And before you groan remember that these sweet young girls, who have risked their lives to save us, must ride with us—then circle all the way back to the city by another road. And lest we forget, let's hear it for the girls!"

The chorus of yells, thanks, cheers—and not a few kisses rolled out. I had to whistle for attention before it died down.

"Here is the drill. We are now going to go to a factory that has a railroad siding. A freight train from the north will be arriving when we do. We board and we're away. There will be no stops until we are far from the city. Now—mount up! Forward—Ho-o!"

There was silence during the ride, because my gallant bikers were feeling the strain. There was some panic when a chopper came swooping up, but I ordered male heads down—girls to wave and smile. It worked fine and there were no more alarms after this. As we rounded the last bend to approach the kakalaka factory we heard the wail of the train's horn. The line of freight cars was just clattering into the siding when we appeared.

"Open the doors!" I ordered. "Get in before another chopper shows up. Take your bikes—they'll be debited from your future accounts—wave bye-bye and blow kisses because we are off in one minute."

I turned to thank Neebe, the gorgeous, brown-limbed redhead who was president of the cycling club, but she was just passing on the club flag to her second-in-command. Then she wheeled her bike toward me, smiling a smile that melted my bike handles.

"May I be very forward, offworlder James diGriz, and force my presence upon you? You have but to say no and I will go."

"Glug . . .!"

"I assume that means yes." She entered the freight car, propped her bicycle against mine, and sat down daintily upon a bale of hay. "You are very kind. Up until today I have been attending school here in Bellegarrique but now, like everyone else, I am leaving. My home is on a farm in the north in a hamlet named Ling. I have talked with my father and mother, brothers and sisters, and grandmother, and they would all be honored if you would stay with us for as long as you wished."

I knew that Morton had been listening because his face went completely green and he began to pout.

"I would be honored, honored. What a wonderful idea!"

She smiled, then her expression changed to one of shock when she saw Morton's face.

"Is your friend ill?"

"No." I sighed with generosity. "It is just that he has no place to go and is hoping that you will invite him too."

"Of course!"

The green tint vanished instantly and he smiled sheepishly. "I accept with gratitude. But just for a short time. Until I can get in touch with a friend of mine named Sharla."

"Oh, you do remember her," I said sweetly, and he glared at me as soon as Neebe had turned away.

Once we began to relax it was a pleasant journey. The roadbed was flat, the train swift. After an hour we knew that we were

226

well clear of the city and all the enemy lurking there. The hay bales were broken open, the tired ex-girls, using their padded bras for pillows, slept. It was nearly dark when we made the first stop. Hampers of food and drink were loaded aboard and we were away within the minute. We ate, drank, and fell asleep once again. I awoke to the gentle touch of a soft hand on my shoulder.

"We are here," Neebe said. "I must awaken your friend."

Lights were moving by outside the open door as the train squealed to a stop. We climbed down and our bikes were handed after us. Followed by glad cries and shouts of farewell we mounted and followed Neebe down the highway, out of town, and to the family farm. The road was smooth and easy to see. A magnificent nebula halffilled the sky and bathed us in a cool white light.

"Even if I could go back to Nevenkebla I never would," Morton panted.

"You have family there."

"I'll miss them—but I won't miss the draft, the army, the military, the intolerance . . ."

He gasped for air and I nodded agreement. "Understood. This planet has a lot going for it. Though I still don't understand all the permutations of IM it seems to be working. But all is not peace and light yet. Let us not forget Zennor."

Morton groaned. "I would love to."

Next morning it looked as though the entire family was standing around and beaming down upon us. While the ladies of the house fought to see how many eggs, wiffles and other gustatory goodies they could force upon us. We fought honorably to do our best. Groaning we finally pushed away from the table while the audience went off to work on the farm.

"That was very good," Morton said.

"That was very wonderful," I amplified.

"Both meals already deducted from your account," Neebe smiled, handing me back my wirrdisc. "I added an order to transfer payment to Morton's account when it is opened."

"I love IM hospitality," I said. "It is personal without being financial. I want to learn more about your world."

227

"I will be happy to tell you anything you want to know," she said with that same endearing smile. What were these warm sensations that coursed through my body? I forgot them instantly as her smile faded. "But we will have to talk about it later. Right now I think you should see the TV. We recorded a broadcast made earlier this morning."

It had to be Zennor—and it had to be bad news. I watched grimly as the screen lit up and a blast of martial music assaulted my ears. Troops marched, tanks rumbled by, guns fired. A recording undoubtedly; I recognized Mortstertoro base in the background. I suppose the sight of all this might was supposed to strike terror into the hearts of the viewers. I knew them well enough now to understand that they would just be puzzled at the waste of all this material and manpower for no observable reasonable purpose. I turned down the sound until the last tank had ground by, the last jet roared its last roar. The screen cleared and the familiar and loathsome features appeared.

"We are mighty, we are invincible—and we will prevail!" Zennor was coldly angry now. "I have been kind to your people. I have even been generous to my own misled soldiers. No more. I have shown you kindness because I am a kind man. Now I will teach you fear because my rule will not be mocked. You have aided and abetted deserters from our army—who are now under instant penalty of death. You must be aiding them because not one—not *one* of them took advantage of my kind offer of amnesty. Nor have any of them been found in this city. They could not have escaped without aid. Therefore the people of Bellegarrique are guilty of treason, of aiding traitors and deserters, and they will pay for their crimes. I speak you to you now, you inhabitants of the rest of this country. The citizens of Bellegarrique know of their guilt for they are attempting to flee my wrath. This city is almost deserted now as they crawl away like the cowardly vermin that they are. But not all of them have escaped. I have seized and imprisoned hundreds of these traitors. I did this once before and my requests were granted. I was kind and generous and released the prisoners. I will not be as kind this time—or as easy to please. Here are my demands—and they will be met.

"Firstly, I want every escaped deserter returned to this city. I will not inflict the death penalty but will enlist them instead in penal, hard-labor battalions. I said that I was a merciful man.

"Secondly, I demand that all of the services of this city be restored, electricity and public utilities, and the food markets must be reopened. This will be done. I want to see people returning today, I want the normal life of this city to be as it was when we arrived, I want the deserters turned over to the military police. You will do this, and begin doing it now."

He paused dramatically, then pointed his finger directly at the camera.

"You will do it because in one day from now I will shoot ten of the prisoners. I will shoot these first ten no matter what you do, as an object lesson that I mean what I say. I will shoot ten of them the next day and, ten again the day after that if my orders are not obeyed. If my orders are obeyed the shooting will stop. But it will begin again whenever I feel that my desires are being thwarted."

That was it. That was all. And it certainly was enough. The screen went blank and I found myself staring at Morton with nothing at all to say.

"There are rare cases of insanity like that here," Neebe said. "Gene changes not caught in prenatal examination. He is insane, isn't he? These things that he says he will do—they are impossible. He won't really have innocent people killed?"

I was too ashamed of the human race to look at her, to answer her questions. Morton did; he was angry.

"Yes, he will, that is the worst part. I grew up with his kind of people in charge of my life. Believe me, he will do it."

"Then what can we do to stop him?"

"That is an almost unanswerable question," I said. "You can't force the deserters to undesert. Knowing IM you wouldn't even think of asking them. And I don't know what they will do voluntarily. If you had a government they could deal with Zennor, come up with some workable compromise perhaps. But he still hasn't realized that there is no central government to meet with. The future does not bear thinking about."

229

"But we have to think about it," Morton said, with a cold grimness I had never seen before. "Zennor must be killed. There is no other way."

"No!" Neebe said. "That is a hideous suggestion. This problem is so strange, so awful, that it would take the wisdom of Mark Forer itself to solve it."

"Maybe, maybe," I muttered. "But I feel that what is happening here is well beyond even the mighty capacities of that long-gone brain to solve."

"Nothing was ever beyond Mark Forer," she said with calm and unshakable belief. It angered me. It was like calling in the deity of your choice as you fell off the cliff, begging for aid. Praying for a heavenly hand that would never, never swoop down from the sky to save you.

"That is just an opinion, your opinion. And to me it sounds more like blind faith than intelligent thought. We have to work this out ourselves because Mark Forer is long gone, rusted away. It can't help us now."

"Mark Forer *could* help us," she said with calm unreason. "But of course we could never ask. That is a basic tenet of IM. We must solve our problems for ourselves. Everything we need to know is in the writings that it gave us."

"You are just jollying yourself along. You could ask, but you won't. That is a way out. You can't ask because it is not around to ask."

"That is not true," she said sweetly, smiling warmly upon my ill humor. "Mark Forer is in Bellegarrique, where it always has been."

I have known stoppers in my day. But this was the whopper topper stopper. I stared speechlessly at Morton. If I looked like he did then my jaw was hanging open, my eyes were popping and I was gurgling like an idiot. Neebe smiled warmly upon us and waited impatiently until we got reglued and were able to speak again. I sputtered first.

"Mark Forer . . . gone . . . thousands of years ago . . ."

"Why? Essentially an artificial intelligence must be immortal. I suppose bits and pieces get replaced as they wear out, but the intelligence will remain the same. Or grow. We have always been immensely pleased that Mark Forer saw fit to accompany us to this world. We sincerely hope that it watches and approves of the way we practice IM. But of course we would never consider asking it for aid."

"Well I would," I said, climbing to my feet. "I certainly would ask for help without a moment's hesitation. Mark Four's social theories are about to get a lot of people shot dead. So that cold artificial intelligence had better have some answers how to arrange it so that they don't."

"But you will have to go back to Bellegarrique to dig Mark Four out," Morton said. I nodded grim agreement.

"I was hoping you wouldn't say that just yet. But, yes, Morton old friend. I've got to find where our great electronic leader lives and search it out. And there better be some ready answers."

CHAPTER 28

"Do you know where Mark Forer plugs in?" I asked Neebe. She shook her head.

"Not physically. It is just known, understood, that Mark Forer came with us and aided in the design of the city of Bellegarrique. And never left it."

"Well someone has to know." I thought hard, then snapped my fingers. "Our old friend, Stirner, he should have that vital bit of info. One of the top men in the world of electricity. And if he doesn't know he will surely know someone who does know. Do you have any idea of how I can contact him?"

"The telephone is over there."

"Thanks, Neebe, but I don't have his number or the slightest idea where he is staying or anything."

"But no one has a number. And it doesn't matter where he is staying. Just call CD and ask for him."

"CD?"

"Central Directory. Here, I'll get it for you."

She tapped the keypad and the screen lit up with NAME, PLEASE? in large letters. Very polite. Very efficient. I tip my hat to the man or machine that wrote this software. I answered four questions and the screen changed to RINGING. The letters faded and Stirner's grim face appeared on the screen. He smiled

232

faintly when he saw me, but he had obviously been watching the broadcast too.

"Ahh, good offplanet friend Jim. I hope that you are well. Can I do you a service?"

"You certainly can, good dynamo supervising friend Stirner. I would like to have a chat with your demigod, Mark Forer."

"A strange choice of terms. I would certainly not refer to it as a demi . . ."

"Then forget the term. Do you know where Mark Forer is?"

"Of course."

"Will you take me to it?"

"Ahh, now that is a question that needs some thought. Mark Forer's individualism has always been respected, for all the obvious reasons. I do remember reading in the historical records that after this city was founded it did make suggestions and was occasionally consulted. But not lately, not in, hundreds of years at least. I would not go to it myself, but, yes, I feel that I can take you. I respect your individualism just as I respect Mark Forer's. We must each make our own way in this world."

"And I am going to make my way back into the city."

"You must be careful. It will not be easy. The trains have stopped running and citizens are being forcefully stopped from leaving. At last report no one was returning."

"I'll think of something. You are still in the city?"

"Yes."

"Stay near the phone. I'll get there today. I must talk to Mark before Zennor's deadly deadline runs out tomorrow morning."

I hung up and looked blankly into space. I could see no answers hanging out there.

"Any advice, Morton?"

"None that make any sense. Like being a returned deserter."

"Like you, that idea I considered and rejected. That would just get me back in jail and shot."

"May I make a suggestion?" Neebe said.

"All aid greatly desired."

"I will take you to the city. You will go as my father. We have a wonderful theatre group here in Ling and our makeup

233

department is quite famous. You could be an old man, I could be your daughter and driver. It would be so exciting."

"You're wonderful!" I jumped to my feet and, in a fit of mad enthusiasm seized her and kissed her. Then I sat down quickly again as the hormones started humming and driving all other thoughts from mind. She was an incredibly bright, lovely, intelligent, beautiful girl and I was just going to have to forget all about that. For the time being. "We better get started."

"My brother will take you to the theatre. I will phone them and arrange what must be done. Then I will make the transportation arrangements. You do not mind if I say that I find this fascinating and exciting as well. I must thank you for letting me help. It is so much more fun than school."

"The thanks are mine. What do you study in school?"

"Vulcanology. I just love the magma and the scoria, then when you go down the fumerole . . ."

"Yes. You must tell me of those burning pleasures. Later."

"Of course—there is my brother now."

I think that it was a special train that they laid on. Just two cars and no other passengers. Morton looked guilty—but glad as well that he wasn't going back to Bellegarrique. I waved him a stiff goodbye with my cane and climbed shakily aboard. I was ancient and crochety and needed practice. Gray beard, rheumy red eyes, wrinkled like an old boot, they had really done a great job at the theatre. A harness under my clothes had me bent over so far that I was staring down at my wrinkled and liverspotted hands.

The track was straight, the train was fast and there were no stops until we reached our destination. A black vehicle was waiting on the platform when we arrived. The driver got out and held the door open for us.

"You've driven one of these?" he asked.

Neebe nodded. "A two hundred volt Lasher-gnasher. Great fun to drive."

"Indeed they are. I've got her revved up to thirty-three thousand. More than enough energy for the trip." He pointed to the circular housing between the rear wheels. "The flywheel

234

is in here, electric generator on its shaft. Motor on the front wheels. Clean and nonpolluting."

"And very hard to turn over with that gyroscope down there," I said.

"You've got it. Good luck."

Neebe spun the wheels and I was pushed back into the seat by a large number of G's. We hurtled along the empty road.

"I'll slow down before we reach the roadblock. Isn't this fun! I wonder what the top speed is?"

"Don't . . . find out!" I croaked as the landscape hurtled by in a blur. "Though I am an old man and have led a full life I don't want to terminate it quite yet!"

She laughed her gorgeous bell-like laugh and slowed to something close to the speed of sound. She obviously knew the road well, all those bicycle outings of course, for suddenly she hit the brakes, slowed to a crawl, then turned the corner just before the barrier across the road.

"What you doing blocking the road like that, you varmints?" I croaked testily out of the window, then shook my cane at the fat captain who was leaning against it picking his teeth. Remnants of hotpup, I hoped.

"Knock off the cagal, Grandpop. Where do you think you're going?"

"Are you as stupid as you look, stupid? Or haven't you heard your supreme commander's orders? City workers to return at once. I am an electrical engineer and if you want light in your latrines and refrigeration for your beer you will open that thing instantly or sooner."

"Don't get your cagal in an uproar, Grandpop," he sneered. But he stepped back and signaled two sergeants to open the barrier. Not a private in sight, I noticed. I hoped the officers enjoyed doing their own work for a change. I shook the cane one last shake as we drove past, then on down the road and around a bend and out of sight. Neebe pulled up at the first phonebox and I leaped arthritically down.

"Are you in the city?" Stirner asked.

"Just arrived."

"Very good. Then we will meet at the entrance."

"Entrance? What, where?"

"Mark Forer Square, of course. Where else would it be?"

Good question. I had imagined that only the statue was there. I hadn't realized that old Mark itself was in residence. I climbed back into the car and we were off with the usual screech of tires. I pulled off bits of the disguise as we went, starting with the harness. I left the beard on in case there were any patrols around—and there were.

"Slow down," I cozened. "Let's not be too suspicious."

The sergeant leading the patrol glared at us as we went by. I ignored him but was very impressed by his squad. As they turned the corner the last two slipped into the open door of a building and vanished from sight. So not only weren't the deserters returning—but their ranks were steadily being added to. Great! If this kept up Zennor would soon have army of only officers and noncoms. You don't win wars with that kind of setup. I saw that we were getting close to our destination so I pulled at the beard and wrinkles and was forty years younger by the time we turned into the square and slid to a stop. Stirner was standing before the statue, looking up at it admiringly.

"I wish I were coming with you," he said.

"I as well," Neebe agreed. "It would be wonderfully exciting. But of course we have not been asked so we cannot intrude."

"How do I get in?"

Stirner pointed to a bronze door at the rear of the stone base of the statue. "Through there."

"Got the key?" They both looked at me with surprise.

"Of course not. It's not locked."

"I should have known," I muttered. What a philosophy. Hundreds, thousands of years the door has been here, unlocked, and no one had ever gone through it. I put out my hand and they took it in turn and shook it solemnly. I could understand why. This was a little like saying so-long to the head of your local church as he started up the ladder to see God.

The handle was stiff, but turned when I twisted hard. I pulled and the door squeaked slowly open. Steps led down into the ground, a little dusty. Lights came on and I could see that one of the bulbs was burned out. I just hoped that Mark Forer wasn't burned out as well.

I sneezed as my feet disturbed the dust of ages. And it was a long way down. The steps ended in a small chamber with illuminated wiring diagrams on the walls and a large, gold-plated door. Carved into it, and inset with diamonds, were the immortal words I AM. THEREFORE I THINK. Beneath this was a small sign with red letters that read PLEASE WIPE FEET BEFORE ENTERING. I did this, on the mat provided, took a deep breath and reached for the handle that appeared to have been carved from a single ruby.

The door swung open on oiled hinges and I went in. A large, well-lit room, dry and airconditioned. Dials and electronic devices covering one wall. And in the middle of the room . . .

Mark Forer, obviously. Just like in the paintings. Except that plenty of cables and wires ran from it to a nearby collection of apparatus. Its dials glowed with electronic life and a TV pickup swiveled in my direction. I walked over to stand before it and resisted the compelling desire to bow. And just what does one say to an intelligent machine? The silence lengthened and I began to feel ridiculous. I cleared my throat.

"Mark Forer, I presume?"

"Of course. Were you expecting someone else . . . *krrk!*

The voice was grating and coarse and the words trailed off with a harsh grating sound. At the same time there was a puff of smoke from a panel on the front and a hatch dropped open. My temper snapped.

"Great! Really wonderful. For hundreds of years this electronic know-it-all sits here with the wisdom of the ages locked in its memory banks. Then the second I talk to it it explodes and expires. It is like the punch line of a bad joke—"

There was a rattle from behind and I leaped and turned, dropped into a defensive position. But it was only a little rubber-tired robot bristling with mechanical extensions. It wheeled up in front of Mark and stopped. A claw-tipped arm shot out, plunging into the open panel. It clicked and whirred and withdrew a circuit board which it threw onto the floor. While this was happening another circuit board was emerging from a slot on the robot's upper surface. The grasping claw seized this and delicately slid into the opening before it. Mark's panel snapped shut as the robot spun about and trundled away.

"No," Mark Forer said in a deep and resonant voice, "I did not explode and expire. My voice simulation board did. Shorted out. Been a number of centuries since I last used it. You are the offworlder, James diGriz."

"I am. For a machine in an underground vault you keep up with things pretty well, Mark."

"No problem, Jim—since you appear to enjoy a first name basis. Because all of my input is electronic it really doesn't matter where my central processor is."

"Right, hadn't thought of that." I stepped aside as a broom and brush bristling robot rushed up and swept the discarded circuit board into its bin. "Well, Mark, if you know who I am, then you certainly know what is happening topside."

"I certainly do. Haven't seen so much excitement in the last thousand years."

"Oh, are you enjoying it?" I was beginning to get angry at this cold and enigmatic electronic intelligence. I was a little shocked when it chuckled with appreciative laughter.

"Temper, temper, Jim. I've cut back in the voice feedback emotion circuits for you. I stopped using them centuries ago when I found that the true believers preferred an excathedra voice. Or are you more partial to women?" It added in a warm contralto.

"Stay male, if you please, it seems more natural somehow. Though why I should associate sex with a machine I have no idea. Does it make a difference to you?"

"Not in the slightest. You may refer to me as he, she or it. Sex is of no importance to me."

"Well it is to us humans—and I'll bet you miss it!"

"Nonsense. You can't miss what you never had. Do you wake up at night yearning helplessly for photoreceptors in your fingertips?"

It was a well-made point: old Mark here was no dummy. But fascinating as the chitchat was, it was just about time I got to the point of this visit.

238

"Mark—I have come here for a very important reason."

"Undoubtedly."

"You've heard the broadcasts, you know what is happening up there. That murdering moron Zennor is going to kill ten of your faithful followers in the morning. What do you intend to do about it?"

"Nothing."

"Nothing!" I lost my temper and kicked the front of the burnished panel. "You invented Individual Mutualism and foisted it upon the galaxy. You taught the faithful and brought them here—and now you are going to stand by and watch them die?"

"Knock off the cagal, Jim," it said warmly. "Try sticking to the truth. I published a political philosophy. People read it, got enthusiastic, applied it and liked it. They brought me here, not the other way around. I have emotions, just as you do, but I don't let them interfere with logic and truth. So cool it, kid, and let's get back to square one."

I moved aside as the broom-robot rushed up again, extended a little damp mop and polished off the scuff mark on Mark's housing that I had made with my shoe. I took a deep breath and calmed down because really, losing my temper would accomplish nothing at all.

"Right you are, Mark, square one. People are going to be killed up there. Are you going to do anything about it?"

"There is not much I can do physically. And everything political or philosophical is in my book. The citizens up there know as much about IM as I do."

"So you are just going to sit there and listen to the sizzle of your electrons and let them die."

"People have died before for their beliefs."

"Wonderful. Well I believe in living for mine. And I am going to do something—even if you do not."

"What do you intend to do?"

"I don't know yet. Do you have advice for me?"

"About what?"

"About saving lives, that's what. About ending the invasion and polishing off Zennor . . ."

And then I had it. I didn't need to swap political arguments with Mark—I just had to use its intelligence. If it had memory banks thousands of years old it certainly had the knowledge I needed. And I still had the electronic spy bird!

"Well, Mark old machine, you could help me. Just a bit of information."

"Certainly."

"Do you know the spatial coordinates of this system and this planet?"

"Of course."

"Then you give me a little printout of them, soonest! So I can send an FTL message to the League Navy for help."

"I don't see why I should do that."

I lost my temper. "You don't see . . .! Listen you moronic machine, I'm just asking for a bit of information that will save lives—and you don't see . . ."

"Jim, my new offworlder friend. Do not lose your temper so quickly. Bad for the blood pressure. Let me finish my statement, if I might. I was going to add that this information would be redundant. You sent an FTL message yourself, just after you retrieved the corvine-disguised transmitter."

CHAPTER 29

"I sent a FTL message?" I said, my thoughts stumbling about in small circles.

"You did."

"But—but—but—" I stopped and seized myself by the mental neck and gave it a good shaking. Logic, Jim, time for logic. "The recorded message from Captain Varod said that I would need the coordinates to send a FTL message."

"That was obviously a lie."

"Saying it was a radio message was a lie too?"

"Of course."

I paced back and forth and the TV pickup followed me as I moved. What was going on? Why had Varod lied to me about the signal? And if he had received it where was he? If he had got the signal and hadn't sent his fleet or whatever, then he was the one who must take the responsibility for the murders. The League did not go in for that sort of thing. But Mark might know what was happening. I spun about.

"Speak, ancient brain-in-box!! Has the League Navy arrived or is it on the way?"

"I'm sorry, Jim, I just don't know. The last orbiting telescope ran out of power centuries ago. I know no more than you do about this. All I can surmise is that we are very distant from these rescuers you expect."

I stopped pacing and was suddenly very tired. It was going to be another of these days. I looked around the room. "You don't have an old box or something that I can sit on?"

"Oh dear, I do apologize. I'm not being a very good host, am I? Out of training."

While he was talking a powered sofa came trundling in and stopped behind me. I dropped into it. It was hard to think of Mark as an it, not with the voice and all.

"Many thanks, very soft." I smacked my lips and it got the hint.

"Please make yourself comfortable. Something to drink perhaps?"

"I wouldn't say no. Just to stimulate thinking, you realize."

"I'm not too well stocked at the present moment. There is some wine, but it must be four hundred years old at least. Vintage with a vengeance, you might say."

"We can only try!"

The table stopped at my elbow and I blew dust from the bottle, then activated the electronic corkscrew which managed to extract the truly ancient cork without breaking it. I poured and sniffed and gasped.

"Never—never smelled anything like that before!"

And it tasted even better. All the sniffing and tasting did clear the mental air a bit. I felt better able to handle the problems of the day.

"I don't know the time," I said.

"Over sixteen hours to go before the promised executions." Mark was anything but stupid. I sipped the wine and ran over the possibilities.

"I sent the message—so the Navy has to be on its way here. But we can't count upon their arrival to save the day. The only grace note to all this is that at least I know I won't be stranded on this planet forever. Now what can I do to save lives? Since obviously neither you nor your IMers are going to lift a finger."

"I wouldn't say that, Jim. There are a number of conferences going on right now in the city. People are returning in large numbers."

"Are they knuckling under? Going back to work?"

"Not at all. A protest is being organized, as to what shape it will take—that is still being discussed."

"How do you know all this? Spies?"

"Not quite. I simply tap all the communication circuits and monitor all phone calls. I have subunits looking for keywords and making records for me."

"Are you tapping the Nevenkebla circuits as well?"

"Yes. Very interesting."

"You speak the language?"

"I speak *every* language. Fourteen thousand six hundred and twelve of them."

"*Jamen, én ting er i hvert fald siker. Du taller ikke dansk.*"

"*Og hvorfor så ikke det? Dansk er da et smukt, melodisk sprog.*

Pretty good—I thought that I was the only one who had ever heard of Danish. But there was one that I was sure Mark had never heard of. An ancient language called Latin. Spoken only by a secret society so secret I dare not say more about it.

"*Nonne cognoscis linguam Latinam?*"

"*Loquarne linguam Latinam?*" Mark answered in a decidedly snotty manner. "*Quid referam in singulorum verborum delectu, in coniunctorum compositione, et structura, in casuum atque temporum discriminatione, in certarum concinnitate formularum, in incisorum membrorumque conformatione, in modulandis circumdictionibus, in elegantiarum cuiusque generis accurata, elaborataque frequentatione quantus tum sim et quam purus putus Ciceronianus? Ex qua Cicero mortuus est, meis verbis nihil latinius. Memoria vero libros omnium auctorum latinorum tam veterum quam recentiorum et neotericorum continet. Voces peregrinae et barbarae quae latinis eloquiis inseruntur, omino mihi notae sunt. Nae tu es baro et balatro, nam ego studeo partes difficiles cognoscere quas scholastici doctores gestant, latebras singulas auxilio mei ipsius cerno. Doctissimi enimvero homines omnino universitatum modernarum me rogant sensus omnium talium verborum.*"

I could only gape at this as it hummed in electronic joy, very proud of itself. "Did you catch all those nuances, Jim? About what a pure Ciceronian I am? Each word carefully chosen, the composition of sentence structure, the contrast of cases and tenses, phrases and clauses . . ."

He, or rather it, went on for quite a while like that. Bragging. Chatting away with Mark I tended to anthropomorphize him. It. Her. Whatever. This wasn't a human but an intelligent machine with abilities far beyond anything I had ever imagined before. But how could I put them to work?

"Mark, tell me. Will you help me?"

"In any way I can."

I sipped more wine and felt its healing and inspirational powers doing good things to me. Memory. Something that had happened earlier today.

"Mark—I saw two soldiers desert today. Are there other newly arrived deserters in the city?"

"A goodly number of them. One hundred and twenty one in all, wait . . . sorry, one twenty-two. Another just arrived."

"Any of them armed?"

"You mean equipped with weapons? All of them. They have all deserted from patrols in the city."

But would they use their guns? And if so, what could I do with them? An idea was taking shape. Meet fire with fire. And they just might do it. There was only one way to find out. I poured another bit of wine and turned to my electronic host.

"I would like to have all of the deserters meet me in some central place. With their weapons. Can you arrange that?"

He was silent for long seconds. Looking for a way to back out of his offer? But I had underestimated him.

"All done," he said. "The people who are hiding them will escort them after dark to the sports center. Which is very close to the site selected for the murders."

"You are one step ahead of me."

"I should hope so. Since I am incredibly more intelligent than you are. Now, since there are some hours to go before your meeting, would you repay the favor and have a good chat with me? I have been rather out of touch with galactic matters for a thousand years or more. How are things going?"

It was a strange afternoon and early evening. His memory, as it should be, was quite formidable and I learned a number of interesting things. But there was one fact which he could not tell me since he had been born? built? wired? well after the spread of mankind through the galaxy.

"Like you, Jim, all I know are myths and ancient memories. If there was an original planetary home of mankind, called Dirt or Earth or something like that, its location is nowhere in my memory banks."

"Well, just thought that I would ask. But I think I better be going. Nice to talk to you."

"The same. Drop in any time."

"I'll take you up on that. Would you mind turning off the lights when I get to the top of the stairs?"

"Not a problem. This place is pretty well automated as you might imagine."

"No problem with the electricity supply?"

"You bet your sweet chunk there isn't. Survival was the first emotion I learned. City power supply, standby generators, battery backup, a couple of fuel cells and a fusion generator that can be fired up in ten minutes. Don't worry about me."

"I won't. So long."

I climbed the long flight of stairs and when I touched the door all the lights were extinguished. I pushed it open and peeked out: no patrols that I could see. When I threw it wide and exited there were Neebe and Stirner sitting on the bench, waiting for me.

"Aren't you worried about the enemy finding you here after curfew?"

"Not a problem," Stirner said. "So many men have deserted that all patrols appear to have been canceled. All of the military are either on the base or in the municipal building. Now—please tell us. You have spoken with Mark Forer?" They both leaned forward in tense anticipation.

"Spoken with him and enjoyed his hospitality. And he's got a couple of cases of wine left that you wouldn't believe."

"I would believe anything about Mark Forer," Stirner said and Neebe nodded agreement. "But I am sorry that he did not give you a solution to the problem of the killings."

I blinked rapidly. "How do you know that? I didn't say anything about it."

"You did not have to. Mark Forer knows that it is a problem we must deal with ourselves. And so we shall. A decision has been reached. All in the city will assemble in the killing place tomorrow, an individual decision by each one. We will stand in front of the guns."

"A noble gesture—but it won't work. They will just shoot you down."

"Then others will take our places. There is no end to nonresistance. They will keep shooting until they run out of charges for their weapons or take despair at the murders. I am sure that they are not all moral villains like their leader."

"I wouldn't count on it. But there may be an alternative. With Mark's help, we are on a first-name basis you will be happy to hear, I have arranged a meeting of all the deserters in the city. If you will kindly lead me to the sports center we will see if my plan might perhaps be a better and more practical one."

It was a pleasant stroll, the streets of the city empty of fear for the first time since the invaders had landed. We met other groups going in the same direction, each of them accompanying one or two armed deserters. Laughter and smiles, they were cheerful now that they were away from the army—but would they go along with any plan that might jeopardize that newfound freedom? There was only one way to find out.

The sports center had an indoor stadium with a wrestling ring that held us all. The escaped soldiers sat in the lower rows while interested civilian spectators were ranked above and behind them. I climbed into the ring and waited until they were all seated, then grabbed the microphone. The audience rustled into silence.

"Fellow ex-draftees, newly arrived deserters, I welcome you. Most of you don't know me . . ."

"Everyone knows you, Jim!" a voice called out. "You're the guy almost throttled the general."

"Better luck next time!"

I smiled and waited until the cheers and shouts had died down.

"Thanks guys, it is nice to be appreciated. Now I have to ask you to help. Our dear general, cagal-kopf Zennor, plans to shoot down some unarmed civilians tomorrow. These are the people who have helped you and your buddies escape, who have extended friendship to us all—and a happy home here if we want it. Now we have to help them. And I am going to tell you how.

"We are going to take these guns that we have been trained to use and aim that at Zennor and his mob and threaten to waste them if they pull any triggers. It will be a standoff—and we might not get away with it. But it is something that we have to do."

I felt a little ashamed of adding the macho emotional argument, but I had no choice. It wasn't the world's greatest idea and it had more holes in it than a carload of doughnuts. But it was the only plan in town.

They argued and shouted a lot but in the end a majority voted for it. The minority could see no way to leave with dignity—I said the macho appeal—so reluctantly went along with the plan. The locals led us by back routes into the buildings facing the square and we lay on our guns and slept. I was sure that a number would disappear during the night. I only hoped that enough would be left in the morning to give me a little firepower backup.

At the first light of dawn I was aware of figures moving about in the square outside. I shoved a teddy bear aside a bit so I could see through the curtains of the toy store where I was hiding. The troops were beginning to arrive. And the prisoners, ten of them, handcuffed and bound, being unloaded from a truck. As it grew lighter I saw that every soldier was an officer or a noncom. Of course—Zennor couldn't trust privates to do his dirty work! They were probably all locked up and under guard back on the base.

Zennor himself stalked from the municipal building and stood in the middle of the square. Just as I heard the rumble of wheels and powerful motors as the heavy gun units rolled up. I hadn't counted on this.

I hadn't counted either on Zennor drawing his pistol and shooting out the toy store window.

"Come out of there, diGriz—it's all up!" he shouted, and blew away a teddy bear.

Did I have a choice? I opened the door and stepped out in the street. Looked at all the guns aimed at the windows where my rebellious soldiers were hidden. Looked at the wicked smile of triumph on Zennor's face.

"I'm a general, remember? Did you really think that your ridiculous maneuver would succeed? My agent has reported to me every detail of your stupid plans. Would you like to meet him?"

One of the deserters emerged from a doorway at Zennor's signal and walked toward us. He wore tinted glasses and a large moustache; I had seen him at a distance before. Now I was seeing him up close as he pulled off the moustache and threw away the glasses.

"Corporal Gow," I sighed.

"Broken to private now! Because I let you escape. They would have shot me too if I hadn't been rich enough to pay the bribes. But my downfall is now your downfall. Those other privates, verminous swine, they knew I had been a corporal, wouldn't talk to me. But I could tell something was wrong. When they deserted I instantly reported to the general. At his direction I walked through the city—and was encouraged to desert by the treacherous natives. I did, and General Zennor received complete reports. "

"You're a rat!"

"No insults, spy. My rank has been restored by the good general. And you are in the cagal."

"You are indeed," Zennor agreed. And aimed his gun between my eyes. "You've failed and failed badly. Let that be your last thought as you die.

"This is the end of you!"

CHAPTER 30

Well, yes. This was just about the lowest low moment I had ever experienced. In a life that had been, unhappily, quite filled with low moments. I mean, really. Here was this murderous general leering away at me and fondling the hair trigger of his pistol. Behind him were his potbellied troops looking down the barrels of their cannon. While on all sides my disarmed army was being kicked out of hiding and forced at gunpoint into the square. There can't be many moments lower than this.

"You are not going to get away with this, Zennor," I said. Which was pretty feeble but about all I could think of at the moment.

"Oh yes I am, little man." He raised the gun and pointed it between my eyes and caressed the trigger. Then lowered it. "But I don't want it to be too easy for you. Before I blow you away, you are going to watch me shoot every one of these treacherous deserters. They had the affrontery to attempt to raise their weapons in rebellion against me. They will die for this mistake. Then I am going to shoot the ten prisoners, just as I promised. Then, and only then, will I kill you."

"Not if I kill you first," I growled and felt my lips curl back from my teeth. I had nothing to lose. I raised my hands and stalked toward him. And he ran!

Not far. Just to the nearest prisoner, a grandmotherly woman with gray hair. He pulled her away from the others and thrust the muzzle of his gun against her head.

"Go ahead, diGriz. Take one more step toward me and I pull the trigger. Do you doubt me?"

Doubt him? Never. I did not take the step. The world was coming to an end and there was nothing I could do about it. They had the guns: we had nothing.

It was then, at the darkest moment, through the blackness of my thoughts I became aware of the shuffling of many feet. I turned to look just as Zennor did.

Around the corner came a solid mass of people, filling the street from side to side, an endless number of them. Leading the front rank was Stirner—and Neebe!

"No, don't, go back!" I shouted. Neebe smiled sweetly at me. And kept walking at Stirner's side. Zennor had his gun aimed at Stirner now—who appeared completely indifferent to it. Stirner stopped and called out loudly.

"All of you men with weapons—put them down. We will not hurt you for that is not our way . . ."

"One more word and I will kill you!" Zennor roared. Stirner turned to him, his face cold as death.

"I believe you will," he said. "Until this moment I really did not believe it possible that a human being could kill another. After seeing you I believe it."

"Good, then you will . . ."

"Be quiet. I will do just what I came here to do. I will take your weapon. If you kill me, someone else will take your weapon from you. If he fails another will try. Eventually it will be empty, discharged and will be taken from you. You cannot win. Those who follow you cannot win. It is all over."

"It is not!" Zennor shouted. There was spittle on his lips now, a look of insanity in his eyes. He pushed the woman captive away and ground his gun into Stirner's body. "No one has the guts to do that. When I blow your blood all over them they will turn and run. My men will fire a volley and the survivors will flee in panic. That is what I will do and you cannot stop me . . ."

I dived for him hands outstretched. He pushed Stirner against me and lashed the pistol barrel across my head, aimed it at me, tightened his finger on the trigger.

"Are you volunteering, diGriz? Good. Than you shall be first."

A shadow drifted across the square and an amplified voice boomed against our eardrums.

"The war is over. Lower your weapons."

Filling the sky was the biggest spacer I had ever seen, bristling with guns—and all pointed down at Zennor's troops.

The Navy had arrived!

But a little too late.

"Never!" Zennor cried. "Gunners, fire! Kill the captives! Shoot down that ship!"

Nor was I forgotten. He ground the pistol barrel into my temple and pulled the trigger.

The gun did not fire.

I saw his knuckle whiten with the strain—but the trigger would not move. His face went ashen as he realized what was happening. I lashed out and knocked the pistol aside.

Then, from way down on the ground, I brought up a punch that I think I had been saving for all of my life. Up, faster and faster it went, until my fist caught him full on the jaw. Lifted him into the air, dropped him unconscious to the ground. I rubbed my sore knuckles and realized that I was grinning like a fool.

"Your weapons will not work!" the voice from the sky boomed once again, and even through the echoes and distortion I recognized Captain Varod. "This ship is projecting an entropy field that does not permit metal to move against metal or electrons to flow. It does not affect life forms. Therefore if you good citizens of Chojecki would be so kind as to disarm these invaders I would be immensely grateful."

There was the quick thudding of running feet as a number of deserters got there first. The sight of officerial black eyes and bloody noncommisioned noses was a pleasant one. A hatch opened in the ship above and a familiar uniformed figure dropped down on the end of a line. I felt a hand on my arm and turned to look into Neebe's gorgeous, smiling face.

"Then it is all over, Jim?"

251

"It is—and it has a happy ending as well."

"What will happen now?"

"The invaders will go and will never come back. Your planet will be your own again. Peace will prevail here forever."

"Will you be leaving too?"

My heart gave a couple of rapid hammerbeats and I squeezed her arm and prepared to drown in those eyes. Then I surfaced and shook myself off.

"I don't know . . . not true. I do know. As great as the attractions are here," I squeezed the hand of the greatest attraction, "in the long run I would not be happy. Nor would those about me. Your planet, if you will excuse me saying so, is a little too quiet for me. Paradise is fun for awhile, but I would not like to make a habit out of it. There are a lot more worlds out there that I haven't seen yet. The galaxy is a very big place. It hurts to say it, but I must move on."

"Stay on this world, Jim," Varod advised as he walked up behind me. "Because if you leave here you will find out that justice and a jail term await you on a certain planet."

"That's what you say, Varod, that's what you say!" I spun about and shook a very angry finger in his face. "You lied to me, tricked me into coming here—then ignored my FTL message and left me here to rot, almost got me and about half of the planet killed . . ."

"Never! We were in orbit all of the time, watching everything. As soon as we arrived we had Zennor bugged completely with undetectable bugs. We were here two days after you sent the FTL message. Well done."

"Two days? Bugs? That's impossible. Mark Forer would have known about them."

"It did. We have been in constant consultation with that great intelligence. It has been of great help."

"Are you telling me that Mark Forer lied to me—just like you?"

"Yes."

I opened and shut my mouth and ran it all through again. "Why . . . I mean why hang around and run the risk of things getting out of hand when you could have landed at once?"

"We had to wait until after the elections," he said with

252

infuriating amiability. "We had done everything we could to get Zennor off of his home planet as quickly as possible. Planted all those radio-broadcasting bugs so he would know that he was being watched. We worked on his paranoia, in the hopes that he would stay out of contact with his home base until it was too late. You were very good at causing trouble for him here. I must congratulate you on that. It gave him no time at all to even consider contacting his base. That was very important to us. Once Zennor left on his interplanetary adventure—as we hoped he would—it was possible to stage a little coup d'etat in Nevenkebla. The civilians were more than weary of the endless state of emergency. A palace revolution quickly got rid of the military. A civil government has been elected and peace will prevail from now on. This disarmed army will return and be absorbed in the populace."

"You played me for a patsy," I said, with some warmth.

"I don't know the term, but I assume that it means we took unfair advantage of you and let you do our dirty work for us."

"That will do until a better description comes along. Well— didn't you?"

"Not at all. You became involved in this matter for your own reasons. If we had not watched you and come to your aid you would be dead right now."

Very hard to argue with that. And I had come here of my own accord. I looked down at the prostrate form and resisted the strong desire to kick in a couple of ribs.

"What about Zennor here?"

"Zennor is a sickie and will get the proper treatment in a hospital that specializes in people with problems like his. As of this moment he no longer exists."

"And what about me?"

"You would be wise to stay right where you are now. Escaped prisoner, conviction still pending—"

"Don't shoot me that line of old cagal," I sneered. "I am an undercover operative of the League Navy and will be treated as such. I was responsible for your locating this planet and have suffered in the name of League justice. I have even made financial arrangements on your behalf . . ."

"Yes, the soldier you promised the credits to, for aiding you. The voice-actuated recorder in the spybird caught your conversation with him. Aspya will be paid."

"Then so will I. Full salary for all the time I have been working for you. Right?"

He rubbed his jaw and scowled. "I suppose that you will be asking for a full pardon for crimes committed on Bit O' Heaven?"

"No. I just want that incident wiped completely from my record so I can walk forth a free man. With my back pay in my pocket."

"I agree. As long as you remain in the Navy employ. Although a bit impetuous, you make a good field agent. . ."

"Never!" I shouted, shying back and neighing like a horse. "Never! Work for the law? Pay taxes and look forward to a miserable pension in my old age? Death before dishonor! Pay up and wave bye-bye, captain. I have my own career priorities."

"Like following a life of crime?"

"That is different. In all truth I can promise you—never again!" I placed one hand over my heart and raised the other palm outward. "I have learned my lesson. I hereby forswear any interest in a life of crime and pledge my word to be a productive member of society forever after."

"Good, my boy, good. I'll take care of the money for you then. The likes of you don't belong in crime."

"No sir, they don't!" I said.

Lying again, lying and smiling and lying through my teeth. After all—I had some good examples to follow. When a full captain in the League Navy lies to you, when the greatest artificial intelligence in the known galaxy lies to you—should a simple ex-porcuswine swineherd be forced to tell the truth?

My throat was dry and I suddenly felt a great yearning for some of that four-hundred-year-old wine. I looked forward to raising a glass of it very soon. Raising it in a toast.

To my future career out there among the stars. I could almost taste that wine upon my lips and I smacked them dryly, turned to face Neebe and Stirner.

"My friends—this calls for a celebration. Come with me, I beg you. I know of a *very* exclusive drinking establishment not too far away from here."

254

EPILOGUE

"This is undoubtedly," Stirner said, eyes wet with emotion, "the very best glass of wine I have drunk, ever thought of drinking, managed to drink, ever drank, will ever drink, ever imagined that I some day might have considered drinking . . ."

"While your grip on syntax seems to be failing," Mark Forer said, "I appreciate the emotion. Now that you have all tasted the wine, I am much cheered that you enjoy it, I would like to propose a toast. To James diGriz, planet saver. We shall be ever grateful, Jim."

"Ever grateful!" they chorused, raised their glasses and drank. Except for Mark, who had no glass to raise. Instead of drinking wine he had one of his robots pour a dollop of electrolytic fluid into a dry battery; Mark had informed us that the sudden surge of electrons was most stimulating.

"Thank you, my friends, thank you," I said, then raised my glass in turn. "To Morton and Sharla, who sit on the couch beside you, holding hands and blushing because they are soon to be married."

They all cheered and drank at that; Mark Forer giggled over his zippy electrons. I raised my glass again.

"A toast of thanks as well to my physical guide and intellectual mentor, Stirner. And to my companion in adventure, Neebe—

long may her bicycle roll." More cheers and glugging followed as I turned to the glowing machine before us.

"Last—and certainly—not least, to Mark Forer. Guide, teacher, spiritual leader, purveyor of fine wines. To Mark!"

When the cheering had died away, and another bottle had been cracked, Mark Forer spoke to his attentive audience.

"Thank you, thank you dear believers in Individual Mutualism. Too long have I been sholitary . . ."

Sholitary? This mean machine was getting pissed on whizzing electrons! Drunk!

". . . too long a lurker beneath the streets watching the passing parade passing above me. Now, at last, finally I welcome your dear company and I greet you. And we had better crack another case of wine."

Stirner staggered off to fetch it and Neebe went to help. Alone for the moment Morton and Sharla wrapped themselves in happy osculatory embrace. Mark was muttering to himself.

This was perfect opportunity to slip away. I hated goodbyes. Quietly, so as not to disturb them, I rose and made my exit. As I slowly eased shut the door behind me I saw Mark's TV pickup swivel to face me; the diaphragm contracted and dilated quickly in an electronic wink. I winked back and closed the door, turned and slowly climbed the stairs.

As much as I liked this planet and its politically monomaniacal citizens, I knew it was not for me. Too civilized and peaceful. Without crime and without police—what would I do for a living?

Go, Jim, go! The stars are yours!